PRAISE FOR *THE PALACE AT DUSK*

"No one writes realistic heart-wrenching, gotta-have-him stories better than Angela Terry. I can't get enough of every one of her books, and *The Palace at Dusk* is my favorite yet. Her skill in unfolding the complexities of life that not only include what a character's romantic heart desires but also other goals in life grip the reader from page one and keep them never wanting to put her books down. This novel is representative of how women's fiction should be—overflowing with soul, empowerment, and full-circle moments."

—C. D'Angelo, award-winning author of *The Difference* and *The Visitor*

"Heartfelt and thought-provoking, *The Palace at Dusk* is the story of one woman's quest to forge a life—and find love—on her own terms. Angela Terry is a fresh, luminous voice in women's fiction."

—Camille Pagán, bestselling author of *Good for You*

"Angela Terry has done it again! *The Palace at Dusk* is a page-turning novel set in the competitive world of Big Law. A portrait of the messiness of life and love, family, and friendship, it's perfect for fans of Emily Giffin and Kelly Harms."

—Andrea J. Stein, award-winning author of the bestselling novel *Typecast*

PRAISE FOR *THE TRIALS OF ADELINE TURNER*

"A perfectly paced rom-com that consistently places you right at the scene; the summer reading escape I didn't know I needed."

—Emily Belden, author of *Hot Mess* and *Husband Material*

"*The Trials of Adeline Turner* is a fast-paced tale of dating in your thirties and learning to trust your inner voice. Brimming with wit, banter, romance, and heart, it has all the ingredients of the perfect beach read. I was charmed!"

—Lindsay Cameron, award-winning author of *BIGLAW* and *Just One Look*

"The verdict is in, and Angela Terry's *The Trials of Adeline Turner* is a must-read! Readers will root for Adeline and enjoy Terry's sparkling writing style, which creates the feeling of catching up with an old friend who has quite the story to tell. This novel has it all—but my favorite part? The ending, which had me smiling from ear to ear, completely satisfied, albeit sad to leave the world of Adeline behind."

—Ashley R. King, author of *Painting the Lines* (Ace of Hearts Book 1)

PRAISE FOR *CHARMING FALLS APART*

"From the very first page, I was hooked on this tale of heart-break, self-discovery, and one woman's charming determination to turn lemons into lemonade. Fans of Emily Giffin and Lauren Weisberger will love this engaging and entertaining debut!"

—Meg Donohue, *USA Today* bestselling author of *You, Me, and the Sea*

"*Charming Falls Apart* is the perfect comfort read. A smart and heartfelt ode to the healing power of friendship and the strength in reinvention. Fans of Sophie Kinsella will root for Allison James as she rebuilds her life on her own terms."

—Allie Larkin, internationally bestselling author of *Swimming for Sunlight*

"A breezy read perfect for a summer day. So many young women rush to make a plan for how they think their lives should go without stopping to think about what will make them happy. We can all cheer for a heroine who loses it all and comes to realize she never wanted it anyway."

—Maria Murnane, bestselling author of the Waverly Bryson series

"Truly beautiful moments in this book and this woman's journey."

—Paperbacks and Coffee Mugs

"If you like *Eat, Pray, Love* or any Christina Lauren novel, this book is for you."

—Wildly Reading

"Angela Terry is a fabulous writer; I enjoyed this pretty perfect rom-com."

—Hannah Reads

"A must read for fans of Elizabeth Gilbert (one of my all-time favorites) and contemporary romance."

—My Darling Bookshelf

ALSO BY ANGELA TERRY

The Trials of Adeline Turner

Charming Falls Apart

A NOVEL

ANGELA TERRY

GIRL FRIDAY BOOKS

This is a work of fiction. Names, characters, organizations, places, events, and incidents are either products of the author's imagination or are used fictitiously.

Published by Girl Friday Books™, Seattle

Produced by Girl Friday Productions

Design: Rachel Marek
Production editorial: Abi Pollokoff
Project management: Kristin Duran

Image credits: cover © creativelement/Shutterstock

ISBN (paperback): 978-1-959411-39-0
ISBN (ebook): 978-1-959411-40-6

Library of Congress Control Number: 2023906926

First edition
Printed in the United States of America

For my parents,
Catherine and Richard Terry

PROLOGUE

PARIS, 2016

"Is this chair taken?" a fellow American tourist asked me, pointing to the extra chair at my sidewalk café table. I shook my head.

"May I?" He then pointed to another table where a pretty young woman sat with a guidebook and a hopeful look. I nodded.

He thanked me, then carried the chair over to the woman's table, and the two of them grinned at each other, so clearly in love. I spied a shiny diamond ring on her left hand and wondered if they were in Paris for their honeymoon. Meanwhile, I was sitting alone in the most romantic city in the world, asking myself, *How did I get here?*

Over the last several years, I had made countless bad decisions in my love life and my career, and now I needed to know if I was about to make the biggest mistake of all. Running away from my problems the first time had only made them worse, and so this time I had to get it right. When I returned to the States, I had a decision to make.

I took a sip of my coffee and opened to the first page in my journal, a gift given to me years ago that I had left blank. I hadn't journaled in a long time, probably not wanting to see my story in black and white. But the only way for me to make sense of it all was to start at the beginning, and so I started writing.

Part 1

2009

CHAPTER ONE

Ten p.m. on a Friday, and I was still staring into my computer screen, working on yet another tedious assignment for a partner I despised. He had asked me to double-check all the real estate titles for one of his deals. It was a reasonable-enough request for a *real estate* associate. But I was a first-year *corporate* associate. There's a difference. The client was a Fortune 500 company that had not only their own offices around the world, but also those of their subsidiaries. And his deal was scheduled to close on Monday.

Or so he said.

If I'd learned anything as a corporate attorney, it was that closing dates were moving targets. I couldn't count how many all-nighters I had pulled because someone told me, "They're closing in the morning! I needed this yesterday!" only to learn that everything had been moved out another week and my sleep sacrifice was all for naught. I was seriously starting to question my decision to be a lawyer at Levenfield LLP.

At least I wasn't alone in the office. Some litigation associates involved in a big document review were toiling away in the conference room a few doors down. And some corporate and real estate associates were still wandering the halls, doing grunt work for whatever deals they were assigned to. I had finished up the US and European real estate holdings, and I just needed to finish up the Asian ones before I could leave. I took a deep breath and redoubled my focus, determined to plow through this last part so I could get home before night turned into morning.

"What are you working on?" an unfamiliar voice said from my doorway.

Actually, it wasn't that unfamiliar. I had heard it before, but that was two summers ago.

"You don't want to know." I groaned and turned away from my computer to face the voice.

Apparently taking that as an invitation, Brad Summers, a real estate associate who had been in my summer associate class but hadn't stepped foot in my office since, sauntered in and took a seat across from my desk.

"So, Miss *Jasmine Phillips*," he drawled out my full name. "How is it we're on the same floor and never talk?" He grinned.

"Please, *Bradley*, call me Jae," I said, mimicking his formal tone with a smirk of my own. "And I don't know."

Two years ago, as summer associates, Brad and I had spoken all the time. On our first day, we had sat next to each other at the Welcome Orientation Breakfast. We were fresh off our second year of law school, and, needing to expend our nervous energy, we took turns cracking jokes to each other over some dried-out pastries. With his hazel eyes, unruly chestnut hair, and a smile that lit up his face, Brad charmed me right from the start, and I mentally noted that he was the best-looking guy in our class.

Later that same day, my office phone had rung, and it was Brad asking if I would be at the happy hour that night. I said, "Of course," since these events were mandatory—part of the two-month interview to secure employment after graduation. As soon as I arrived, Brad must have spotted me because he was immediately at my side, whispering conspiratorially, "Steer clear of the shrimp skewers, but load up on the stuffed mushrooms when they come around."

"Duly noted."

Even though we were supposed to mingle, I noticed that Brad hovered in my orbit. When the event was over, he asked me if I wanted to grab a drink. That was when I casually, but reluctantly, mentioned that I had promised to call my boyfriend before it got too late on the East Coast. Brad took the hint. Although we still included each other in lunches and hung out at events, Brad respected that I was in a relationship, and our office friendship was easygoing and fun. Though I knew it was best for my career not to get involved in an office romance, there had definitely been times that summer when I wished I didn't have a boyfriend.

A year later, on our first day back at Levenfield as attorneys, I had been excited to reconnect with Brad, but he kept his distance, and so I kept mine. I figured that maybe the reality of lawyering was beating him down, because the real estate associate I knew as Brad Summers never socialized, never smiled, and always looked tired. But now, sitting across from me, Brad had a sparkle in his eyes and sported a grin I hadn't seen since our summer-associate days.

"We should change that," he said, his eyes twinkling merrily.

"O-kay," I said, still wondering what had suddenly possessed him to brazenly make himself at home in my office. Then, on closer inspection, I realized he seemed a little unsteady. I suspected that he had hit up the firm's on-site happy hour earlier in the evening and may have snuck some alcohol back to his office.

"We should get a drink," he declared.

"It's after ten."

"So? It's Friday." He leaned forward and put his elbows on my desk, as if challenging me on this fact.

It was a Friday. And sadly, this was probably the most exciting thing to happen to me on a Friday in a long time. But even so, I was a first-year lawyer before I was a twenty-seven-year-old single woman. "I can't. I have to finish this project for Meyers."

"Mr. Potato Head?"

"The one and only." A couple other associates and I had privately nicknamed him that, but I hadn't realized it had made the rounds. Frankly, it was much too kind for a nickname. But his face distorted itself into such a wide range of fits of rage and displeasure that when someone randomly compared him to a "Mr. Potato Head" late one night in a conference room, all of the overtired, slap-happy associates burst out laughing, and the moniker stuck. "He needs me to finish this by tomorrow morning."

"I can help," he offered cheerfully.

"But you don't even know what I'm doing." Also, I didn't trust an inebriated colleague to be able to get the job done.

"Oh, come on, Jae. What is it?"

"I have to confirm the title on these Asian offices." I held up the list.

"That's it? Sounds like the perfect job for a real estate lawyer." He stood up. "We'll split it," he said, grabbing the paper from my hands and running out of my office with it.

"Hey!" I called after him as I stood up. Yes, he was cute, but I was tired and really wanted to get home by at least two o'clock in the morning. I walked out of my office and followed him down the hall.

By the time I caught up to him, he was already at the copier, and the list was zipping out of the machine. He grabbed the copy and handed me the original. "Here. You do the first half and I'll do the second," he said.

"I don't know. . . ." I frowned. But then Brad looked at me as though in disbelief that I'd refuse his offer. And what the hell? Why not? Mr. Potato Head should have given the task to a real estate associate in the first place. Plus, Brad was right—it was Friday night, and I deserved some fun. "Okay, deal."

With the prospect of drinks looming, I managed to rush through my portion in an hour. Brad was just as fast. When he sent me an email with Done! in the subject line, I responded a minute later with an impulsive, Me too!

Within seconds Brad was at my door. "Let's go," he said, and tilted his head toward the elevators. A passing thought that I should check his work before leaving floated through my mind. But worried about losing my mojo, I instead grabbed my purse, and we headed out into the night. Though it was after 11:00 p.m., it was July and the LA air was still warm.

"Where should we go?" I asked. I was afraid to offer an opinion in case my selection wasn't "hip" enough.

Brad was already leading the way. "I know a place."

Excited to be out of the office and for once not headed straight home after work, I followed him. Even though I told myself it was just two colleagues going out for a drink after a long week, I felt an air of risk about it all as I tucked back some hairs that had escaped from my low bun. We walked a couple blocks and then crossed the street to a hotel. When we walked inside, Brad headed straight for the bustling bar, which had a spacious lounge area and a long dark wood bar along the entire back wall. Brad looked around until he spied a seat. "Over there." He pointed to a spot in the corner.

I followed him over to a brown leather sofa, and we each took opposite ends. As Brad stretched out and put his arm on the back of the sofa, I leaned forward to pick up the menu off the table and began to study it, surreptitiously sneaking a peek at Brad. With his long limbs and broad shoulders, he looked too fit to be a lawyer, and I mentally noted again that he still was the best-looking male specimen in the office. This thought, coupled with the fact that other than a general acknowledgment in the hallway or kitchen, we hadn't really spoken for the entire year we'd been working together, set off a fluttering in my stomach. *What would we talk about?*

Despite the extensive drink selection, I requested the first cocktail listed on the menu, and Brad asked for a vodka tonic. After ordering, I was about to ask him what inspired him to come into my office, but once the server left, Brad turned to me and said, "Did I ever tell you about the time I got my pants stolen on the beach?"

I laughed at the ridiculousness of the pants-stolen-on-beach scenario and shook my head. "No, you've never mentioned that story."

"It was in Thailand, and unfortunately they stole more than my pants." He repositioned his arm on the back of the sofa and crossed his ankle onto his knee, getting comfortable and settling into his tale. "I had just arrived that day, and it was too early to check into my hotel. Since I'd heard there was great surfing, I went to the beach to watch. I met some other tourists, and they agreed to keep an eye on my bag while I took a quick swim. But when I came out of the water, the tourists, my backpack, and my pants were gone! Stolen!"

"That's crazy!"

"I know."

"I didn't realize Thailand had such good surfing."

Getting my joke, Brad laughed and knocked his knee against mine. "That's not the point of the story."

I smirked, and he shook his head and laughed again.

"Really, that's terrible," I said. "So what did you do?"

"Well, I wandered to the road with no money, credit cards, ID, phone, or *clothes* and hitchhiked back to my hotel, hoping they would believe I was a guest checking in there."

"At least you had your swim trunks. Unless you're more of a Speedo guy?"

Brad winked at me in response, and I laughed and said, "Well, considering that you're sitting across from me and not still in Thailand, I assume everything worked out?"

He related to me the rigmarole he went through with the hotel, until the server interrupted us with our drinks.

Drinks in hand, we clinked our glasses and said, "To Thailand!"

As I took a sip of my cocktail, I wondered if Brad was as nervous as I was and if his "no pants" story was his usual icebreaker. Lacking a similarly ridiculous story to share and not sure what to say next, I said, "Thanks again for helping me out tonight. It's great to be out of the office." After I said it, I realized I sounded a bit pathetic.

"Yes, you work too hard." He tilted his head toward me. "I always see you in your office at night. You should get out more."

Even though it was an innocent observation, his concern made me shift in my seat. "If you always see me working at night, then that means you're working late too. So what were you doing in the office at ten o'clock on a Friday?" *And why did you come into mine?*

"I wasn't working," he said, again with that same twinkle in his eye.

"Okay," I said slowly, squinting at him. "Then what were you doing?"

"Waiting for you." He fixed his gaze on me with his gorgeous eyes.

"Funny," I said, then looked down at my cocktail and took another sip. *Was that a come-on, or was he joking?* Warning bells went off in my mind, and a little voice shouted, *"Danger, danger."* Though I was still attracted to Brad, I wasn't going to date a colleague. Luckily, I didn't have to think of something else to say because Brad, maybe sensing something in my hesitant pause, changed the subject.

"What's your dream vacation?" he asked.

"Easy answer—Paris."

"Nice. I've never been. You?"

"Yes, several times. In fact, I studied there for a semester during my junior year of college and loved it," I said, reminiscing. "It's my favorite city in the world."

Brad appeared impressed. "What do you love about it?"

"What's not to love? The museums, the parks, the cafés, the bookstores." I ticked off each item with my fingers. "When I retire, I plan to move there. I'm already saving my money."

"Really?"

"Oui."

Brad smiled and looked at me in a way that made me feel like the most charming, interesting person he'd ever met. But his gaze was also making me flush, and I needed to take his attention off me.

"What about you? What's your dream vacation?" I asked.

"Any beach where I can go surfing and then lie in a hammock with a beer." He stretched out his legs alongside the table and leaned his head back on his hands, as if he were already in his imaginary hammock.

"Even after your terrifying pants experience?" I widened my eyes in mock horror. "You're a brave man."

He laughed, and I felt as if I had the most amazing sense of humor on top of my charmingness.

We continued to talk nonsense about dream vacations and where we would love to live, and totally ignored all the obvious conversation points that we had in common, such as how things were going at Levenfield and whether we liked our departments, or, *again*, what exactly had inspired him to pop into my office that night. Instead, we entertained each other with random stories of trips gone awry and childhood antics (Brad had been raised in a small town in Wisconsin and loved to rib me about how I'd grown up in a "tony" part of Los Angeles), story after story, tumbling out in an easy flow.

Last call arrived too quickly, and soon we were back outside in the 2:00 a.m. summer heat.

As we stood in front of the hotel, Brad asked, "Where should we go now?"

"Um, it's two a.m. I'm going home," I said. "Why? Where do you want to go?" I gave him an amused look.

He shrugged, and for a second I wondered whether maybe he thought he was coming home with me. I felt an uncomfortable flutter of excitement.

"I don't know." He put his hands in his pockets and looked down at the ground. "I guess I'll head back to work."

"You're going back to the office? Are you serious?"

He looked up at me and grinned. "Unless you want to go somewhere else?"

I shook my head. "Sorry, but I need my beauty sleep." Luckily, I spied a cab coming up the street toward the hotel and flagged it down. When it pulled up, I opened the door to get in. "See you Monday," I said.

Brad shut the door behind me. He stood back and waved, and I gave a little wave back as I told the driver my address. My gut told me that if I had invited him back to my place, he probably would have taken me up on it. I let out a deep breath. I'd managed to keep a clear head and do the responsible thing—even though everything in me wanted to do the opposite.

CHAPTER TWO

On Monday afternoon, Mindy, the only other female first-year corporate associate, and I walked to our usual lunch spot. We never actually ate there, but instead carried our salads back to our offices to eat alone at our desks to maximize our billable hours.

"So how did your last-minute project for Mr. Potato Head go?" Mindy asked. "Were you in the office all night?"

We usually used these walks to vent about the same nefarious partner we worked for, but that afternoon I had something else on my mind.

"I stayed pretty late, and since he hasn't bothered me at all today, I assume everything went well," I said with a shrug, wanting to share the more interesting news of that night. "But, hey, you'll never guess who stopped by my office Friday night."

"Who?" Mindy asked, her voice eager, telling me she was primed to hear some good office gossip.

"Brad Summers."

"Huh?" she said, her eyebrows knitted together. "How strange."

I couldn't really read her tone or expression, so I continued. "Um, yeah. It was kinda crazy. He was like, 'We never talk. We should go out for drinks.'" I paused, waiting for Mindy to say something. When she didn't, I said, "So, we went for a drink."

"Really?" Mindy's eyes widened. "I'd be careful, Jae."

"Why's that?" I kept my tone neutral, instantly regretting mentioning it.

"For one, you two clearly had a thing for each other when we were summers. But since we started, he's ignored you and the rest of us for no reason. It's weird. And two," she said, looking at me pointedly, "last I heard from my UCLA friends, he has a girlfriend."

Thud. I swallowed and said, "Well, he helped me out with my assignment, and so I wasn't going to turn down a drink. But I just thought it strange, too, that he finally deigned one of us with his presence." My instincts told me that if we continued talking about Brad, my outing might appear to be something more than it had been. So I changed the subject to Mr. Potato Head's latest inane assignment.

Back at my desk, I could barely eat my salad as I was still unnerved by Mindy's reaction and warning. Mindy and I had gone out for happy hour before with Jeff, another associate in the real estate department on our floor; so what was the big deal with my having drinks with Brad? And while I suspected that, yes, he had been hitting on me at the end of the night, nothing had come of it, and I hadn't spoken to him since. And as for a girlfriend, based on my history with Brad, I was sure it would have come up in conversation, and it didn't. *Not that it mattered.*

All I knew was that I was never, ever mentioning my Friday night outing to anyone ever again, if only to stay off the gossip radar. And later that afternoon, as I passed Brad in the hallway, he simply acknowledged me with a nod, so I wrote off our night as a drunken fluke.

***

Tuesday afternoon my office phone rang.

"Hey," I answered when I saw that it was Mindy calling.

"Hey. Did you see this email?" she asked, her voice perplexed.

"No. What email?"

I clicked over to my inbox and saw an email from Brad to Mindy, Jeff, and me, asking if we wanted to grab some beers after work.

"Huh," I said, hoping that his asking all of us out made my drink with him less suspect in Mindy's eyes.

"I don't know what to say," she said.

"Seems to call for a yes or no answer." And I was especially curious what hers would be after our conversation the other day.

"In that case . . ." She paused for emphasis. *"No."*

I was taken aback at her dramatic response, and my gut told me not to press her. And then I worried that if I said yes, Mindy would take it to mean I was interested in Brad. For an associate, navigating law firm politics was a bit like an episode of *Survivor*, only more treacherous. Maybe Brad had been onto something by not socializing with his fellow associates until now?

Jeff appeared in my doorway. "Mindy, I have to go. Jeff is here."

I heard her say something that sounded like "put me on speakerphone," but I just hung up. Another etiquette point I had learned my first year in Biglaw—no one said goodbye on the phone.

"What's up?" I said to Jeff.

He closed my door and sat down on a file cabinet. "Did you see Brad's email?"

"Yup. Are you going?"

"Uh, *no*," Jeff sniffed, taking off his glasses and polishing them on his button-down shirt. "It's weird. I'm in the same department as he is, and he's barely spoken to me. We've had all year to hang out, so why now?" The four of us were the only first-years on that floor, and even I had to admit Brad's sudden interest in socializing was strange.

"I don't know. Maybe he realized he's set himself up as an outcast on our floor and is trying to rectify the situation?"

"Sorry, Dr. Phil"—he shook his head—"but ever since we've started, I've just gotten a weird vibe off him."

It wasn't like Jeff to be unfriendly or get "vibes" off people, which made me wonder if I was missing something about Brad. Acting more nonchalant than I felt, I leaned back in my chair and said, "All vibes aside, I'll go if you go. It could be fun." While I said this, I could hear the new-mail alert on my computer. I glanced over to see that Mindy had replied to all.

Sorry, I can't make it tonight.

I didn't say anything to Jeff and waited for him to make up his mind.

"I have plans tonight, so I can't make it anyway," he said, giving me a smug smile.

"How convenient." I tapped a pen on my desk, not sure if I believed him. He just wiggled his eyebrows at me and left my office.

I really wanted to go, but if Mindy and Jeff weren't, then I knew my response.

I typed to everyone: Wish I could, but I have too much work tonight.

Brad replied only to me.

Too bad. Is it anything I can help with?

The too-much-work thing was a lame excuse, and I hated myself for giving in to peer pressure, or law firm paranoia, whatever you wanted to call it. True, there was always too much work, but I didn't have any hard deadlines. So I replied vaguely.

> Thanks, but it's a bunch of loose ends I need to tie up. Can't really use help.

Brad emailed back.

> Okay. If you finish early, the invite is still open.

I felt like a jerk.

I felt even worse around five when Brad stood in my doorway and asked, "How's it going?"

I jumped a little in my seat but quickly regained my composure. "Good," I said.

"Are you still swamped?"

"Yeah." I slumped a little in my chair to show defeat. The truth was that I could go home any time, but now I had to put on a show. I seriously disliked myself in that moment, since normally I'd never been someone who followed the crowd, or was even really part of the crowd. If I had, then I probably wouldn't have been top of my class in law school; but maybe I would have had more friendships.

"Are you sure I can't help?"

"Yeah, it's not really anything I can delegate—"

"I find a beer can make me work better," he interrupted, grinning at me. "Why don't you take a break?"

"I really shouldn't. I need to get this stuff finished."

"Oh, come on. One beer?" He gave me a playful incredulous look. "You have to take a break for dinner anyway."

"I don't know. . . ." I shouldn't have used the work excuse because it gave him an opening. The trouble was I *wanted* to go. I just didn't want to be talked about.

All of a sudden, Brad's face clouded over in defeat as he said, "I'm not going to beg you to have a drink with me."

His statement was so unexpected that it jolted me for a second. For the first time, he had reached out to the associates on our floor, and we all shut him down. I took a deep breath. "You're right. I could use a break. One beer won't hurt me," I said.

"Great!" he said, his eyes bright again, the cloud lifted. "When do you want to go?"

"Give me twenty. I'll email you when I'm ready."

Brad left with a smile on his face. I knew I was outcasting myself by not being one of the sheep. But what else was new? And maybe I'd solve the mystery of Brad's standoffishness.

A minute after Brad left, Jeff appeared at my door with a smirk on his face. He had heard our exchange from his office next door.

"Yeah, yeah. I know. I wimped out," I said.

Jeff continued to smirk and then shook his head. "Shut up," I said as he walked away chuckling.

Whatever. I had had fun on Friday. It had been energizing not to talk about work and remember that I had a personality outside of the office. Jeff, Mindy, and I bonded by complaining about our workloads and the latest crazy partner demands. But I had enjoyed discussing fantasy vacations and swapping funny stories with Brad a great deal more. What harm could one beer do?

***

Brad and I walked over to a nearby brewpub that was popular with our firm for low-key lunches. We bypassed the tables and sat up by the bar. I'd never been much of a beer drinker, but I ordered what I hoped was a decent selection. Sitting close to each other, practically shoulder to shoulder, on our stools at the crowded bar, we launched into small talk about our current work assignments. But once we had found our conversational footing and imbibed some liquid courage, Brad abruptly changed the topic.

"I'm thinking of buying a new camera," he said.

"People still use cameras?" I teased.

"Some of us, yes." He smiled at me. "I've always been drawn to photography, but I only recently started getting into it. All those art classes, I guess."

"Art classes? When did you take those?"

"In college." He took a sip of his beer. "In between my engineering requirements. My dad thought an engineering degree would be more practical than an art degree. He was probably right."

"Wouldn't that be more practical if you were actually an engineer? Or a patent attorney? How'd you end up in real estate, anyway?"

He shrugged. "I never liked engineering, but I like the structure of buildings and spaces. And I like the transactional side of real estate law. Seeing a deal come together and all that. So it seemed like a good fit."

This was my opening to ask if he liked his department and find out why he kept to himself. But away from the office and with a beer in front of me, work politics seemed a lot less interesting. Instead, I said, "So tell me about these art classes and photography."

His eyes lit up, his face and hands became animated. He began by telling me the similarities between art and photography and how the "eye" his drawing classes had given him helped him think about the type of pictures he wanted to take. "The difference between drawing and photography is that with a camera, you are out in the world, but viewing it in an entirely new way. It's almost like seeing everything for the first time." He suddenly stopped himself. "Sorry. Am I talking too much? Are you sure you want to hear all this?"

"Not at all!" I waved my hand in a gesture to say, "Keep it coming." How did we not talk about this before? *What a dark horse he is,* I thought as I sipped my beer while he told me about his first forays into photography.

I didn't know if it was the beer or the topic, but we became so engrossed, we ordered another round.

While we talked, we faced each other on our barstools, and our knees kept accidentally bumping together in the tight space. Brad was a little buzzed on his third beer, while I continued nursing my second. He looked thoughtfully at me and blurted out, "You remind me a lot of a girl who used to live down the street from me."

"Oh?"

I suddenly became very aware that my right knee was resting between his legs, and I didn't bother moving it. To do so would acknowledge that it had gotten there in the first place.

"Something about the way your hands move and the way you talk." He tilted his head and studied me. "She's small like you and has dark hair." He took my hand and held it, looking at it, perhaps comparing it to the one of this girl from his past. I let him.

After a few seconds, he released my hand and grabbed his pint. "She was nice. But we lost touch when my family moved."

I nodded. I liked him holding my hand; it had felt warm and solid, and I wasn't sure I wanted to hear a story about some girl he knew way back when. Mindy's comment about Brad's maybe having a girlfriend came back to me. I swallowed and averted my gaze from him, looking down at my almost-empty glass.

"Should we head back to the office now?" I asked.

"I don't have to go back to the office."

"I do," I said, even though I didn't.

Brad looked at me for a beat too long, but then waved to the bartender for our bill and silently downed the rest of his beer.

After we settled up, Brad walked me back to Levenfield. Our easy camaraderie had shifted, and we were quiet. I hoped he just read it as my reluctance to go back to work. As we stood outside of the building, I asked, "How are you getting home?"

"I drove."

"Do you think you should be driving now?"

"I'll take a nap in my car first."

I shot him a skeptical look, considering that he could have easily taken a cab home. But I felt I needed to get away from his presence, so instead of questioning his decision, I just shook my head and said, "Okay. See you tomorrow." Before he could respond, I turned around, headed into the building and up to my office to call a cab.

In the elevator, I congratulated myself at again leaving Brad when I felt things were getting too murky. And his slightly strange behavior aside, it was a good drink. Other than some accidental knee touching and a hand inspection, it was an innocent night, and nothing happened to give Mindy or Jeff any fodder. And while I hadn't learned the reason for his sudden interest in hanging out, I wouldn't peg him as the weirdo they seemed to think he was, and I could see us rekindling our friendship.

***

Sitting at my computer at nine thirty the next morning, I remembered why I didn't like beer. Although I had only had a couple pints, I was feeling pretty rough. I had a dull headache, and the loud knock at my office door didn't help it. I looked up to see Jeff walking in with a large coffee. He sat down across from me. It was our usual morning ritual. "How was last night?" he asked.

I put my hand to my forehead. "Don't ask."

"I see." He took a sip of his coffee. "You got drunk with Brad?" He raised an eyebrow at me. I could take teasing from Jeff, and I was glad it was him asking and not Mindy. Maybe because Jeff was in a different department, we had a better dynamic; whereas I suspected Mindy viewed me as competition, so at times my "friendship" with her felt more like the keep-your-friends-close-and-your-enemies-closer type.

"Only two beers, but I guess I can't handle my liquor anymore." I purposely changed the subject. "How was your night?"

"It was good. I paid some bills, got my laundry done."

"Are you kidding me?" My mouth dropped open. "Your 'plans' last night were with laundry?"

"That's right." He gave me an amused smile.

"You suck." I narrowed my eyes at him, giving him a disgusted look.

Jeff laughed. "So, come on, spill."

"It was fine. We just went to the pub across the street, and then I came back to work." Jeff continued to smirk at me. "Oh, please. Don't give me that look. And, anyway, you and Mindy are the ones who ditched me."

"You could've said no."

"No, I couldn't, because I'm a nicer person than you. I felt bad that we all tried to blow him off."

Jeff guffawed. "You're not *that* much nicer."

I narrowed my eyes at him again and took a sip of my coffee. I was about to change the topic, but of course at that moment Mindy came scampering in. "How was your date with Brad last night?"

"Oh my god. What's wrong with you two? It's not a date if he invites everyone." I rolled my eyes at her. "So how was your night?"

Ignoring my attempts to deflect, Mindy perched herself on the corner of my desk. "So what did you guys talk about?"

"I don't know." I shrugged. For two people not keen on hanging out with Brad, they seemed awfully interested in what had gone on. "The same stuff we all talk about. If you had joined us, then you would know."

My email pinged, and I was saved by a message from Mr. Potato Head, who wanted to know my status on a research project. I had never been happier to hear from him. "Sorry, you two. I have to respond to this."

"Later," Jeff said while Mindy "harumphed," and they both exited my office.

I muddled through the day as best I could, though I noticed that Brad never made it into work. If it had been Jeff or Mindy, I wouldn't have thought twice about emailing them to make sure everything was okay, but I wasn't comfortable enough with Brad to do that. For some reason, it seemed intrusive. But I couldn't stop worrying. *What if something happened to him and I'm the last one to have seen him alive?* I felt guilty somehow, yet I did nothing and hoped for the best tomorrow. Perhaps Jeff was right; I wasn't that much nicer.

***

The next day I breathed a sigh of relief when I walked into work and glimpsed Brad alive and well in his office. Not like I was his keeper or anything, but I was a little irked. I had managed to show up to work the next day with my hangover, so it felt a little unfair that he chose to stay home with his.

I walked into his office. "Hey."

"Hey, yourself," he said, spinning in his chair toward me, grinning.

"I see that someone didn't come in yesterday," I said mock sternly.

He laughed. "Yeah. Sorry, I don't have much going on assignment-wise."

"So you pressured me into drinks, knowing that I had to come back to work while you got to go home and relax the next day?" I shook my head at him. *"Jerk."* I was teasing him, of course, and I could tell by the twinkle in his eye and smile he was enjoying it.

Not only was he enjoying it, but he was actually starting to blush.

While I had suspected it, in the bright light of day without the fuzziness of drinks, I could see that Brad Summers had a crush on me. I felt a sudden lightness, and my limbs tingled. He was adorable and boyish with his messy hair and innocent eyes, and, god, I was still so attracted to him. *It's so unfair!* my heart silently screamed. Given that he was a colleague and I couldn't do anything with this secret realization, it was once again time for me to exit.

"Well, I should go because some of us have work to do," I said mock haughtily, standing up straighter and pulling my shoulders back to look big and important.

Brad laughed. But when I turned around to leave, he said, "We should do it again."

"Sure." With my back to him, I waved my hand to say goodbye, knowing I was sporting a huge smile.

As soon as I exited Brad's office, Jeff walked by and raised his eyebrows. Since his office was next-door, I was sure he had heard our exchange. But he had only heard it. He hadn't *seen* the evidence that Brad Summers liked me. So I also waved my hand at Jeff and said brightly, "Morning, Jeff!" to deter him from making any snide remarks.

The rest of the day, I couldn't shake Brad out of my mind, nor could I quite believe that someone as good-looking as him would be into me. Not that I had a horrible self-image problem, but I grew up in Los Angeles where at the time everyone around me seemed blonder, tanner, and more surgically enhanced. I went to college and law school in Boston where I felt I fit in better. But I wanted to take only one bar exam, and California's being the hardest and longest exam, and being fresh off my law studies, I decided that was the one to take. Plus, I saw how people on the East Coast worked and, frankly, it was a lot. Not to say that I didn't work long hours. As an associate at Levenfield, I was always aware of my billables, so a billable eight-hour day sometimes translated into at least ten to twelve physical hours in the office. But when it's snowing outside, it makes it easier to stay inside and continue working.

Although I returned to California, reuniting with my family, I still felt like a bit of an outsider. My father was a well-known entertainment lawyer, and I liked how he commanded respect. My mother was a housewife, a term I use loosely, since she spent her days directing other people to work on her house when she was not at Pilates class or the spa. My younger sister, Saffron (nicknamed "Saffie"), was like my mom—bubbly, blond, and groomed to marry well. She was twenty-two and worked as a hostess-slash-aspiring actress, meaning she was having fun until she settled down. We didn't have any brothers, so I guess we each adopted our role in the family from the parent we more resembled.

My poor mother, though, didn't understand me, and had said on one too many occasions regarding my ex-boyfriend from law school, "It's a shame you and Trey couldn't make it work."

To which I always replied with an eye roll, "We couldn't make it work because he stayed in Boston." And where he met someone else. We had tried to do the long-distance thing when I first took the job in LA and went back and forth every other weekend. But eventually, law firm life took its toll, and after too many canceled trips *and* a cute paralegal in his office, we finally canceled the relationship.

"You know what I mean, darling. It's too bad you didn't find someone to marry before you graduated."

What I always wanted to retort was that I didn't need anyone to marry because I could afford to take care of myself, which I suspected was what she really meant. Of course, if my mother did have a point, it was that it was hard to find time to date with my work schedule. (I'm sure that's why office romances and hookups are so prevalent in my field.) But every time she uttered that dreaded statement, it made me feel like there was something wrong with me. So Brad's attention, although I didn't dare dream of acting on it, gave my ego a little boost, and I found myself smiling the rest of the day.

CHAPTER THREE

Drinks tonight? the email said. My smile widened.

Jeff and Mindy were not included in this invite.

Drinks twice in one week with Brad? For appearances' sake, I knew the right answer was no. And though it had been innocent so far, I felt uneasy now, since I was pretty sure he had a crush on me. My hands hovered over my keyboard, ready to decline his invite.

Then again, the deal I'd been working on had just closed, and work had been slow that week. And I had fun hanging out with Brad, and I always knew when it was time to end the night.

What's the saying about idle hands? I found mine typing, Sure. What time?

Within seconds his response appeared.

5:30. Same place as Friday. I'll meet you there.

I couldn't concentrate for the rest of the afternoon. I tried to avoid Jeff and Mindy so I wouldn't let my plans slip. I had promised myself that I wouldn't date anyone at the office. The problem was that I wasn't dating anyone outside the office either—so there was nothing and no one to rush home to. When 5:20 p.m. rolled around, I left the building quickly without saying goodbye to anyone.

Although I was a few minutes early, I found Brad already sitting at a table by one of the large windows. He didn't notice me right away. Instead, he was looking out the window where a sultry young woman in a minuscule tank top and bohemian peasant skirt was passing by slowly, her hip sway exaggerated by her clothes. An unexpected wave of jealousy hit me as his eyes seemed to follow her.

"Hi," I said, dropping my computer bag on the floor and intentionally interrupting his reverie.

He turned to me with a slow smile. "Hi, yourself. Glad you could make it."

His sluggish movements made me wonder if he had been there awhile. An empty glass on the table answered my question.

A server appeared as soon as I sat down, and I ordered a sauvignon blanc. It seemed a sensible choice for a weekday.

Brad nodded toward his empty glass. "I'll have another."

Waiting for our drinks, I started second-guessing my decision to come and briefly considered taking out my BlackBerry to fake a reason to leave. Brad was silent and looking out the window. Since he had been the one to suggest drinks, I decided to let him break the ice. In the meantime, I followed his lead and stared out the window until he finally spoke.

"I need an adventure," he said, still not looking at me.

"Yeah? Don't we all," I replied with a short snort.

Brad turned to me, perhaps surprised by my tone. Maybe he had been about to share something personal, and I'd hurt his feelings. Wasn't my mother always telling me I could be a bit harsh? So I cleared my throat and asked, "What type of adventure?"

Brad tilted his head, the look on his face thoughtful.

"I'm not sure." He gazed out the window again, his voice wistful. "Something to give me inspiration, though. Maybe just to go to different places."

I shifted in my seat. "What type of inspiration are you searching for? Something for the Richardson contract?" I said, trying to return to our usual easy banter.

Brad, though, answered me seriously. "I don't know. I want to do some sketching or take some photos. Maybe put together a series. You know, to tell a story."

No, I didn't know. But this was getting interesting. "What sort of story do you want to tell?"

He turned back to me and smiled. "I don't know. That's why I need inspiration."

"Can I help?" I smiled back, though I was having a hard time taking this conversation seriously. Most attorneys I knew didn't look for inspiration but saw life in billable hours.

"You can be my muse," he said, which made me wonder if he'd been joking the whole time just to get a reaction out of me.

"I hope you're not asking me to pose naked in your studio?" I thought I was being funny, but as soon as the words were out, I felt my cheeks burn.

I worried that Brad noticed my face reddening, because he looked at me for a second too long before responding. "Would you? Pose naked?"

I regretted my joke, but it was too late—my only choice was to carry on. I volleyed back, "Would you?"

He shrugged. "Sure. In fact, I have."

"Seriously? For who?"

"For myself." He grinned, probably enjoying the surprised look on my face. "I did some self-portraits for a project once."

"Are these portraits hanging in a gallery somewhere?" I

raised an eyebrow. I didn't want to flirt, but somehow I couldn't help myself. I tried to rationalize that I would have joked the same way with Jeff. But talking to Jeff didn't make me blush.

"You want to see them?"

I shook my head. "I'm just teasing you." I pulled out my ponytail holder to let my hair fall and shield my face a bit. My complexion tended to give away every emotion, and I didn't want Brad seeing what I was feeling.

"You can still be my muse. And," he added, leaning toward me, "you don't have to be naked."

I knew he was joking, but I couldn't look him in the eye. "We'll see."

I drank my wine too fast and ordered another. Brad told me about how he wanted to visit Peru and Namibia to photograph the landscapes in those countries. As we returned to our familiar and comfortable territory of travel and escape, I realized that the subject matter struck a chord. My life was good, but it was unimaginative. I'd traveled some with my parents, but I wasn't what you'd call adventurous. A study-abroad program here. Annual trips to Europe with my family there. All "adventures" in controlled settings. The most adventurous thing I'd done was to go to school on the East Coast for seven years, and even after that, I'd returned home. Listening to Brad talk about his post-bar trip backpacking through Asia and sleeping on beaches, and the various landscapes he wanted to see, made me realize that this—having secret drinks with a male colleague on a Thursday—was the riskiest thing I'd done in a long time.

As the wine hit me, I decided to embrace this adventure and escaped into the moment. I drank in the way Brad spoke, each word chosen carefully. I loved watching him stretch his long legs alongside the table. I loved the way he raised his glass to his lips, and I let my gaze linger too long. But mostly, I loved the way he looked at me—absorbing my every word and movement, making me feel truly seen in a way I never felt before. With each drink, the smiles between us were taking on new meanings. That evening something had shifted.

After I recounted a funny story about a trip to Napa where I was late for my flight and, having forgotten to move the bottles of wine in my carry-on into my suitcase before checking in my luggage, had a mad race around the airport to ship them home, Brad asked, "Do you still have some of this wine?"

"Actually, yes, I do."

"I'd like to try it." He looked at me seriously, and I thought I understood his meaning. I'd also made my decision. I made it long ago.

"Okay," I said. "But first, I'm going to find the ladies' room." *To catch my breath.*

In the ladies' room, I assessed myself in the mirror. As I reapplied my lip gloss, I reassured myself. *Nothing has happened yet, and who's to say anything will. No one has made any moves.* I refastened the cap on my lip gloss and took a last look at my reflection before walking out into the unknown.

Brad was already standing over the table and tucking a receipt into his wallet. He must have paid our bill—did that mean we were on a date? He suddenly seemed incredibly tall to me.

"Are you ready to go?" he said, his tone low and intense. His hazel eyes had turned dark with purpose.

My heart pounding, I looked straight into his dark eyes and said, "Yes."

We took a cab from the hotel and rode in silence to my house, each looking out our respective windows, but Brad's hand found mine and he entwined his fingers with mine, only letting go to pay the driver when we arrived at my place.

When we walked through the front door of my small Venice

bungalow, I gestured to the sofa in the front room. "Make yourself at home."

Brad looked around, but rather than heading to my sofa, he wandered over to my bookshelves, which were bursting with titles—all of which I'd read. My tastes ran to the eclectic. When it came to books, I'd been to more places than most—Elizabethan England, World War II–era Japan, turn-of-the-century Mexico—and perhaps those were my adventures. I stood in the entry, watching the smile playing at his lips as he examined my collection.

He turned to me. "So where's this wine I heard about?"

"Oh yes!" I said, feeling caught out staring at him. "Red or white?"

"Red."

I opened my bar cabinet and selected a cabernet sauvignon. I couldn't remember if I had actually bought that particular bottle on the trip, but that was a minor detail. I was more than a little buzzed, and after a few failed attempts at aiming the corkscrew at the cork, I held out the bottle and opener to Brad. "Would you mind?"

Brad took the bottle from me, and I went into the kitchen to get two glasses.

He followed me a moment later with the open bottle. "Here you go," he said, handing it to me. His proximity in my tiny kitchen made my hands shake as I tried to pour the wine. When I handed him his glass, we held them up and he touched his to mine, holding my gaze as he did so. Without saying a word, we both headed over to the sofa and sat at opposite ends. I kicked off my heels, tucked my legs beneath me on the cushion, and turned to face him.

"You have a lot of books." He gestured around the room, to the shelf and the precarious piles on my floor.

"Oh!" I also looked around and acted surprised, as if I were seeing them for the first time.

He laughed. "Have you read them all?"

"Pretty much. I don't like to put a book on my shelf that I haven't read. That's my to-read pile over there." I pointed to my armchair, which was stacked with some thirty volumes. Since I used my armchair as an extra shelf, it was probably clear that I didn't entertain much. Whenever my mother visited, she just shook her head. "Sweetheart, do you really *need* all these books? Really, let me bring Julia over. She could do wonders with this place." Julia was my mother's interior designer-slash-best friend-slash-therapist. I would not allow her in my space.

"What about you? Are you a big reader?" I asked Brad.

"Not really. In fact, I don't think I've read a novel since high school English."

"How awful." I made a face, and he laughed.

"Yeah, with all my science and engineering classes, there weren't many chances to read literature in college. Then there was law school, and now there's work."

I was incredibly attracted to Brad, but it was already clear to me that other than Levenfield, we didn't have much in common. He was an engineer who liked adventure and physical activities like hiking and surfing. I preferred sitting in coffee shops and perusing my way through bookstores. He backpacked around Asia and slept on beaches. I traveled to European cities and slept on four-hundred-thread-count hotel sheets. I felt we were complete opposites even physically. He was tall and light-eyed, with golden chestnut hair and lightly tanned skin. I was petite with dark eyes and hair. It amused me that he looked more like the stereotypical Californian than I did. But Brad seemed different, too, like he didn't quite belong. There was an unaffected quality and earnestness about him that was different from the other guys

I'd met in LA. Maybe that was why we found ourselves sitting on my sofa drinking wine. Perhaps he recognized that I didn't quite fit either.

"You mentioned you like to draw. Have you worked on anything lately?" I asked.

"When I have time, I like to sketch. I even keep a sketchbook and some charcoal in my car. I recently did a nude, a picture of a woman on a beach."

Oh no, back to the topic of nudity. If I was embarrassed at the bar, I was even more so sitting alone with him in my home. Yet I couldn't help but pursue it.

"Really? Anyone you know?"

I took the last sip of my wine and felt it burn my throat, fueling my jealousy toward some unknown woman whom he had once been inspired to sketch.

I wondered if he could tell I was jealous, because he laughed and said, "No, just an image in my mind."

He reached for the wine bottle on the coffee table and refilled both our glasses. When he sat back, he moved in a little closer so that he was sitting in the middle of the sofa. Then, suddenly it seemed, he was sitting right next to me. I wasn't drunk, but I'd consumed enough wine by that point that his closeness didn't faze me. In fact, I leaned back on the armrest and comfortably stretched my legs across his lap. As we talked, he stroked my legs, running his hand under the fabric of my skirt. My nerves blunted by wine, I watched him, fascinated, as he expertly slid off my skirt. There was no fumbling or asking me to shift one way or another. I had never been with someone so smooth and practiced.

"Are you hitting on me?" I asked, even though we were obviously well past that point. But a part of me wanted to make sure this was happening. He smiled and pulled me on top of him so that I was straddling him. Then he gently pulled my shirt over my head and set it down where I had been sitting. He ran his hands down my back and whispered, "You are so beautiful."

"So are you," I said as I began undoing the buttons of his shirt. That was the perfect word for him—beautiful. Sexy could mean so many things. Handsome sounded generic. Brad was beautiful. I carefully slid his shirt off him and then pulled the T-shirt he wore beneath it over his head, only briefly breaking eye contact. As if reading my thoughts, he swept me up and said, "Where's the bedroom?"

In one motion he laid me on the bed. I watched his every move as he slipped off his shoes, then his belt, and slid off his pants. We kept our eyes on each other the entire time. He fell over me, our mouths and hands seeking out each other as if we were long-lost lovers finally reunited—insatiable and greedy.

***

Afterward, we lay in my bed, the sheet over us, my head resting on Brad's chest and his arm around me, his fingers absent-mindedly stroking my arm; my fingers doing the same on his chest. In every television show, this was the point where someone asks, "What are you thinking?" But I wasn't that person. I preferred this contented silence, as one word might break the spell.

Brad, however, chose to break it. "Jae, I'm sorry," he said, his voice uneasy. "I have something to tell you."

My hand that was lightly tracing circles on his chest froze. *This can't be good.* Had Mindy been right about a girlfriend? I felt a confession coming, and I wished I could close my ears.

I rolled off him and slid farther under the covers, trying to protect myself from what his words might be. But when Brad didn't say anything for a minute, I wondered if maybe he had planned to make a bad joke and then thought better of it. So I turned back to him and rested my head on his shoulder where it was before. He wrapped his arms around me, and I let my arm fall across his chest.

"This feels nice," he said into the dark, again breaking the silence. "This feels right."

I nodded but didn't say anything. It did. It felt like we belonged together. I didn't want to ever move. I didn't want the sun to rise. And I didn't want him to tell me anything unless he was feeling exactly how I was feeling at that moment, which was that I wanted us to lie there forever.

"But, Jae, there's something you should know," he started again, holding me tighter, so that I couldn't turn away again.

"Can it wait till tomorrow?" I looked up at him and he was staring at the ceiling, but I couldn't make out his expression in the dark. "We've had too much wine tonight for talking."

He took a deep breath and nodded. "Okay." He kissed the top of my head, and it seemed like I had just bought us time between the before and after.

In that moment, I felt the warmth of his skin enveloping me. Nothing mattered but this feeling. I reached up and kissed him. He turned over and was on top of me again. His mouth closed in on mine. His hands ran through my hair and traveled down my body. His kisses followed his hands, and I could feel that he was ready again.

With every thrust, every movement of his body over mine, I quickly moved toward my brink, then reached it. I had never felt so unselfconscious, so completely in the moment. I felt him explode inside me, and then his body collapsed on top of mine. His breathing was heavy, his heart racing against mine. We remained silent, simply breathing. Our breath slowed in tandem until we fell asleep, our bodies melded together.

CHAPTER FOUR

When I woke up, it was to soft velvet kisses slowly teasing my lips. My lips awakened and teased his back. His body lay over mine, and he slowly began to move his hips against me. Three times in one night was a new experience for me. My hips slowly began to move in the same rhythm, and soon he was inside me again—this time much slower, but still just as intense. When he came, it was much quieter. It was intimate; it was gorgeous; it was as if Brad were finally mine. I loved his body in the dark. I loved his body melted with mine. The term *soulmate* flickered through my mind.

He stroked my hair, my face, and looked into my eyes and kissed me again. He then stood up without saying anything and went into the bathroom. I lay there listening to him and the shower running in the other room. When he returned to the bedroom, he began collecting his things. The backlight of the bathroom showed off his long, lean figure, and I watched him get dressed. In order to tie his shoes, he placed them one at a time on the bed frame. This posture showed off his muscles, strong and perfect. His anatomy defied his career—I could imagine him as a carpenter or an outdoorsman, his body in perfect symmetry with his vocation.

I wanted him to stay, but was too shy to ask. Besides, it was already four o'clock in the morning, and we needed to be at work in a few hours. Of course, he had to go home and change clothes. I closed my eyes, feeling sleep closing in again. I could hear him near me and then felt his lips on my forehead. I opened my eyes to look at him. "Good night," he whispered. I smiled and closed my eyes again. I didn't want to watch him walk out the door.

***

When I opened my eyes, it was seven thirty. I dreaded facing the workday on only a few hours of broken sleep and a red-wine hangover. But with the knowledge that I'd see Brad again soon, I resolved to make an effort. In the bathroom mirror, I didn't completely recognize myself and this particular brand of dishevelment. Eyeliner smeared, hair tangled, lips swollen from the night's activities—I had never felt sexier.

Fueled on Advil and coffee, I was walking out my front door when my BlackBerry buzzed with an email.

Left my watch at your place.

I smiled at this first contact the "morning after." I searched around the living room and sofa, moving the cushions, bringing back memories of him moving closer to me. Next I went to the bedroom, where I found his watch on my nightstand. I wished I could keep it there as a happy memory, but it was not mine to keep.

I typed back: Found it.

Within seconds my BlackBerry buzzed again: Leave it. Will collect later.

My pulse quickened as I wondered whether he was as concerned as I was about gossip and didn't want to take any chances. But considering that I could easily hand it off to him at the office, his message made it clear that he wanted to see me again outside work. So I placed his watch back on the nightstand. I liked the idea of Brad's personal items spending the day in my home.

At work, everything was business as usual. Brad and I did not exchange emails or even run into each other. Which was just as well, since it took all of my concentration simply to stay awake. Getting my work done was no easy feat. Images from the night before kept reappearing in my mind—a flash of naked skin, Brad carrying me to bed, Brad's body moving in sync with mine.

A little after four o'clock, my office phone rang. Brad's name showed on the screen. I picked up.

"Hello?" I said, my senses suddenly alert.

"Hey," he said softly, and then cleared his throat; I couldn't tell if the need was from nerves or exhaustion. "How are you?"

"I've been better. You?"

He let out a groan. "Surviving."

"I hear that." I laughed in sympathy, but his groan made me warm. "So when would you like to pick up your watch?"

"Can I pick it up tonight?"

My heart skipped a beat, knowing I would see him again soon. "Sure. What time?"

"Now?" He laughed weakly.

"I wish," I said, also ready for the workday to be over. "How 'bout we both leave at five and meet at my place?" I gave him my address.

"Okay. You go first and I'll follow you. Just email me when you leave."

At exactly five o'clock, I shut down my computer and packed my laptop and some files to work on that weekend, as it hadn't been one of my more productive days. Before I closed the door to my office, I emailed Brad on my BlackBerry.

Leaving now.

On my way out to the elevators, I passed Brad's office and glanced in. He looked up right as I was passing. I felt an electric shock go through me when our eyes met. Just a simple look from him and I was on fire. He gave me a small smile and wave, and I returned a slight nod, then continued to the elevators. I felt myself blushing with memories of the previous night, and in the elevator, I focused my gaze on the ground while I glowed inside.

Brad appeared at my door only ten minutes after I had arrived home.

"Hi." I smiled as I let him in.

"Hi." He smiled tiredly back. He stepped into my bungalow and gave me a hug. Although this hug was tamer than the night before, I could feel the memories in his arms as I breathed him in.

"Come on in." I gestured to the living room. "Would you like something to drink?"

Brad groaned and dramatically put his hand on his forehead. "No, thank you."

I laughed. "I was thinking more along the lines of water."

"Oh," he laughed back. "Sure." He sat down on my sofa and leaned back, stifling a yawn. "Ugh. What a day."

"Yeah, it was pretty rough. Thank god tomorrow is Saturday." I walked over to hand him his glass of water, and then collected his watch from the bedroom, placing it on the coffee table in front of him.

"Thanks," he said, looking up at me from the sofa.

"You're welcome." I sat next to him but perched myself at the edge of the cushion.

Brad reached for the water and took a sip. Neither of us said anything for several seconds, but it felt longer. I wrote it off as the awkwardness of the morning after.

Brad turned to me, his eyes serious. "So," he started, then paused.

Something unreadable flickered across his face.

Then he took another sip of water before asking, "So, uh, are you going to be in the office tomorrow?" At Levenfield, first-year associates typically spent most of their weekends in the office, conspicuously trying to out-bill each other.

"No. I brought stuff home, so I think I'll just work from here tomorrow." I patted a sofa cushion.

His eyes followed my hand, resting there a moment before he raised them back to mine. "Would you be up for coffee or lunch tomorrow?"

I nodded. "Sure. Just shoot me an email in the morning and let me know what time." I tried to play it cool. *He wants to spend time with me outside the bedroom. So definitely not a one-night stand.*

"Okay, I'll do that." He finished the last sip of his water and then said abruptly, "I should get going."

"Oh? Okay," I said as we both stood up, my small hope of last night's repeat performance extinguished. He grabbed his watch, slid it into his pants pocket, and headed toward the door. I followed to let him out. When I opened the door, he turned and hugged me again before leaving. It was more than a friendly hug and less than a passionate hug. I felt that there was some meaning behind it, but my sluggish brain couldn't discern what the meaning was. I was too exhausted.

***

Saturday morning I woke up early, having fallen asleep around eight. Rather than tackling the pile of mail that had been collecting on my kitchen table, I drank my coffee and dove right into work, making up the billables I should have done the day before.

By one o'clock, I still hadn't heard from Brad, so I emailed him: Lunch?

It took a few minutes before he responded.

> I'm on a roll. How about coffee later?

I felt a small stab of disappointment but shook it off.

I emailed back.

> I'm about to run some errands down your way. How about a coffee then? Around 3:30?

> Cool. I'll need a break then.

Later then, I typed back happily. I closed my laptop and decided to grab something to eat while I was out. That night I was meeting my family for an early dinner to celebrate Saffie's twenty-third birthday, before she met up to party with her friends. One of the tasks I'd put off was buying her a present, so I planned to head to her favorite store to buy her a ridiculously expensive candle.

As I drove up to Santa Monica, everything was bright and in clear focus—the blue of the sky, the green of the leaves, and the white of the clouds—the type of day I imagine people think of when they hear *Los Angeles*. Near the pier, the waterfront was populated with people biking, skating, running, and making the most of the day. Instead of feeling detached, today I felt like my fellow Angelenos as I cheerfully ran my errands, stepping in and out of stores, purchasing a smoothie, birthday card, and the candle, as well as popping into a bookstore to pick up a new memoir I'd heard about. Around three o'clock, I was back at my car, and so I emailed Brad.

> I'm about 30 minutes away. Is it almost time for that coffee break?

He must have been right at his computer because his response came a minute later.

> Sorry but I'm making lots of progress. Don't want to lose momentum. Can we meet later?

My cheerful mood evaporated as I typed back.

> Sorry, later is too late. I'm meeting my parents at 6 for dinner.

Brad responded: What are you doing after dinner? Can we have coffee then?

I wondered whether he still meant coffee or drinks? But it didn't matter because I replied: We'll see. I'll email you when I'm done with dinner.

After being blown off twice, I wasn't in the mood to make any promises. I figured if I was still upset later, I could give him the same treatment. With that thought, I started the car and drove home.

CHAPTER FIVE

Given that I was attending a celebration dinner, I decided to wear a red sundress and wrap that my mother had bought me. Unlike my mother and sister, I normally shied away from bright colors and had adopted a rather muted-colored, conservative wardrobe to fit in with my fellow associates at work. And though I was still undecided about meeting Brad later, I figured I wouldn't mind him seeing me in something other than my usual black skirt.

My parents arrived fifteen minutes earlier than I expected. "Hello! Hello!" I answered the door, and said quickly, "Let me just grab my purse."

"No rush, darling," my mother said as she pushed the door open wider and walked inside, my father right behind her. Although in her early fifties, my mother still resembled a Beach Barbie—blond and spray tanned with the figure of a twenty-year-old. My father's dark blond hair was peppered with gray, but his daily runs kept him young looking as well.

My mother stood in the middle of my living room, assessing

it. "It looks like you've made an effort in here," she remarked while I inwardly bristled.

Never mind that her daughter had graduated from Harvard Law School and made a healthy $100K-plus per year at a prestigious law firm—sometimes it felt like all she cared about were my looks, my single status, and my ability to keep house. I tried not to let it bother me, but there was always that part of me that wanted my parents' approval, something they seemed to generously grant my sister.

"Yes, I had the afternoon off today, so I was able to do some straightening up."

My mother turned to me. "As you should! It's ridiculous how much they work you young attorneys." She shook her head. "I blame your father for this career choice."

My father and I shared a smile, and he shrugged. Although I knew he was a shark at work, at home he let my mother run the show.

Her eyes wandered to my kitchen, where she spied some dirty glasses in my sink, and she clucked her tongue. Then she looked up and studied the ceiling.

"This ceiling is so outdated." She sighed dramatically. "You should really paint this place. Or at least hang up some artwork." She waved a hand in the direction of my living room.

"My living room is fine, Mom. And I didn't know a ceiling could be 'outdated.'"

My mother shrugged. "Well, I guess you're never here to enjoy it anyway, so what does it matter?"

I shot my father a pleading look, and he gave me a sympathetic smile. And so, before she could walk farther into my place, he said, "Come on, Diane. We don't want to be late."

***

When we arrived at the restaurant, Saffie was already there and seated at the table with a cocktail, merrily texting on her phone.

"Here's the birthday girl," my mother said, giving my sister a wide smile. "Hello, darling."

"Hey, Mom!" They gave each other an enthusiastic kiss on the cheek. Not an air-kiss, but an actual one, and I felt the usual stab of envy at their easy affection.

Once we all greeted Saffie, wished her a happy birthday, and sat down, my father asked, "Should we order a bottle of wine?"

"Ooh, how 'bout champagne?" said Saffie, clapping her hands.

"Sounds great," I chimed in. "And only one glass for me because I'm meeting someone after dinner." I'd made up my mind to see Brad after all.

"Oh?" said my mother and Saffie in unison, clearly interested in hearing more. I didn't even have to look at them to know that their eyebrows were raised, their eyes shiny and curious.

"Just a friend," I said, keeping my eyes on the menu. I would have loved to say it was a date, but I didn't want to raise their hopes, or mine.

Though we were technically a close family, our time spent together always left me vaguely depressed. Looking around at their golden heads, it was sometimes hard not to feel like the outsider. My dad is really my stepfather who adopted me when I was one year old. My biological father died in a car accident when my mother was newly pregnant with me, and I take after his dark hair and eyes. My dad was his best friend from law school, and he and my mother initially bonded together in their grief, eventually fell in love, and married. Sometimes I wonder if my father had lived, whether my mother and I would have had a totally different relationship, complete with teenage angst and door slamming. While we have that typical mother-daughter push-and-pull relationship, since I'm all that remains of her first love, there is always a restraint, almost a politeness between us, and at times I would almost relish a full-on fight. Instead, she mildly finds fault, and I get somewhat irritated.

And while I love my sister, we were very different individuals growing up, without a lot in common. We were five years and worlds apart. She was the fun one; I was the serious one. When people met us for the first time, they were always surprised to learn we were sisters. Though we were close when we were younger, Saffie seeming to copy everything I did and always wanting my attention, things started to shift when she was entering junior high and I was finishing high school; she was discovering boys and clothes and popular culture and had figured out that though her older sister may have been smart and got good grades, she definitely wasn't cool. Then because I was living on the East Coast during her high school and college years, when I returned home, we never really reconnected.

After we had ordered and Saffie filled us in on her plans later that night, our mom told us the family gossip, and I pretended to be interested. Mostly the talk was about my cousins' marital statuses, pregnancies, and children; and since my sister was only twenty-three and more like my cousins than I was, I felt like these details were meant to remind me that I was the only one who wasn't married with children. Most of my cousins met their future spouses in college or had a "career" of being a salesperson in some clothing boutique or the equivalent before snagging their husbands. I couldn't help but feel—quite snidely—that theirs wasn't the kind of "success" I wanted to achieve in my life.

One Christmas, as my cousin Lisa reached for a cookie, her husband gave her a disapproving look and said, "Are you sure you want to do that?" and she put the cookie down. That was their marriage? Not being able to have a cookie on Christmas because it could ruin her size zero figure? I felt lucky to have other options in my life. I wished my mother could see that.

After our entrées but before the dessert arrived, I excused myself to go to the bathroom. Once there, I emailed Brad: Dinner is ending earlier than I thought, so I can still meet up for that coffee.

I waited a couple minutes for Brad's response, freshening up my makeup, but nothing. I didn't want my mom or Saffie having to come find me, so I gave up and went back to the table.

After our dessert came, I felt my BlackBerry vibrating in my purse. Though doing so was rude, I pulled it out to check it—as I'd hoped, the message was from Brad.

"Sorry," I said to my parents, although my family was used to it as they'd watched my father do the same constantly over the years. "I just need to respond to this."

Brad wrote, Okay. Can you meet me at the office?

Sure, I typed. And you're still at the office???!

> Yes, but I'm ready for a break. What time will you be done?
>
> We're finishing up dessert. I'll be there in the next 30 minutes.

Brad didn't respond immediately, but I figured we were on for that night, so I slipped my BlackBerry back into my bag.

"Everything okay?" my mother asked.

"Yeah. Just work stuff."

My mother shook her head. "On a Saturday night? Don't they know you have a life?"

Saffie grinned and said cheekily, "It's not work. It's her date tonight."

I rolled my eyes at her, but I couldn't help the grin spreading across my face.

My mother, who had been noticeably silent on the subject earlier, finally asked, "So who is this friend you're meeting?"

"He's a friend from work. Another lawyer."

"What type of law?" my father chimed in.

"Real estate," I answered my father, and then turned to my mother. "It's just some colleagues hanging out on a Saturday. Associate bonding and all."

When I caught Saffie's eye, she mouthed, "Yeah, right," and smirked.

My parents offered to drive me to my office after dinner, but I insisted on taking a cab. When the valet brought their car around, my mother leaned in and hugged me. "Have fun with your friend tonight." Her hopeful tone stirred up both affection and mild annoyance in me, as if I would be disappointing her if I didn't enjoy my night.

In the cab, I emailed Brad to let him know I was on my way and asked him to meet me outside. It was a Saturday night, and while there would be fewer people in the building, that meant it would be more noticeable and suspect if I went up to Brad's office. But when I arrived, there was no Brad outside. I paid the cab driver and waited in the night air. That part of town was dead in the evening, and I wondered whether to go inside. I emailed Brad again: I'm here. Should I come up?

He swiftly responded, No. Packing up now. Coming down.

A new office building was being built across the street, and I walked over to the construction site. At the moment, it was a large hole in the ground surrounded by a high chain-link fence. I entwined my fingers with the links and leaned into the fence, looking down into the hole. I thought to myself, *What if I lean too far?* If I fell, I would surely die. Suddenly, a large boom startled me, and I looked up to see colored light bursting into the black sky. Fireworks. It brought me back to myself, and I laughed, thinking, *What's wrong with me? One moment I'm morose, thinking of how it would feel plunging to my death; in the next, I suddenly feel alive and exhilarated.* I would come back to this moment again and again.

"Hey," Brad interrupted my philosophical musings.

I spun around, smiling. "Hey!"

My excitement faded when I saw his face. He wasn't smiling and didn't look at all happy to see me. For someone who had originally suggested meeting up for coffee, he looked rather miserable.

"Where should we go?" I asked, suddenly unsure of what the evening held.

"I'm probably going to keep working tonight, so someplace close."

Ah! So he's miserable about work, I told myself. That was something I could understand.

"It's nine o'clock. You're really coming back to work?" I asked.

"Maybe." Brad looked around, appearing tense.

"Um, there's a Starbucks not too far from here," I said. "It might still be open."

"No." He didn't look at me but instead kept nervously looking around us, as if uncomfortable being seen with me.

Okay. Brad was starting to piss me off. *He* had invited me out for coffee. But now he looked like this was the last place he wanted to be. *And* he'd rejected my suggestion, which I'd only made with his workload in mind. He was quickly ruining my Saturday night, and I was about to say as much.

But then he said, "I have my car. I know a place."

Since I was already there and with no cabs in sight, I figured I might as well see where the evening went. We walked to the garage without talking until he stopped at a silver Porsche. I was surprised. I guess I shouldn't have been, since it was LA, where what you drive is who you are, and he was a young attorney at a big firm making big money. Wearing a plain gray T-shirt, jeans, and leather flip-flops, Brad seemed so unassuming that I just assumed he'd be driving a silver Honda or Prius or something else fuel efficient.

Perhaps sensing my unspoken question, Brad said, "It's my dad's car. Mine is in the shop."

Instead of showing off and driving too fast in a sports car, like I would expect most twenty-something guys in his position would, Brad drove us quietly, carefully focused on the road and our destination.

He took us to an Italian-style coffee-slash-wine bar that I had never been to before. It was dark and half-empty. We sat at a small rustic-looking table, and a server came by and handed us menus.

"I haven't eaten yet. Do you mind if I get dinner?" Brad said.

"Go for it." I wasn't hungry, but I scanned the menu anyway. I turned it over to the wine list. "I'm just going to have a glass of wine. Since I'm not working tonight, for once I'm not really in need of caffeine."

For someone who was adamant earlier about going back to work, Brad seemed easily swayed now that we were out, and ordered a beer.

But he still didn't seem relaxed. I filled the conversation by commenting on the café and asking how he'd found it. "I noticed it on my way to work," Brad said, but didn't elaborate.

When the server arrived with Brad's food, Brad tried talking to him in Spanish, and I knew enough of the language to know he was asking him about the aquarium that was part of the bar's decor. I wondered if this was an attempt to avoid conversation with me.

But after a few bites of his dinner and finishing off his beer, he finally relaxed and became more animated, the way he'd acted the other times we'd been out together. I asked him what he was working on, and he said it was a pro bono case that he was helping with, trying to stop an eviction situation for an elderly woman who had lived her whole life in the same apartment.

"Wow, good for you. She's lucky to have such a dedicated attorney," I said, and then took a sip of wine as I felt the tips of my ears go red.

Our firm encouraged us to take on pro bono matters, and I had yet to. And so while Brad had been busy all day trying to help people, I had been focused solely on when our next date was.

Talking about the case seemed to energize him as he told me what case law he'd found so far to support his arguments and what he still needed. We brainstormed some possible searches to try, and then when Brad was finished with his dinner and me with my wine, he offered to drive me home.

In the car, sitting next to Brad, with two glasses of wine in me, the windows open and the warm night air whipping past us, I was happy.

It was almost eleven o'clock when Brad pulled into my driveway, and I guessed that he probably wasn't going back to work.

"Would you like to come in?" I asked.

Brad waited a beat, enough for insecurity to gnaw at me. "Okay," he said in a tone I couldn't discern, and turned off the ignition.

Once inside my place, I offered him something to drink.

"Thanks, I'll just have some water."

I felt a slight shrinking in my heart, as maybe it meant he

didn't intend to stay long and needed to be sober to drive home. I poured him a glass of water and then turned on some music, hoping to cover up any awkwardness, and we each took a corner of the sofa.

As I was trying to think of something to say, Brad suddenly said, "I want to run away."

"What do you mean?" I braced myself, confused by his unexpected statement.

"Sorry. Forget it." Brad's hazel eyes were large and vulnerable.

I stared at him for a second too long, not knowing what to say. Brad stared back at me sadly, and I would have said anything if I knew what words would make him stop looking at me like that. He solved my dilemma by leaning over and wrapping his arms around my waist and placing his head in my lap. "I'm so sorry, Jae."

I gently caressed his hair. "Sorry about what?"

"About everything. That I just said I wanted to run away and for what I have to tell you. You're going to hate me."

My hand froze and I took a deep breath, remembering that he had wanted to tell me something after we had sex. I wanted to make him sit up, but I also didn't want to look at him.

"What is it?" I said carefully, my voice belying the buzzing in my brain.

"I have a daughter."

"Okay," I said slowly. It wasn't the worst news in the world. Therefore, I knew there was more.

"She's only three months old. Her name is Ivy."

Reflexively, both my hands flew up and away from Brad. *Three months?*

Mindy had said Brad might have a girlfriend, and I now suspected he had more than a girlfriend—he had a *family.*

I moved and tried pushing Brad off my lap. "You need to sit up to tell me the rest."

Brad gripped my waist tighter for a second, but then relented and sat up, his back against the arm of the sofa. He ran his hands down his face and then looked at me.

There was whirring in my brain, and I started, "Brad, are you . . ." I paused, not quite believing I was asking this, and not sure I wanted the answer. "Are you *married*?"

He stared at me, silent, his eyes forlorn.

"Oh my god!" I said, wanting to jump off the sofa and shove him out the door, but was frozen to my spot.

"We were broken up when I found out she was pregnant," Brad said quickly, probably guessing from my horrified look that he had only a few seconds to explain. "She had told me she was on the Pill, but something went wrong. I don't know. She said she wasn't going to have the baby, but time passed, and nothing happened. And the longer she was pregnant, the more responsible I felt—"

"Stop," I interrupted him. While he had been talking, my mind was spinning with various scenarios. "If you're going to tell me this story, you need to start from the beginning. I mean, who is she? You were single two years ago, and now you're *married* with an infant daughter?"

"She was my law school girlfriend. I met her at a party my first year, and she was an undergrad at UCLA. While everything was great during the first few months we were dating, after that it was like she either loved me or hated me, and we'd break up, but then get back together, and it went on like that for three years." He swallowed. "When I first met you that summer, we had broken up."

"But you're together now," I said.

Brad looked up at the ceiling and blinked a few times. I wondered if he was going to cry.

"My last year of school, she stole my credit cards, pretending that she thought they were hers. She charged outrageous amounts, and with that on top of my school loans, I didn't see how I would get out of debt for years. Right before graduation, it was the final straw, and I broke up with her, thinking we were finally over. But then when I was studying for the bar, she was at my apartment crying and apologizing, and honestly, it was just easier to get back together those months to keep some peace so I could focus on studying. And during that time, she really supported me, making sure I ate, cleaning my apartment . . . ," he trailed off, and swallowed. "It seemed like she had really changed."

Brad finally looked at me, likely wanting to see my expression, but I kept my face neutral because I just needed to hear everything. When I didn't say anything, he continued. "So after the bar exam, we went on a month-long trip to Asia. Any truce we'd had was over in the first week, and we spent most of the trip arguing. And when we got back, that's when we found out she was pregnant."

"*Clearly*, you didn't spend the entire trip arguing," I said, not sure what to believe.

"Not the entire trip, but most." He shrugged weakly. "And we only had sex once, but that was it."

"Well, once was enough. And you *married* her? You didn't *have* to get married to support your daughter."

"But I did," he said, his eyes boring into mine. "When Kathryn first learned she was pregnant, she wanted to get an abortion. I said I would support whatever decision she made, and that if she wanted to keep it, I'd help provide for them. She waited another month, and then told me that the only way she would have the baby would be if I married her. And during that time, waiting for her decision, the more responsible I felt, and I wanted to know my child. So, even though I knew I was probably making a mistake, I agreed, and we got married at city hall."

I didn't say anything as my mind tried to make sense of his story.

Brad swallowed. "And, Jae, I'm sorry. You're the last person I should be looking to for sympathy. But between the credit card debt, my law school loans, and now supporting her and my daughter, and the complete shit show of my marriage, I feel lost all the time. I never could have imagined that my life would get this out of control."

Considering the Porsche in my driveway, I said, "I don't know their situation, but could you ask your parents for help?"

"Oh god, no." Brad shook his head, then turned it to the side away from me, his eyes tightly closed. "I'm their only child. I couldn't possibly let them know that they raised a total fuckup."

I sighed. While I know women should support other women, I knew Brad, and I didn't know her. And so from what he omitted, I filled in the blanks and created my own story. Brad's girlfriend had been taking advantage of him financially in law school. When she recognized that her cash flow was about to disappear, she decided to get pregnant in order to keep him supporting her. It appeared that her plan had been wildly successful—but it was also so transparent. And given the fact that he had too much pride to tell his parents, I doubted Brad's ego would let him admit that he'd been duped.

I wanted to shout, *"Come on! All the years you were dating her, and she didn't get pregnant? How convenient that it happened when you were breaking up with her but still took her on an all-expenses-paid-by-you trip to Asia. She knew what she was doing. Why did you let her take advantage of you?"*

But I'd also been duped. Brad and I weren't in the early stages of a relationship. I was a one-night stand for a married man.

"So you were just drunk that night," I said, not looking at him.

"Oh, Jae, I'm sorry." He came closer to me on the sofa and

took my hands. "I'd been drinking, but that wasn't it. I think about you all the time. It's why I can't hang out at any associates' events. And I try to stay in my office as much as I can so as not to see you. But this week, I let myself drink and, god, I don't know. Hanging out with you reminded me of who I was even just a year ago, and that if I hadn't been so stupid, I could have been with you and had a totally different life. And now I feel so horrible and guilty toward you, and toward my daughter."

As you should, I thought.

I pulled my hands away. "It's late. You should go."

"I'm so sorry. I'm an asshole, and I would never want to hurt you."

"But you did," I said quietly. "So you need to leave, and we need to pretend this never happened."

I stood up reluctantly. Brad looked at me sadly but stood up too. I let him put his arms around me and hold me close for a last goodbye. I wrapped my arms around him as well. He started to rub his hands along my back and, even after everything he told me, I savored the feeling, knowing I wouldn't feel his hands again. Finally, Brad pulled back. "I'll let myself out," he said, his voice slightly husky.

Unable to think clearly, I simply mumbled, "Okay."

Even so, we still stood there for several more seconds, looking at each other. Brad sighed and then pulled me in one last time, holding me tight and stroking my hair.

"Goodbye, Jae," he said. He then let go of me and let himself out.

Once the door shut, I fell back onto my sofa, pulling the throw blanket over me, and closed my eyes as I felt a heaviness in my heart and brain.

CHAPTER SIX

When I opened my eyes, morning light was streaming through my windows. It was a new day, and everything had changed. I wasn't sure if I was glad I had the twenty-four-hour buffer between Brad's confession or disappointed that I would have too much time to think before going into work on Monday.

That Sunday I caught up on some assignments, cleaned my place, and took a novel off my almost-ready-to-topple-over to-be-read pile. But it was all a distraction, and not a very good one as I went over various *what if* scenarios. I believed Brad, which made it so much worse. If I thought he was simply a player, then I would have felt angry and hated him. But instead, I knew he felt the same way about me as I did him, and there was absolutely nothing that could be done about it—and I would have to avoid him at the office for totally different reasons than I had a week ago.

On Monday, Brad made it easy to evade him, since he didn't show up to work. That was unusual, and after what he had communicated to me Saturday night, I was a little scared. He had held onto me and said he wanted to run away—*What if that was a cry for help? What if Brad crashed his car or did something crazy after leaving my house?*

I shot off an email from work.

Everything okay?

I used his Levenfield email, and I realized that I didn't know his phone number or personal email.

Monday came and went with no word from Brad. Tuesday morning, he was back in the office, and I felt I could finally breathe easily even though I was annoyed that he had ignored my email. Adding to his unusual behavior, he kept his door shut all day. Three days had gone by since he had unburdened his soul to me, and now I was getting the silent treatment. Even though we agreed it was for the best, by Wednesday I felt a little pissed; so I doubled down on work, determined to forget Brad Summers.

This decision was easily supported by what was happening at work. I had just been assigned to a new deal that had a tight turnaround for closing. That meant lots of tedious document review and due diligence in my immediate future. And for the next two weeks, I stayed in my office until 2:00 a.m. every night and woke up at 7:00 a.m. the next day to do it all again. My grueling schedule allowed me to bury my pain and keep my distance from Brad, who kept his as well.

On Friday afternoon at the end of that period, we had a team meeting scheduled to discuss the status of the project and an upcoming site visit. Most lawyers dreaded business travel, but being young and not having any family or home responsibilities, I viewed it as a refreshing change of scenery, even if it involved sitting in some other office's conference room, reviewing documents. Plus, the proposed trip, on the firm's dime, was to San

Francisco, where Maya, my best friend from law school, lived and worked.

I was one of the first to arrive in the conference room. One by one the usual players entered the room as well as a couple new ones. Then Brad walked in.

My stomach clenched, and my palms started sweating. I wasn't sure of the expression on my face, but as he walked past me, he nodded. I looked down at my BlackBerry, pretending to check my email. Yes, I had known that the project was a joint effort between the corporate, intellectual property, and real estate departments—but he hadn't been involved up to that point. He sat two seats down from me, so he was out of my line of vision, but I was in his. I could feel my cheeks beginning to burn, and I shifted my focus to my notepad to try to control my emotions. Fortunately, Mitch, the head partner in charge of the deal, began talking.

"As you can see, we're adding to the team today. Apex wants a closing date in the next month. In order for that to happen, we need to get people up to San Francisco to start collecting and reviewing Aventis's files."

Mitch paused and looked around the room.

"Jasmine, Oliver, and Brad, start packing. You're flying out Sunday to hit the ground running on Monday. Aaron will be in charge of the due diligence and will work with Aventis's management." Aaron was a young partner in the corporate department whom I liked, and I had assumed he'd be going to San Francisco with me. Oliver was a mid-level IP associate whom I didn't know very well, but he regularly assisted with our department. "Aaron and Jasmine have been working with this client and deal, so you two can bring Brad and Oliver up to speed on the details."

"Okay," Aaron and I said in unison.

"No, it's not okay," every fiber in my being wanted to scream.

But that's what happens in my world—I'd never worked with Brad before, and most likely never would in my career, but because I slept with him, I was going to be punished by having to face my mistake every day for the next two weeks. Even though most people (including me) know it's a bad idea to sleep with your colleagues, you never quite think the worst will happen to you. *Ugh.* I hated him for turning me into a cliché.

***

I flew into San Francisco Sunday morning. The rest of the team would be arriving in the late afternoon, and Aaron had arranged for us all to have dinner together so we could discuss the game plan for Monday morning. I didn't want to risk being on the same flight and having to spend one more second in Brad's presence than necessary. Also, I needed a morale booster in the form of my friend Maya.

Maya was a first-year real estate associate at a large firm in San Francisco, and we had only managed to see each other once in person since we started our respective positions. She was just as busy trying to shine as an associate and getting in as many billables as possible as I was. To maximize our time together, she said she would meet me at a coffee shop near my hotel once I checked in.

Maya had been a go-getter in law school, and we spent many a late night together in the law school library studying. She was the first in her family to go to law school and had received a scholarship. Maybe it was because we were both from California, serious about succeeding, and each had something to prove—that she was deserving of her scholarship and that I could be as successful as my father—that we instantly bonded.

When I opened the door to the coffee shop, I immediately

spotted Maya at the counter even though her back was to me. Physically, she was an inch shorter than me, but her corkscrew curly hair gave her an extra two inches, making her appear an inch taller; and her big personality made her seem a full foot taller than me.

I came up next to her. "Hey, you."

She jumped, and I laughed.

"Oh, Jae!" she said, lightly punching my arm. "You scared me!"

"Sorry about that. That wasn't the impression I was going for."

She laughed and said, "Come here," pulling me in for a quick hug.

"It's so good to see you," I said, giving her a little squeeze, and pulled back.

"You too. Let's order and catch up." She quickly ordered a large mocha latte, and I ordered a decaf chai tea, skipping the caffeine. My anxiety was already at an all-time high because I knew what lay ahead of me for the next two weeks.

We quickly found a table in the half-empty space, where there were some tourists, but it clearly catered to the weekday work crowd.

"So." She slapped her hand on the table. "How are you?"

"I've been better." I looked up to the ceiling and gave a sad laugh, before looking back at her. "And how are you?"

"I'm fine. I mean, I bill, sleep, eat, and repeat." She cocked her head. "But back to you—what do you mean you've been better?"

I had debated telling her the story. In truth, there wasn't much to tell, but there was much to be embarrassed about. Even with a friend. But I needed to say it aloud to someone, because the weight of carrying a secret was too much.

"Remember back when I was a summer associate at Levenfield, and there was that other associate who asked me out?"

"Yeah." She nodded. "You liked him, but you were with Trey."

"Exactly." I swallowed. "Well, the short-story version is the other week we went out for drinks, had sex, and then he told me he was married."

Maya's eyes widened, and her mouth formed an *O* before she choked out, "Oh my god! *What?!*"

I cringed. "And it gets worse. He's flying in tonight, and we're working together for the next two weeks. I can't avoid him."

Maya just stared at me, and I couldn't figure out the look on her face. Finally, she said, "I actually don't know what to say. I mean, this is so not *you*."

"I know." I shook my head. "And honestly, I'm not sure what I want you to say, other than that I was stupid."

Maya looked at me more compassionately. "Tell me what happened."

So I recounted my earlier drinks with Brad, leading up to the night of our one-night stand, and then Brad's belated confession.

After she listened without interrupting, she said, "As your friend, I can tell you still like him, and so I'm sorry this happened. But after that prick Trey cheated on you in Boston, you deserve someone good and *not* another cheater." She took a deep breath. "But also as your friend, I have to ask, *why* would you do something so stupid? Law firms are gossip mills. Why jeopardize your career right out of the gate? And for a guy? You don't even want to get married."

One of the things Maya and I bonded over early on in our friendship was how we wanted to put our careers before marriage. We knew some women in our classes who we suspected came to law school to leave with a JD and a ring on their finger. And it wasn't so much that I never wanted to marry, but I didn't have a particular desire to either. That didn't mean I wanted to be alone for the rest of my life, though.

"Obviously, it's not something I'm proud of." I deserved her judgment because if I were hearing this story about someone else, I would think the same. "Maybe I'm lonelier than I thought. And, well, as you said . . . I *like* him."

"But how can you? He led you on."

"Okay, I'm furious with him, and with myself." I was furious because, yes, I still liked him *and* I had liked myself when I was with him, and the thought of *what if* tore at me.

This statement elicited Maya's sympathy again. "Oh, Jae. I'm sorry. That really, really sucks." She leaned forward. "Just be professional this week. And on Friday we'll go out for a drink and hang out the whole weekend so you can forget about this mistake and move on."

I smiled. "Let's make that *many* drinks, and deal."

CHAPTER SEVEN

I was the first to arrive in the lobby. Not sure how business or casual this dinner would be, I had changed from my travel clothes into a black jersey wrap dress. I would have preferred to stay in my hotel room until the last possible second, but Maya was right—I needed to be a professional during this trip, which meant playing the eager-to-please associate.

I sat on one of the sofas, nearest the elevators and farthest from the hotel bar, in order to be spotted quickly. The hotel we were staying at had a large open lobby, and the decor was contemporary but bland, probably catering more to the conference and business crowds. I've always loved hotels, particularly nice ones. There's something compelling about disparate souls all sleeping under the same roof, everything provided for you, and the complete anonymity of it all.

I was lost in these thoughts when Brad arrived. Standing in front of me, he was a complete stranger. On the surface, I knew that Brad was a terrible man for cheating. Yet, I also wasn't 100 percent sure he was totally a bad person, and he wasn't helping me to figure it out.

"Hi." He shifted uncomfortably on his feet, hands in his pockets.

"Hi," I said from my seat on the sofa.

His eyes met mine for a second, and I detected fear. He turned away from me and began looking around for the others. My muscles tensed, and I thought how it was entirely his fault that we were in this awkward situation. Suddenly I wasn't feeling very professional and was about to say something, but was saved when Aaron and Oliver joined us.

Aaron had made reservations at an Italian restaurant in North Beach, and we took a cab that was waiting outside the hotel. I sat in front with the driver, which was a relief, because no one could see my face and the competing emotions I'm sure were on it. At the restaurant, Brad sat directly across from me. Aaron ordered a bottle of Chianti for the table, and during dinner I kept holding either my wine or my water glass, mostly to hide my nerves and to avoid Brad's eyes. Whenever I laughed or inadvertently caught his eye, I could see him looking at me with a sad puppy-dog expression. I wanted to punch him. *He doesn't get to look at me like that.* Or was it my imagination? Whatever it was, it was making me self-conscious. Sometimes I would find myself looking back at him, and our eyes seemed to lock for longer than necessary.

Luckily Aaron and Oliver didn't seem to notice. Aaron was fun and gregarious and a great storyteller. He was in fine form that night, and after he gave us an overview of the types of documents and notes we should be taking during this due diligence project, he then regaled us with some of his misadventures as an associate.

"So whatever you do, if a partner invites you on his boat, don't drink any alcohol. And if you do decide to go ahead and drink despite my wise counsel, then I suggest you refrain from throwing up on his shoes." Aaron held up his hand as if taking an oath. "True story."

Though Aaron's stories mostly managed to distract me during dinner, when I went to bed that night, I could not stop picturing Brad's face across the table.

***

Monday morning came too quickly. Our hotel was walking distance from the company, so at eight o'clock, we all met in the lobby, grabbed some coffee at Peet's, and headed down to Aventis's offices. There they had two conference rooms ready for us to use. Being more senior, Aaron and Oliver set up in the larger one while Brad and I were in the other that was already filled with boxes of documents. While I had been mentally prepared to spend the two weeks with Brad in a conference room, I hadn't thought I'd have to do it *alone* with him.

We had sent the client a list to let them know the categories of documents we needed to review, so luckily, all day Aventis's paralegals and assistants came in and out of our room, bringing us various binders, meeting minutes, and agreements. Brad and I worked quietly. He would once in a while clear his throat to say, "I'm going to get some coffee. Would you like some?" The break in the silence startled me every time, and I would shake my head to indicate no without looking at him. And I wondered if Brad's frequent coffee runs were his way of avoiding the tense silence in our room.

Apparently, someone else must have noticed that Brad was constantly in Aventis's kitchens, because the next day a coffeepot was set up in our conference room. When we first walked in, we both glanced at it and then at each other. Brad had nowhere to run. Even though we were both reviewing documents, his were real estate related and mine were mostly corporate contracts and financials, and so there wasn't any reason for us to talk or ask each other questions. But when he went to pour himself a second cup of coffee, he asked, "Would you like a refill?"

His innocent question startled me, and I forgot to be mad for a second as I said, "Uh, sure."

Brad walked over with the pot and carefully topped off my cup. Although there was nothing to read into this except a sign of good manners, it felt oddly intimate. "Thank you," I said while keeping my eyes on the papers in front of me so I wouldn't have to look at him.

"You're welcome," Brad said, his voice so close to me, it sent my nerves tingling.

If this was how my body reacted to his pouring a cup of coffee, I already knew I was in trouble.

When he got up for his third cup and asked me again if I would like some, I said, "No, thank you. I think I'm done with coffee."

"Done with coffee???" Brad said in a voice of mock horror.

His joke, which wasn't even that funny, made me laugh if only because I needed a break from the tension of the last two days. "I'm actually more of a tea drinker," I said, forgetting my promise to myself not to engage. "I'll take a dirty chai latte over a regular latte most days."

"I see," Brad said, but didn't follow up. And like Monday, we continued to work in silence the rest of the day.

Late Wednesday morning, after I returned from a visit to Aaron and Oliver's conference room, I found a white paper coffee cup sitting on a napkin next to my laptop.

I looked at Brad and pointed to the cup. "Did you give me this?"

He looked up from his papers, his eyes wide as if not sure of my response. "Yes. I ran out to Starbucks for something stronger than the drip coffee in here and got you a dirty chai latte. It's soy milk. I hope that's okay?"

"Yes. Thank you." I quickly sat down and opened up my laptop, focusing intently on the screen and letting my hair fall in front of my face.

It was a small gesture, an act of kindness to a colleague, something Mindy, Jeff, and I did regularly if one of us went out for a coffee break. But from Brad, I felt some significance behind it, and I tried to ignore that feeling. I mean, what was he getting at? *I slept with you; I'm married, but here's a chai latte.* I didn't want him to be courteous to me, just professional. And I wanted to dislike him, or better yet, not think of him at all, but that clearly wasn't possible.

***

On Thursday afternoon, Aaron told us that he had made plans for another team dinner that evening, as everyone but me would be departing Friday night to return to LA to spend the weekend with their families.

At five o'clock, we walked back to our hotel to drop off our computers and meet back in the lobby in twenty minutes. After spending yet another entire day with Brad, I wasn't thrilled with another group dinner. But starting Friday night, I would finally have a break, and so I mentally told myself, *You can do this,* while brushing my hair and touching up my makeup in the mirror in my room.

When I got down to the lobby, Brad was there, wearing a different button-down shirt, and his hair looked a little damp. As I approached, a fresh woodsy scent that was the hotel's shower gel confirmed that he must have stepped out of the shower minutes ago. He smelled and looked so good that I felt my legs go a little wobbly, but I concentrated on keeping my composure.

"Hey," Brad said, watching me walk up to him.

The elevator's doors dinged, and I saw Brad look over my shoulder and nod. "Hey, Aaron." *Thank god,* I thought. *I can't spend another second alone with him.*

"Hi, you two," said Aaron, walking quickly toward us. "Change of plans tonight. Everything's gone to shit on the F&D closing, and Oliver and I need to get on a conference call with Russ at six." Aaron's slumped face and shoulders told me he was worried he was looking at something close to an all-nighter. "So we're just going to order room service tonight."

"Sorry about F&D," I said, secretly thankful I hadn't been assigned to that deal. The word *shit* came up a lot around it.

"Yeah, thanks." Aaron grimaced and then quickly said, "We'll talk first thing in the morning at eight to review where we are with Aventis, and come up with our game plan for next week."

"Okay," Brad said. "And room service is fine with me."

"Oh no," Aaron said, holding his hands up in a gesture of surprise. "You two should go to dinner. It's supposed to be one of the best Chinese restaurants in the city. You've been working hard all week, so enjoy one of the few perks of the job. The reservation is under Silverman."

I froze, not sure what to say. Although Brad's gaze was focused on the elevator straight ahead, his eyes were still burning through me.

When neither Brad nor I said anything, Aaron waved his hands as if shooing us out the door. "Go! Have fun. And remember to keep the receipt and submit it to my secretary." He then gave us a final wave off as he headed straight back to the elevator and to work.

Brad and I stayed silent for what felt like an eternity but was probably only seconds.

Finally, Brad said, "So I guess we're going to dinner," but with a question mark in his tone.

"I guess so." We had no choice, because if we didn't after Aaron's insistence, it would look suspicious.

It's only dinner, I told myself.

We took one of the taxis that was in front of the hotel, and I tried my best to forget what happened the last time we were alone in a cab. Neither of us said anything on the way there, and it made me wonder if Brad was trying to repress the same memories that I was.

When we opened the restaurant's door, Brad approached the host stand, and said, "We have a reservation for Silverman."

"Silverman. Party of four?" the hostess asked.

"Yes, but it's only going to be two of us."

"Oh." The hostess seemed to frown slightly as she consulted the screen in front of her. But when another hostess came, she handed her two menus and said, "Table forty-one."

The other hostess smiled at us and said, "It's downstairs. Follow me."

As she walked us down a set of stairs, the lighting grew dimmer and the music louder. I immediately noticed that it looked different from the typical high-end LA places with their clean lines and contemporary appeal. This place was designed with dark mahogany walls and red velvet drapes, and what sounded like a live jazz band playing. Brad shot me a confused look, and I responded the same way, as it wasn't clear whether this was a restaurant, jazz club, or opium den.

The server led us to a rounded booth that looked over the rest of the restaurant. While it would have been fine for four people, it felt oversized for the two of us.

Once the server left, as I held my menu, I pulled it close to my face, squinting, and said, "It's so dark in here, I can barely read this."

"What's that?" Brad leaned toward me. "It's so loud in here, I can barely hear you."

This made us both burst out laughing. The situation and this strange but lively restaurant atmosphere were so surreal that the tension between us evaporated. "Are you getting a drink?" Brad half shouted across the booth.

"I think we have to," I half shouted back, pointing to a tray of colorful umbrella-embellished cocktails headed to the next table over.

Once we ordered our drinks and food, Brad moved closer to me and said, "Sorry if I'm too close, but I don't want to have to shout the whole night."

I responded by moving slightly closer to him. "Agreed."

Once our drinks arrived and we had finished commenting on the restaurant's decor, we relaxed into discussing what we had been reviewing that day, then moved on to talk of previous client matters, then to light gossip regarding our colleagues, as if we were simply two associates bonding on a business trip.

But after our second round of drinks, like magnets, our thighs rested against each other's in the booth. After sitting for days with a conference table between us, unconsciously our bodies sought out each other. I had to admit to myself that I had never desired someone so intensely.

When we had finished with our entrées, and the server came back with dessert menus, I said, "I can't eat another thing."

"Same here," Brad said. He turned his head toward me and rested it on the back of the booth, gazing at me. "But I'm also not ready to leave."

The way he was looking at me made my heart hammer,

and I could feel my cheeks turning hot. When I didn't say anything right away, he took my hand, holding it lightly in his, and stroked my palm with his thumb. Every nerve ending in me came alive.

"We could have another drink," I said tentatively. "Enjoy the music a little longer?"

Brad nodded, and then entwined his fingers with mine under the table.

I could almost feel a miniature Maya on my shoulder screaming, *What are you doing???* The thing is, I knew exactly what I was doing, and I didn't care. I didn't want the night to end either. I could feel the heat of Brad's body radiating next to me, and all evening I couldn't help noticing how sexy he looked in his dark gray pants and crisp white button-down shirt.

After our last round, we paid our bill and hailed a cab outside. In the cab, he ran his hands up my skirt, and I began undoing the buttons on his shirt, and at the hotel we were in his bed, naked once again. My skin hot against his skin, his face above mine as he slowly and urgently moved inside of me, erased all the hurt and anger from the last few weeks. In that moment, nothing else existed. Afterward, despite my better judgment (it was already too late for that), I fell asleep in his arms. When I next woke up, I caught a glimpse of the digital clock on the nightstand. It was 4:00 a.m. I slipped out of bed, got dressed, and quietly left, returning to my room before anyone was awake to see me.

When my alarm went off a few hours later, I was still in my clothes from the night before. The memory of the night played over in my mind, and I lay in the bed in a swirl of conflicting emotions. I didn't know Brad was married when we first slept together; but this time I had known and did it anyway. *Oh god, what is wrong with me?* I thought. And, worse, why didn't I feel more guilty about it? At least it was Friday, and all I had to do was get through the day, and then Brad would be on a plane to Los Angeles, and I could reset.

***

For once, that Friday morning, Aaron and Oliver were waiting for me in the lobby.

"You look chipper," commented Aaron, and I blushed, not sure how to take his observation.

"Thanks." I had taken extra care with my clothes and makeup to hide my mild hangover. "How was the restaurant?" he said.

Relief spilled through me as I realized his remark meant that he probably worked all night and wasn't feeling that "chipper" himself.

"It was incredible," I tried to say casually. "Thank you for pushing us to go."

"Good to hear." Aaron glanced at his watch. "And so I guess we're still waiting on your partner in crime."

"Guess so," I said, again willing my cheeks not to turn crimson.

At ten minutes after eight, Aaron sent Brad an email. No response. Aaron then went to the front desk and called Brad's room. I couldn't hear the conversation, but when Aaron returned, I saw the annoyed look on his face and guessed what had transpired.

"Brad overslept, so we're heading over without him," Aaron said, confirming my suspicion. "He'll be in a little later."

Brad ruined the game plan for our eight o'clock meeting. While I was alone the first hour in the conference room, my culpability in the reason for Brad's tardiness made me work faster than usual, as I flew through documents, flagging important sections and typing as fast as I could to take notes. The fact that Brad had overslept was believable, yet from past experience, I couldn't help but wonder whether he was avoiding me. If that was the case, then it was a bad career move.

A little before ten o'clock, Brad finally showed up, looking rather sheepish, and at the sight of him I felt a quick flutter in my chest that I tried to ignore.

"Good morning," I greeted him, keeping my tone neutral.

"Good morning." He looked unsure whether or not he should smile. He decided on not and sat down with his laptop.

"Did you see Aaron?" I met his eyes over my laptop and raised my eyebrows, worried.

"Yeah. He had to let me in." He turned on his computer. "It wasn't good."

Brad poured himself some coffee and settled in to work in silence for the next half hour, until Aaron and Oliver came in for our rescheduled status meeting.

"Get through as much as you can today," Aaron told us. "Take shorthand notes on anything important, and write up more detailed notes in your memos this weekend. As long as we continue at this pace, we're on target to finish by next Friday." He turned to Brad. "And Brad, no lunch break for you. We'll bring you back a sandwich so you can make up what you missed this morning."

The rest of the day Brad and I didn't talk and focused on our respective document boxes. Even though Aaron and Oliver were in the next conference room, I felt like they were watching us, and it was easier to stare at a contract than at Brad and wonder how he felt about our night together.

***

At five o'clock, we closed our laptops, and the four of us walked back to our hotel. At the elevator, Aaron said, "So I guess Oliver and I will see you both Monday morning."

I looked at Aaron and then Brad. "You're not all on the same flight tonight?"

"No," Brad said, without looking at me. "I changed my flight this morning and am going to stay over the weekend."

"Oh," I said, still looking at Brad but imagining a look passing between Aaron and Oliver. *Oh my god, right after we have dinner together, Brad is suddenly late in the morning and changes his flight. This looks bad.*

As we all got in the elevator, and I frantically wondered what expression my face should be wearing, Aaron said, "So, Jae, what plans do you have this weekend?"

Relieved at my chance to quash any suspicions, I said, "I'm meeting up with my best friend from law school. She's an associate at Gilchrist."

Before anyone could ask Brad about his weekend plans, the elevator doors opened, and Brad and I exited on our floor. Our rooms were in opposite directions, which we both headed in. But once I heard the elevator doors close, I turned around and followed Brad to his room.

"Why the sudden change in plans?" I asked.

Brad turned around. "I wanted to finish cleaning up my notes, and I figured I'd get more work done here than at home. And this is my first time in San Francisco, so I figured why not check it out?"

I narrowed my eyes at him. If that was the case, then why didn't he mention his change of plans to me earlier? Especially after last night. Was he staying because of me? And did I want to know the answer?

"Here," he said, sliding his keycard into his door and opening it. "Why don't you come in?"

As we stepped inside, my phone rang. "This is the friend I'm meeting. I need to take this." I headed over to the desk in his room and sat down. "Hey, Maya," I answered. "What's the plan?"

She groaned into the phone. "Don't kill me, but the plan is that I'm stuck in my office all weekend. I'm getting pulled into an emergency document review for the project I've been working on. I'm so, so sorry," she said. "They need to get it done by Monday, so at least I know"—she paused—"or should say *hope* I'll be free next week and can make it up to you."

"Don't worry about it. I'm bummed I won't see you, but I understand. I've been there." It was the reason we hadn't managed to see each other in so long. As I said this, I looked up, and Brad was in the process of unbuttoning his dress shirt and hanging it up. I swallowed. Seeing him in a T-shirt, his arms bare, made me want to reach out and touch him.

After a couple more apologies from Maya and promises made for the following weekend, we hung up.

"Everything okay?" Brad asked as he sat on the edge of the bed, across from me.

I took a deep breath and debated whether to say anything to Brad. I'd barely had a chance to process the night before; now here I was alone with him in his room with no weekend plans.

"Uh, yeah," I started, hoping I'd find my answer once I started talking. "So what are you up to tonight?" I said.

"I don't know yet." He leaned back on his elbows. "I'm pretty tired. I'll probably just watch a movie and go to bed."

I waited a beat before saying, "It's just that my friend had to cancel on me. Work."

"Ah, sorry to hear that." But his mouth twitched up at the sides, and he didn't look very sorry. "So now what?"

"I don't know exactly."

Brad tilted his head at me, speaking the unspoken, and the

room suddenly seemed a lot smaller. So I asked the question I hadn't before.

"Did you change your flight to be with me this weekend?"

"You know the answer to that, Jae." His eyes and tone were serious.

He was right. I did know.

"Okay, then," I responded. "So what movie are we watching tonight?"

CHAPTER EIGHT

We woke up to the hotel phone ringing around seven o'clock. Brad let it ring, and I slowly began to uncurl my body from his. Even drowsy, he managed to foil my attempts and wrapped himself around me in a different position. I wasn't going to resist.

We dozed for another hour, and then I forced myself to get up. As I sat up, holding the sheet against my chest and scanning the room for items of clothing, I spied my dress and made an awkward reach for it and then pulled it over my head. Semiclothed, I stood up and then tracked down my undergarments and, when found, slipped them back on. I kneeled back down by the bed and gave Brad a quick kiss on the forehead. "I'll see you later," I said.

"Nooo . . ." With his eyes still closed, he grabbed my arm, gently pulling me closer. "Don't go."

I laughed as I disengaged my arm. "I have to. I have some work to do before we hang out this afternoon." I stood up again. "By the way, you have a voice mail," I said, pointing to the red blinking light on the hotel phone.

Back in my room, I quickly showered, ordered coffee from room service, and got to work tidying up my notes from the week so that I could spend as much time with Brad as possible. Last night we had made a plan to go sightseeing in the afternoon. Brad said he brought his camera with him and was hoping to take some photos over the weekend. We debated various sites to visit, like Golden Gate Park, and I told him about the conservatory of flowers and described the Victorian building that housed them. But for views of the hills and ocean, I suggested that we walk the Lands End Trail. I also mentioned that I would like to revisit the Palace of Fine Arts, one of the remaining structures from the World's Fair in 1915.

"The last time I was there, it was nearly dusk. I didn't want to leave because I had never seen such a beautiful sunset before with the sky all pink," I said, remembering. "I felt like I was part of a painting."

"I'd love to see that park," he had said, kissing my forehead. "And I'd love to see it with you."

Something inside me bloomed in that moment, and I knew that it wasn't just lust.

Maybe if I had spent the weekend with Maya as planned, or had some time alone to think of my actions on Thursday night, I would have made different decisions. But I didn't have time to think, and so I only followed my heart, even though I knew that once we were back in LA, whatever this was would be over.

***

At noon, I headed down to the lobby to meet Brad. When I spotted him, he was eagerly talking to the concierge who was pointing at different places on a map. I felt a surge of nervousness that I hadn't allowed myself back in my room while rushing through my notes. I was about to spend the whole day, not night, with Brad. Outside of the office, and without the effects of alcohol or sex . . . What if he realized I wasn't as interesting as he thought? That in the daylight, I wasn't the person who lived up to his office crush?

I swallowed and wanted to turn around and get back into the elevator. But it was too late because Brad looked up and saw me. He smiled, and my desire to be near him trumped these new insecurities. When I approached the desk, Brad folded up the map, tucking it into his bag, and said, "Hey, you. Are you ready to go?"

"Yes," I said.

"Have fun, you two," the concierge said, smiling and giving us a friendly wink, probably presuming we were a couple on a romantic weekend in the city. I swallowed again and nodded, feeling a small stab of guilt that I tried to force out of my mind.

It seemed that Brad and the concierge had already planned out our day's itinerary. Brad was serious about getting in as much outdoor photography as possible and wanted to start at Lands End.

On the bus en route, Brad took out the map the concierge had given him.

"From here, we can visit the Sutro Baths, and then walk over to the Lands End Trail," Brad said as I watched his finger trace the path. "Then here's China Beach. And then farther up is Baker Beach. I'd like to see both and get some shots of the Golden Gate Bridge." He then moved to a patch of green on the map. "We have to crisscross some of this neighborhood here, and then we walk through these trails in the Presidio and end up by the Palace of Fine Arts." He looked up at me and grinned, and warmth flooded through me. "Are you up for the hike?"

I wasn't much of a hiker, or that active in general, but I was up for spending as much time as possible with him, so I said, "Of course."

Outside of the office and Los Angeles, and with the entire afternoon stretched out ahead of us, the air around Brad felt lighter. His eyes seemed to dance taking in the views from the bus, and in his seat he lightly bounced his knee. His energy was at odds with the tired-looking, slumped-shouldered Brad I typically saw in the halls at Levenfield. My earlier nervousness about whether he would find me boring dissipated as we commented on the passing scenery and different neighborhoods, and our conversation had an easy flow. Although whenever I noticed someone glancing our way, my uneasy thoughts returned, while I wondered if people on the bus assumed we were a couple. So I just avoided their eyes by keeping mine focused on Brad.

While it had been sunny by the hotel, the sky was a little overcast on the other side of the city. There was a cold breeze coming off the ocean, and I pulled my sweater tighter around me, wishing I had brought a jacket too. We headed to the Sutro Baths, which had the air of ancient ruins even though they were really just old remains of swimming pools from a Victorian bathhouse. Some parts of the path down to the baths were tricky, and Brad held out his hand to help me. After the baths, we walked up to a lookout point and then followed the well-worn coastal trails toward Lands End, which were fairly wide and flat and didn't require any chivalrous assistance.

Truth told, I was already pretty familiar with the landscape—the cypress and eucalyptus trees, the bursts of colorful wildflowers on the paths, and the vista points for the bay and ocean—as I had been to some of these sites before with my law school boyfriend, but I didn't mention it. I couldn't help but compare the two experiences. My boyfriend and I had held hands while walking, and he would put his arm around me whenever we paused to admire a view. We were completely comfortable with each other, believing we knew everything there was to know about the other, and at the time, I considered the experience as one of our most romantic dates and took lots of grinning photos of us with the Golden Gate Bridge in the background.

Brad and I made our way along the trails to both China and Baker Beaches with no handholding, but instead, we would stand a little too close, appreciating the beauty around us. And I found Brad's attention and listening to my stories much more romantic than my ex's handholding. There were many still moments, and it felt natural to lean into each other, almost touching but not quite. I longed to reach out and let my fingers brush his, but sudden feelings of guilt stopped me. And as Brad took his time, trying to perfect a shot in the distance, I would take a mental picture of the moment. There were no overt romantic gestures, no cheesy couple photos, nothing that gave us away to the outside world as more than just friends touring the city, and yet it felt so much more poignant than my previous visit. Maybe because I knew it was fleeting?

We finally reached the Palace of Fine Arts around five thirty, having stopped for a coffee in the Presidio to refuel after four hours of walking. As it was summer, the sunset wouldn't start until closer to eight. Over coffee, Brad said, "I made reservations for dinner at a restaurant called Greens in Fort Mason nearby."

"You know it's a famous vegetarian restaurant," I said, wrapping my hands around my hot coffee cup. Though it was July, it had been windy and chilly by the water.

"I know. The concierge suggested it when I asked for a vegetarian-friendly place." Brad grinned. "I've never seen you eat meat, so I thought this might be your type of place."

The warmth in my hands spread through the rest of me as I grinned back at him. "Thank you." I'd been a vegetarian since college, but it wasn't something I made a big deal out of, and so had never mentioned it to Brad. But, of course, he noticed. I wanted to lean over and kiss him; but I didn't because, as I constantly had to remind myself, we weren't in a real relationship.

Once at the restaurant, I went to the restroom to do some damage control. When I assessed myself in the mirror, my outside seemed an apt reflection of my emotions. I was pretty wind-blown from the day. My mascara had rubbed off and my cheeks were red. Most of my hair had escaped its elastic and was frizzed and sticking out wildly. So I freed my hair from its messy ponytail and brushed it, and then applied a fresh coat of lip gloss. When I came out, Brad commented, "You look nice. You should wear your hair down more often."

"Thanks," I said. "I would, but it's much too high maintenance." Embarrassingly, I could feel a blush rising at Brad's compliment and was saved when the host said our table was ready and to follow him.

He seated us at a small table by the windows that had a view of the bay, hills, and bridge, placing Brad's menu on one side next to the window and then mine kitty-corner so that I was directly looking out on the water. *He definitely sees us as a couple,* I thought.

As we studied our menus, Brad made some jokes about what he as a carnivore was in for. I lightly kicked him under the table. "As long as you stay away from tofu, you'll survive the evening," I assured him. He laughed and let his knee rest against mine.

After the waiter served us our drinks and took our orders, we admired the view. The water in the bay gleamed as it lightly lapped at the pier, very different from the whitecapped, crashing ocean waves earlier in the day by the Sutro Baths. I felt myself relaxing, giving in to my glass of wine and my physical exhaustion from walking around all afternoon.

"I've always wanted to live by the water," Brad said, and took a sip of his beer.

"Me too."

Brad looked at me, surprised. "You seem like someone who has to live in a city."

"We're in a city now. And there you go." I pointed to the water.

Brad laughed. "I meant you don't seem like much of a beachgoer."

"Fair enough. Lying out on a beach isn't my idea of a good time."

"Even with a good book?" Brad joked.

I laughed and shook my head as I leaned forward, resting my folded hands on the table. "But I've always imagined a house on the water. Not a beach house. More like a house on a cliff with big ocean waves below me, with no one around, where I could read and maybe write a little," I mused.

"You write?" he asked, his eyes curious.

I shrugged. "Not really. Just some journaling here and there, some stories started but never finished. But doesn't every lawyer secretly think they have the next *New York Times* bestseller in them?" I grinned. "Anyway, I like having a roof over my head."

I'd always been a voracious reader, but writing was different. Too personal. While I liked the idea of writing something, maybe even a book, I wasn't crazy about putting it out in the world. Besides, it was a lot easier to write legal memos where one basically recited and organized what others had written and followed a formula regurgitating others' legal opinions.

"Can I see something you've written?" Brad said.

I shook my head. "No. Like I said, I don't really write. It's more of a fantasy."

Even though Brad had seen me naked, even though we'd had sex, and even though the night seemed promising, sharing my journals or unfinished stories with him was too intimate. It would be akin to sharing my soul.

Brad must have registered the look on my face. "Are you afraid I won't like it?"

"No, it's not that." I tried to laugh it off. "It's just that there's nothing to like or dislike, since I don't really write." I held his eye a little longer than necessary to prove I wasn't lying.

I couldn't tell whether he believed me, but he did say sincerely, "I bet you'd be a good writer."

"Ha! And I bet you say that to all the girls." But I still felt a slight swell in my chest at the compliment.

"Just the ones who would be good writers." Then thankfully he dropped the subject.

After dinner, we walked along the waterfront until we zigzagged across the freeway entrance to reach the Palace of Fine Arts. We got there still in the daylight and wandered around the building and the small lagoon it sheltered. I stood at one end of the lagoon while Brad walked around taking photos. We had arrived just in time because as I stood there, the magical transformation began. The sky became pink tinged with bits of silver, and suddenly I found myself in a magical fairy-tale garden, with the Palace looming a dusky rose above me and the surrounding green leaves becoming darker and richer as the water shimmered in front of me. The city ceased to exist. All human nature ceased to exist.

I looked around to find Brad. I wanted to share this moment with him, but he was nowhere to be seen. It seemed fitting. My thoughts turned to my last visit, my last boyfriend, and the fact that I was here with someone else's husband, a shadow falling over my mood.

As navy was beginning to overtake the pink in the sky, I heard the soft crunch of footsteps on the leaves behind me. I turned around to see Brad. "Hey, I was getting a little worried you disappeared," I said.

"I was just taking some photos," he said, looking at me in a thoughtful manner as if studying me. Maybe I was romanticizing it, and maybe he was simply looking at me; but whenever I saw that look in his eyes, I felt that I saw so many emotions unsaid behind them. The sunset obviously moved him as well, and I was secretly proud it had lived up to my description.

He walked closer to me and reached out, brushing some stray hairs out of my face, and kissed me lightly on the lips. "You're very beautiful," he said sadly.

It was the first time we had kissed in a public place, and I was too surprised by his actions to say anything. He then took a step back, aimed his camera at me, and snapped several photos. I resisted the urge to cover my face and say no. Because what was the point? He could never show these photos to anyone.

But I, too, wanted the moment memorialized, even if the pictures just ended up hidden in the back of a drawer. Even with the guilt, it was still the most romantic day I had ever spent with anyone.

Once it was dark, we walked to a busier street and found a cab. At the hotel, Brad asked, "Nightcap?"

"What would the night be without a cap?" I answered.

In his room, Brad headed straight for the bath and turned on the water. He came back and took a bottle of red wine out of the mini fridge, opened it, and then carried the opened bottle and two glasses into the bathroom.

I stayed rooted to my spot in the room. "You know, that's not the most hygienic place to drink."

He walked back out of the bathroom and stood in front of

me. "It's not?" he asked, his tone innocent but with a mischievous glimmer in his hazel eyes.

"No, it's not," I said, trying to sound serious, but a grin sneaked through.

Brad then snuck his hands around the bottom of my shirt, and I shivered as he pulled it over my head. Following his lead, I pulled both his sweater and T-shirt off. Then we slipped off each other's jeans. And in one movement, Brad unclasped my bra, and what little remaining clothing we had fell to the floor. He took my hand and led me into the bathroom where two glasses of wine waited on the edge of the tub.

I stepped into the bath first, and then he got in and sat across from me.

"The hotel bubble bath is a nice touch," I laughed, and as he reached across to hand me my wine, I kept thinking of our hands slippery with soap and wondering how we would explain it if an accident occurred.

Brad laughed and said, "C'mere."

I slid over to his side and rested my back against his chest, my head leaning back on his shoulder. While I sipped my wine, under the water Brad's hands traveled over my body. I closed my eyes and tried to remember the last time before him that I had experienced such pleasure. I couldn't. So I carefully placed my glass on the far ledge of the tub and turned my face up toward his as he leaned down and kissed me. As our kissing grew more passionate, Brad managed to lift us both out of the bath and onto the towel on the floor. Our bodies still warm and wet against each other, we couldn't even make it to the bed. Afterward we simply lay there, and Brad repeated his new favorite phrase, "You're so addictive."

When the cold of the hard tile started to seep into our bodies, we peeled ourselves off the floor and climbed into the bed.

Once in bed, Brad put his arm around me, and I found the nook between his shoulder and neck and fell blissfully asleep.

CHAPTER NINE

I was the first to wake up. The digital clock read 8:01 a.m. I tried to sneak out of bed, but my rustling woke Brad, who pulled me back to him.

"Where are you going?" he asked.

"My room."

"No," he murmured, and snuggled in closer to me.

I couldn't argue with that. After a little more dozing, we finally forced ourselves out of bed and ordered some coffee. While waiting for it to arrive, Brad took a shower, and I padded around the room in the hotel robe. On the desk, I noticed a sketchbook. I picked it up and flipped through. There was a sketch of a mountainous landscape and another of a woman on a beach. It was impressive, but the last one sent a stab of jealousy through me. I remembered Brad mentioning that sketch the night he first came over to my place, and I wondered whether it actually was of a stranger. When I heard the water turn off in the bathroom, I quickly shut the book and decided I didn't really want to know.

When our coffee arrived, we drank it in silence in front of

the window and watched as the morning fog burned away and the sun appeared.

Brad was the first to break the stillness. "What should we do today?"

"What would you like to do?"

"I'd still like to see that photography exhibit at the SFMOMA. But we did all my camera stuff yesterday. We should do something you want to do."

We decided to see the photography exhibit first because I was also curious, and then head over to North Beach for coffee, book browsing, and dinner.

The sun looked promising, so I wore a sundress, but paired with a light velvet jacket, just in case the weather turned. I met Brad in the lobby and noted how good he looked in his faded jeans and a navy-blue V-neck sweater.

At the photography exhibit, Brad asked me to show him which photographs I liked, and he listened carefully as I described what attracted me to each picture. When I stopped in front of one that showed a little boy on the pavement with some pigeons, Brad explained the "rule of three" and framing, and why my eye was drawn to the little boy in the photo. In another photograph, the same little boy was sitting at a table looking out the window. Brad talked about the use of light, and I watched his finger trace an outline of where the light was coming from in the picture. He asked me which ones I didn't like and then decoded why I didn't like them—too many focal points, or my eye was drawn to something else in the background, or the way the light shone.

"You seem to be attracted to the shadows in photographs," Brad commented.

"Yes. They seem more interesting to me because they let my imagination wander. I guess I like their mysterious and secretive qualities." Though after I said that, it sounded foretelling, and I changed the subject.

After the photographs, we moved on to the contemporary art, wandering around and looking only at the pieces that interested us. And I was interested in anything Brad wanted to see, as I could listen to him talk about art all day.

We ended our visit at the museum shop, where Brad went inside while I went in search of a water fountain. When I returned, he was at the register, and the salesperson was handing him a bag.

"What did you get?" I asked.

He smiled. "I'll show you later."

From the museum we steadily meandered our way to North Beach. We drank coffee at Caffe Trieste and visited City Lights bookstore. Brad perused the art and architecture sections, while I slowly went through the fiction shelves. When Brad caught up to me, he asked, "So what's your favorite book?"

I laughed. "That's impossible to answer."

But I looked at the selection around me and spotted *Giovanni's Room* by James Baldwin on a table. I picked it up. "I love this book. This is definitely one of my favorites."

"Yeah?" Brad said, and held out his hand, and I gave it to him. "What's it about?"

I stumbled. I didn't want to say that it was ultimately about an affair, but Brad was already reading the back. "It's, um, a very important book. Groundbreaking at the time."

Brad looked up from the back cover and grinned. "Then I guess I should buy it."

His smile felt like sunlight and warmed my insides. Brad had already told me he didn't really read, but he was willing to read something I said I loved. "I can't wait to hear what you think," I said.

Since we had missed lunch, we grabbed an early dinner at an Italian restaurant in the neighborhood. While we waited for our pastas, Brad handed me the bag from the museum store. "This is for you," he said. "A memento from San Francisco."

I tilted my head at him, giving him a confused look. I then looked in the bag and pulled out a journal. On the cover was one of the photographs I had admired in the exhibit. I flipped through and saw blank white pages.

"Thank you, but you shouldn't have." Though the giant smile I gave him belied my words.

"You're welcome. It's for your writing."

"But I told you I don't really write."

He shrugged, smiling. "You do now."

All during dinner, we grinned at each other and held hands under the table. I could not remember the last time I had felt so high. Brad was right. Whatever we had was addictive.

***

Because it was Sunday night, and Aaron and Oliver were returning to start work on Monday morning, when we got back to the hotel we split up and went to our separate rooms with the intention of finishing some work. Although we didn't explicitly make plans, I expected Brad to come over, or email me, but there was no message. I was about to call his hotel room, but instead I emailed: Still working?

There was no response. I waited until a little after eleven o'clock and, finally, somewhat deflated from the high of the last forty-eight hours, went to bed alone.

***

In the morning, I checked my BlackBerry and saw that Brad had responded to my email at midnight. We need to talk, he wrote.

The hairs on my arms stood up. Was he going to say he regretted our weekend together? That he realized how much he loved his wife? That I shouldn't read anything into our time together?

I did not respond.

When I made my way to the lobby, Aaron and Brad were already there waiting. As I approached, I overheard Aaron saying to Brad, "So, your wife is here?"

I froze. Aaron's words were like a simultaneous slap in the face and stab in the heart.

"Yes, she surprised me last night," Brad responded, but there was no emotion in his voice.

Physically I had to focus on staying upright and putting one foot in front of the other, appearing calm despite the emotional earthquake happening inside of me.

"Good morning, Jae," Aaron said, spotting me. "We're still waiting for Oliver."

"Morning," I managed. Brad mumbled a hello, and I couldn't bring myself to look at him to see if he was avoiding my eyes or searching them. I addressed Aaron, "In that case, do you mind if I run to Peet's first? I really need that coffee. I can get you guys something if you'd like?" I said all this quickly.

"Rough weekend?" Aaron joked, smiling. I tried to smile back but could only manage a small nod. "Go get your coffee, and we'll meet you there."

I gave him a rushed thanks and fled the lobby.

Brad's wife is here, I kept repeating in my head. *That's why he didn't come over. Was she the early-morning hotel voice mail the other day, suspecting her husband was up to no good?* My thoughts raced.

I was such an idiot for having spent the weekend with Brad. *We're not a couple and never will be,* I thought.

When the guys met up with me at Peet's, I went outside to wait for them while they ordered their drinks. I couldn't be near Brad more than necessary that day.

We walked to the office together, my soul sick with shame and a heavy sadness cloaking my shoulders. The weather Monday mirrored my internal struggle. The sky was dark with clouds gathering and threatening to open up.

Once we were inside and in our separate conference rooms, Brad said in a low voice, almost a whisper, "I'm sorry, Jae. Kathryn surprised me last night with Ivy. I had no idea she was coming up here."

I swallowed. Was he apologizing that he was married or that his wife showed up? And was I in a position to accept his apology?

"I understand," I said. "She's your wife."

"But I got your email and wanted to—"

"Brad." My head snapped up, and I stared at him. "She. Is. Your. *Wife*." I let some anger linger on the word *wife*, though again, not sure I had a right to be angry and with whom.

Brad's wife was real. Before that afternoon, she was simply an idea and had never really existed for me. But that day, for the first time, she had entered the room and made herself known to me. No matter what I felt over the weekend, I couldn't ignore the situation any longer.

Brad looked at me, seeming stunned at my words, and then bowed his head down over his papers and got to work.

Around late afternoon, the sky finally made good on its threat, and rain poured down. The building actually shook as the rain beat against the windows. Thunder rolled and lightning flew across the sky. The rarity of thunderstorms in San Francisco, combined with the strength of the storm, put me even more on edge. During a particularly ferocious lightning display, Brad walked over to the window to observe the spectacle. With his hands in his pockets and his back to me, he stood at the window, looking out into the dark sky.

"When I was a kid, I loved thunderstorms," he said, speaking to me for the first time since that morning. "In Wisconsin the lightning would race across and light up the whole sky."

He turned to me shyly to see if I was listening, caught my eye for a second, and turned back to the window.

His look and words unexpectedly pierced my soul. In those hazel eyes I saw innocence, and I could imagine him as a little boy with chestnut curls and eyes full of wonder. My anger at him dissipated in that vulnerable moment, and I wanted to go to the window and put my arms around him. Instead, I stayed seated, and a fierce blush came to my cheeks. I looked back down at the documents I was reviewing and cleared my throat. "Yes, I used to watch thunderstorms with my dad when I was little. They're pretty rare in LA."

Although I could feel him turn around and his eyes on me, I couldn't look up to meet them, afraid he'd see my emotions on my face. I didn't elaborate or engage in any more conversation. After a few minutes, he came back to the conference table. I looked up at him then, and he smiled at me before bending his head down to work. I felt as if he had read my thoughts.

Fuck. I still wanted him.

***

Before we left Aventis's offices, Aaron said to me, "Oliver and I are going to try a Mexican restaurant tonight. Are you interested?" My mind whirled. *Did they already invite Brad too?* But Aaron saved me. "Brad is having dinner with his family."

I tried to hide the relief in my voice. "Sure. That sounds great."

At dinner and after a sip of tequila, I couldn't help myself and said, "So that's weird that I didn't know Brad was married or that his wife was visiting. I mean, we've been sitting in the same conference room for days, and he's never mentioned it."

"Yeah, I didn't know he was married either," Aaron said, putting his hands out in a *Who knew?* gesture. "But she was on our flight and seemed to know who we were."

"Yeah," Oliver said, surprisingly engaging in our gossip. "She approached us at the gate and was like, 'Hey, you guys work with my husband, Brad Summers.'" He made a cringing face. "It was so strange, since he's never mentioned having a wife or a kid, and doesn't wear a wedding ring."

"Right?" Aaron chimed in. "I wasn't sure whether to believe her, but since she said Brad's name, we played along. She must've looked us up on the website or something. But how crazy that he talks about us to his wife, but has never mentioned her to us? And we were all in first class together, so it wasn't like we could ignore her."

"It's so weird," I said, playing dumb. "And he has a kid too?"

"A baby!" Aaron said while Oliver shook his head in disgust. "Like a really tiny one."

"And she was ordering drinks the whole flight. Not a glass of wine, but bottles of hard liquor. You could tell the airline attendant was judging her," Oliver said, "as were we. At least it was a short flight."

"Yeah, but then we kind of felt responsible for her, and so we ended up all sharing a cab from the airport. I mean, drinking heavily while traveling alone with an infant?" Aaron spread out his hands as if to measure his incredulity of the situation. "That's not right."

"Unbelievable," Oliver said.

"Very. My guess is *all's not well* on the home front," Aaron said meaningfully.

I shook my head in reply. I wanted to ask so much more, but my throat was thick with guilt, and my mind raced. *Okay, so Brad's wife is depressed and an alcoholic. But who wouldn't be when married to a cheating spouse while caring for a baby?* She obviously cared enough to fly up to see him, so I wasn't sure whether Brad's story of their relationship matched up. I was doubting Brad and hating myself.

I couldn't sleep that night knowing that Brad and Kathryn were under the same roof, and, worse, on the same floor. I thought of calling Maya, but she would probably ask me what was wrong. I tried to immerse myself in a Henry James novel, *The Wings of the Dove*, that I had bought on Sunday. But the book was complicated and sad and just brought my thoughts back around to Brad. I turned on the news to take me out of my head and into the troubles of the world, which were much bigger than my pedestrian one. Eventually I dozed off, but I had a fitful sleep, mostly because Brad kept appearing in my dreams and my anger would shake me awake. Every time I woke up, I remembered that he was sleeping in a bed with her just down the hall.

I didn't feel tired from my troubled sleep because my adrenaline ran high that morning. I even woke up early and went for a walk while it was still dark. When it was time to leave for work, as I left my hotel room and stood by the elevator, I heard Brad's voice. "Do you need anything? Do you have a room key? Okay. I'll see you later."

My eyes stung and my throat burned, and I begged the elevator doors to open and take me away. But it was too late, as Brad was already at my side. From my peripheral vision, I could tell he was surprised to see me, but he quickly masked it with a neutral expression.

"Good morning," I said.

"Good morning."

At that moment the doors opened, and we stepped inside. I stood across from him and finally looked at him properly, noticing the dark shadows under his eyes.

"You look exhausted," I said.

He gave me a small shrug and weak smile in response.

When we reached the lobby, it was still a few minutes early, and Aaron and Oliver weren't down yet. There was no way I was going to stand in the lobby with him a second longer than I had to.

"Tell Aaron I went to get a coffee," I said. "I'll meet you guys in front of Aventis."

"Okay," said Brad, his eyes dead looking at mine.

As I stood in the Peet's line waiting for my latte, I wondered how I was going to get through the day.

At the office, I thought of changing my flight from Sunday to Friday night to get the hell out of there, but an email from Maya popped up saying that she was excited to see me on Friday and sent me the address for the bar we were meeting up at for happy hour. Somehow I managed to get through the week without speaking to Brad, unless absolutely necessary. I directed all my questions to Aaron and Oliver, which gave me a chance to leave the room.

But by the end of the week, I still had *a lot* of questions that I wasn't sure I wanted the answers to.

CHAPTER TEN

When five o'clock hit on Friday, the weeklong anxiety trapped in my chest finally released its viselike hold and almost caused me to bolt for the door—the torture was officially over, and we were leaving that conference room. The walk back from Aventis's office to our hotel seemed quicker than usual, even though it had been the same trek for the last two weeks. After our goodbyes in the lobby and "see you back in LA" between the four of us, and our ride up the elevator, I actually said a cheerful goodbye to Brad as we stepped off the elevator on our floor.

He surprised me when he smiled and waved back pleasantly. "Good night."

But, whether real or feigned, his casual tone (even though it mirrored my own) plunged me back into the despair I had felt all week. *Is he just as relieved to get away from me as I am from him?* I wondered. I walked quickly to my room, not looking back at him. Since I was meeting Maya for happy hour, I had no choice but to shake off my morose feelings.

As soon as I walked into the bar, Maya spotted me and

waved me over. Maya was already standing at a high-top table full of drinks with several of her colleagues, fellow associates from her firm. When I reached her table, she gave me a quick hug and said, "So glad we're doing this!"

"I know. Finally!" I squeezed her back.

"Now, what are you drinking?" she asked.

I ordered the same wine that she had, and then she introduced me to everyone there.

I had worried I would end up unloading on her everything that happened with Brad, but we had no time alone together. Maya was holding court at the table, telling a story about how she outwitted another associate who tried to worm his way onto her deal, and it reminded me of how she was always the center of attention at parties in law school. My introverted nature couldn't help but be both attracted and impressed by her extroverted personality. While we were both serious students, she would make sure I left the library and books behind when I needed a break. So that night, drinks led to dinner with a smaller group, and then post-dinner drinks and then back "home" to my hotel room where I promptly passed out and fell into a sound, dreamless sleep.

In the morning, I checked out of the hotel and stood outside with my luggage, waiting for Maya. The night before, we had planned to drop my bags at her place, grab her dogs for a hike in Marin, and have dinner with a couple of her friends, and then I'd stay at her place and fly home on Sunday.

While keeping an eye out for Maya's car, I also kept looking back at the hotel entrance, wondering whether Brad and his family were still inside or had flown back to Los Angeles. Thankfully, Maya picked me up at exactly ten o'clock, as she had promised.

At the Marin Headlands, Maya, knowing that I wasn't a

big hiker and since we had her two dogs, stuck to an easy trail, which also made it easy for us to finally catch up.

"So . . . ," she started, and I knew by her tone where she was going.

"So," I said, not giving anything away. When she had asked me briefly what I had done the weekend she was working, I had told her about my walk from Lands End to the Presidio, and then also told her about visiting SFMOMA, and didn't mention Brad. But ever since I woke up that morning, I had been debating whether to tell her about my weekend with Brad, his wife showing up, and everything.

"*Sooo* how was it working with that guy?"

"That guy?" The guy with whom I never ran out of things to talk about, whose mind and body I craved? The guy who told me I was beautiful and bought me a journal and told me I'd be a good writer? The guy I was falling for and whose wife had appeared?

"Yeah, the married guy," she said, a distinct edge in her voice.

While I was sure it was because she was worried about me, her friend, my humiliation was too fresh for the judgment in that sentence not to sting.

That settled it. I wasn't going to tell her anything.

"Ugh," I groaned. "It wasn't the best two weeks of my life, but at least it's over." *But it was also the most romantic weekend I've ever spent with anyone,* I thought.

"So did anything happen? I mean, did he try hitting on you again?"

I shook my head. "Nothing happened," I lied, keeping my eyes on the path rather than looking at Maya. "And, frankly, I just want to forget about it." I then veered us away from Brad. "So tell me about your friends we're meeting tonight."

"O-kay," Maya said. "If you're sure you don't want to talk about it . . ." She paused.

This time I looked her in the eye and said, "I don't," so she started telling me about her friends Heather and Matt whom we were meeting that night, basically giving me their full life stories, until I laughed and said, "Okay, I don't need to know *that* much about them. So what else is up with *you*?"

And from there, our conversation turned to work, family, mutual friends from law school, and of course, dating . . . or in our cases, the lack of dating. "I'm just so busy," Maya complained. "And the trouble with dating is that I'm too tired to care."

But the entire time we spent catching up, a gnawing anxiety prevented me from really enjoying our conversation. Not only had I knowingly slept with a married man, but now I was also lying to the person I considered my best friend.

***

We met up with Maya's friends at a Mexican restaurant in the Mission. They were both second-year associates at her firm, but in different departments. Heather was tall and frail with wispy blond hair and a friendly smile. Matt was tall and lanky with unruly brown hair. He wore a tweed jacket with elbow patches that gave him an English-professor look. When we shook hands, I was immediately struck by his green eyes, bright and clear as emeralds, and felt my own dilate in response. Matt was attractive, no doubt. There was only one problem—he wasn't Brad.

When we finally sat down at a table, both Matt and I ordered the vegetarian enchiladas. "Are you vegetarian?" Matt asked me.

"Yes, but not vegan. You too?"

"I am. I started last year, and I'm actually trying to lean more vegan these days." This set us off on a private conversation of why we chose not to eat meat—I just never really liked it, so it was easy to give up; whereas Matt's reasons were more based on the environmental impact of the industry.

Since Matt was on my right, and Maya on my left was engaged in an intense conversation with Heather about a current work situation Heather was navigating, I ended up talking to him for most of the dinner. I learned his blazer was from a vintage shop in the Haight. When he asked where I had visited in San Francisco and I told him City Lights bookstore, he asked me what I liked to read. It turned out he had also been an English major in college, and we compared notes on our favorite authors. While we chatted, I found myself thinking how much we seemed to have in common.

After dinner, the four of us headed back to Maya's place. She was renting a room in a house in Noe Valley that had a big backyard for her dogs. We let the dogs outside in the yard, and we all sat outside huddled around an electric firepit, drinking wine and laughing. And for the first time in ages, I felt relaxed and happy.

Other than my work friend Mindy, I didn't have any close female friends in LA. After being away for seven years in Boston, I had lost touch with my few high school friends, most of whom had also moved away. Maya kept telling me I made a mistake by going back to Los Angeles, and had tried to persuade me to find a job in San Francisco. Sitting in her backyard, I thought, *Maybe Maya was right.* Other than my family and comfort in the familiar, what was tying me to LA? As I took a sip of wine, I promised myself to seriously consider the idea of moving. Of course, deep down I knew my real reason had nothing to do with friendship and everything to do with my inability to work with Brad any longer—I just couldn't stand the idea.

"What time is your flight tomorrow?" Matt asked me.

"It's not till two."

"And what are you doing before then?"

"Not much. Maya has to go into the office, so I'll probably head out to the airport early."

"Yuck. Who wants to hang out in an airport?" he said, shaking his head. "Would you be up for brunch?"

"Um, sure," I said after a pause. True, we had been bonding all night, and in different circumstances he would have been exactly my type, but his asking me out still surprised me.

Then Matt addressed Maya. "Hey, Maya, since you're bailing on your friend tomorrow"—he gave her a smile to show he was joking, and in response Maya good-naturedly narrowed her eyes at him—"how about I take her to brunch and then the airport?"

"Sounds like that's up to Jae, not me." She looked at me, and I shrugged and then nodded.

Late that night, after Heather and Matt left, and we were putting away the wine glasses, Maya asked, "Did I detect a spark between you and Matt?"

"I don't know. I think he was just being friendly."

Maya cocked her head and gave me a look. "Please tell me you're not this obtuse."

I laughed. "Well, then how about just, *I don't know*. I mean, we have a lot in common, but I wasn't exactly feeling a spark." I wished I did, but no matter how attractive Matt was or how well we got along, Brad was still lodged in my mind.

Maya stared at me for a second, then shook her head. "Whatever you say."

***

In the morning, I got up at the same time as Maya, and we shared a coffee before she headed into work. At her door, as she was leaving, she gave me a hug and said, "It was so great having you here. I really miss hanging out in person."

"Me too," I said, and the idea of moving to San Francisco flitted through my thoughts again.

Once Maya was gone, I was by myself for the first time since I last saw Brad; I was already dreading seeing him the next day at Levenfield, and my mind started going to a dark place. I also couldn't help thinking I should have told Maya the truth about my weekend with Brad. It was the first time I had kept a secret from her. Luckily, I didn't have much time to brood before Matt picked me up.

During brunch, I tried to focus on Matt's conversation. He had taken me to a quaint, bustling old-timey San Francisco café in Hayes Valley. There were gray-haired men reading their newspapers, groups of young twenty-somethings retelling the details of the night before, couples having a leisurely breakfast, and a few nervous-looking couples who were leaving their food untouched. My food was also untouched.

My stomach still felt twisty about accepting Matt's brunch offer. While I told myself it would be a good distraction from thoughts of Brad, I didn't want to lead Matt on, in case Maya was right that he felt a spark that I wasn't capable of reciprocating. These thoughts kept me from being totally present.

Matt must have been trying to figure out where I had gone, because he finally asked, "Jae, are you okay?"

I put down the slice of toast I kept picking up and then dropping. "Yes, why?"

"I hope you aren't offended, but you just seem really out of it."

"Oh?" My cheeks flushed. "I'm sorry. I guess I didn't sleep well last night."

Matt eyed me critically. "Bad dreams?"

"No." I gave a little laugh. "Maybe too much wine?" All of it was a lie.

"Or maybe your dog got run over?"

"What? That's horrible," I said. "And I don't have a dog."

"Not anymore," he deadpanned.

His offbeat sense of humor brought me out of my slump. "Hey, I'm really sorry. I don't know. I'm not normally like this. Like I said, I guess I just had a hard time sleeping."

"If you say so. You just seem different from last night. So I can't help but think you got some bad news or something since then."

I wanted to tell him the bad news happened days, if not weeks or months, before our dinner. I wanted to say that dinner the night before had been the first time I was able to forget the bad news.

"Jae." Matt leaned forward. "Sometimes the best person to confide in is a stranger."

I looked up at him over my coffee and felt myself coming round. "Yeah, you're right." I put down my cup. "So what do you think? Does he look like a good confidant?" I nodded toward a man in his sixties with a very distinguished handlebar mustache. Matt looked surprised for a second and then got my joke.

"See, this was the person who was having fun last night," he said, smiling at me.

"I know, I know. I'm sorry." I shook my head. "You're right."

"That's okay. But if you want to talk about it, I'm a good listener."

I did want to talk about it. Matt had such kind eyes and was proving to be a nice person. And I was being the absolute worst company, so I shook my head, no.

"Are you sure?"

I nodded. I needed to snap out of it. Here was this great guy sitting in front of me, and I was upset over someone who had lied to me and whom I would never have a future with. I had to make an effort. "So tell me your favorite story about Maya," I said.

"Only if you share one too." He raised his eyebrows conspiratorially.

I raised my eyebrows back at him. "Of course."

Even though it was hard to concentrate, even though I wanted to have some space and cry, I was determined to enjoy or at least try to enjoy the rest of our brunch. I wasn't sure whether I fooled Matt or not, but he still seemed in a good mood on the way to the airport.

***

Once I made my way through security and found a seat at my gate, I could finally let myself be alone with my thoughts. I didn't want to smile. I didn't want to talk to anyone. At the same time, I wanted to announce to those seated around me, *My heart is broken!* But I never had anyone's heart to begin with, so how could mine be crushed?

Seated across from me, a mother who looked about my age read to her young daughter. I wanted to get up and move. I thought of Brad's wife. I imagined her reading to their daughter, and I wondered how Brad felt when he saw them. Did his heart swell with tenderness? The little girl looked at me. I hadn't realized I was staring. As I looked away, I heard the girl say to her mother, "Is she going to cry?" First called out by Matt and next by an unknown child, I picked up my bag and went to the restroom. When I returned to the waiting area, I made sure to sit at the opposite end.

Once on the plane, I closed my eyes but could not sleep. I tried to read but could not focus. How could I have let myself get into this whole situation with Brad in the first place? I decided that when I got home, I was allowed one night alone to be sad. I would crawl into bed and pile the duvet around me. I would open a bottle of red wine and drink straight from it. I would lie there in misery and self-pity and cry until my eyes were swollen and face puffy. And then I would wake up in the morning and wipe the slate clean. The night before was to perform a lobotomy. In the morning, my life would return to normal.

CHAPTER ELEVEN

Monday morning was LA weather at its best—bright, cheerful, sunny—which belied my mood. The tears had left their mark, as had the wine. Despite my banging hangover, I decided it was nothing Advil, coffee, and some serious eye cream couldn't handle. The weather and the day would not let me indulge in self-pity. By the time I reached the office, I felt ready to be productive and move on.

The first few hours were exactly that. Having been gone for two weeks, I had other lingering assignments that needed my attention. After those first industrious hours that morning, I headed to the kitchen to refill my coffee cup and ran right into Brad, who was doing the same. Although my plan was to be as professional as possible, I found myself looking away, unable to say anything. The pained expression on his face indicated that he was just as surprised and wasn't sure how to act. Finally, he said simply, "Good morning."

I couldn't help myself and muttered, "It was." I avoided eye contact and made a mental note to start getting my coffee on a different floor. So much for my Brad lobotomy the night before.

Since ignoring him was impossible, I vowed to stay in my office as much as possible that day, and the following, and for the rest of the week . . . or for however long Brad and I worked on the same floor. On my return to my desk, there was an email from Matt, responding to mine earlier thanking him for brunch and the ride to the airport.

> Hi Jae—
> You're welcome! I had a lot of fun with you Saturday night and on Sunday. It's only an hour flight between SF and LA. What if I flew in this weekend? Are you free?
> —Matt

Before I could process this email, there was a knock at my door. I turned from my computer.

"Brad?" I stared at him while I felt a flush work its way up my neck. Apparently, even my office wasn't safe from him. "What do you want?" I asked.

Taking my question as an invitation, he walked in and carefully shut the door. Every nerve ending in me tingled; my senses were on high alert.

He approached my desk. "We haven't talked since San Francisco," he started tentatively. "And the way you just looked at me in the kitchen . . ." He swallowed. "Can we meet after work? I really need to talk to you."

I felt the blood rising to my face, my temples pounding. "No," I said, horrified. "We *cannot* meet after work. You're *married*, Brad."

Brad made a motion with his hands as if to say others could hear us. He came toward my desk and leaned over. He was about to say something, but his eyes flicked over to my computer screen where Matt's email was. He paused, his eyes widened and then narrowed. Then he leaned back from my desk, standing up straight, and said, "You work fast." He considered me for another second. "Must be nice." He then turned and walked out the door.

Must be nice? I thought. *What the hell does that mean?* I told myself that he wanted to say something mean but didn't know exactly what to say. *Still. How dare he be upset at me!* He was the one who lied. I began to shake with fury and got up and shut my door. *Fuck Brad Summers.*

Then I sat down and started composing an email to Matt.

***

At home that night, my cell phone rang, and the caller ID said Levenfield. My stomach sank, wondering what work emergency warranted a phone call.

"Hello?" I answered warily.

A long drunken drawl resembling a "Hello" answered me. I recognized the voice immediately.

"Brad?"

"Yeeeess . . ."

There was a muffled noise I couldn't make out. I thought he was saying my name.

"Brad? Are you okay?" I asked again, my wariness turning to worry.

"Nooo . . ."

"Are you at work?" *This is bad. Is he drunk at work?*

When he didn't immediately respond, I said in my best no-nonsense voice, "What's going on? Why are you calling me?"

Again, an incomprehensible response. I could not decide whether to be concerned or disgusted at the fact that he was in his office at eight o'clock on a Monday night in such condition.

"I need you," he mumbled. Those were the words I had wanted to hear before, but now they had a different meaning. With Brad wasted, they sounded like a booty call.

"You should probably call your wife," I responded coldly. "And take a cab home."

"Nooo . . . I need to talk to you. . . ." I wanted to hang up, but his insistence was starting to soften me, or at least piqued my curiosity. *Could it be he's leaving her? That he's sorry for everything?* Then sounding determined, he asked, "Where are you?"

"I'm at home."

"I'm coming over," Brad said, and hung up.

Fifteen minutes later, my doorbell rang. A taxi had delivered Brad to my house in one piece. He was slumped in my doorway and looked in terrible shape, and his eyes were so pleading that I had no choice but to invite him in.

"Just go to the sofa, and I'll get you some water," I said, opening the door wider to let him through.

In the kitchen, my hands shook as I filled up a water glass. He had left my office so abruptly that morning, and now he was here in my house. What was so important that he had to say? And why had he been drinking?

I set the glass down on the coffee table, then took a position on the far end of the sofa and watched him. Rather than facing me, he just stared straight ahead.

"Are you going to tell me what happened?" I ventured.

He shook his head and then let his chin drop to his chest. A cloud of despair seemed to hang over him.

"Something happened," I said, stating the obvious.

He continued to shake his head. "I don't know. I just don't know."

I still wanted to hate him. He used me. He cheated on his wife. The facts were there, but my hate for him was quickly evaporating, and instead, I hated myself again for feeling sorry for him.

"Brad." I leaned forward and put my hand on his shoulder, shaking him to make him respond.

"Oh, Jae, I'm sorry . . . ," he trailed off, and crumpled under my hand.

I didn't know what to do, and I couldn't form words to ask my questions.

We sat in silence while he drained the water glass. The muffled ring of his phone vibrated from his bag. It carried on incessantly. "Are you going to answer that?" Even though I knew the answer already, he shook his head no. We sat on silently as the phone continued its angry buzzing.

When it finally stopped, Brad spoke. "This is not how it should be."

"What do you mean?"

"I . . . I want my daughter to grow up with two parents." Brad took a deep breath, concentrating on his words. "B-but my marriage isn't a marriage . . . and it never will be." He stared down at his lap, faltering. "And if I try to divorce her, I'm sure she'll take away Ivy, and I won't be able to fight it."

Taking another deep breath, he groaned. "And the debt . . . I just don't know when or *if* it will end. And I feel so guilty that I feel this way. I love my daughter. I really do. And then there's you. . . ." His voice went from morose to tender. "I'm so, so, so sorry if I've hurt you, Jae. I can't stop thinking about you. I wish I had the answer to all of this, but I don't."

He looked up at me pleadingly as if I had the answer. I didn't. Instead, I put my hand on his knee to let him know that I didn't hate him and that I had forgiven him. Listening to Brad's rambling, I tried justifying to myself that I was simply being kind and listening to someone who needed help.

"I'm a horrible person," he said sadly, looking up at me. "That weekend in San Francisco with you was the best time I could remember. That's how it should be. That's what love is supposed to feel like."

My heart began to pound and ache at once. I was too scared to say anything right away. I worried I was letting myself be pulled in again.

"You're not a horrible person," I finally said.

Brad shook his head. "But I am." He looked up at me and moved closer to my side of the sofa. "Because the thing is . . ." He swallowed. "I've fallen for you."

The words I wanted to hear.

"And I know it's selfish of me. That I shouldn't tell you this," he said, tentatively placing a hand on my cheek and gazing into my eyes, "but I think I'm in love with you."

I felt dizzy.

Brad is in love with me! But what does this mean? How hopeless is this?

As he was speaking, I noticed little things like the length of his hair that needed a cut, the stubble on his face, the green in his hazel eyes, and could sense the warmth of his body radiating under his button-down shirt.

"I'm sorry, Jae. B-but . . . ," he stammered. "But I don't know what to do."

I knew what the right thing to do was, and so I couldn't believe the words that came out of my mouth. "Come to bed with me."

That's all it took. Our arms flew around each other. We kissed as if breathing for the first time. Our hands pulled off each other's clothes while we made our way to my bedroom. We never turned on the lights. We just found each other in the dark and took each other in body and soul, and the moment felt inevitable.

Afterward, we lay in the tangle of sheets, my head on his chest, his hand stroking my hair. There was no right or wrong. There was only this.

In the darkness, I said, "I missed you."

"Me too," he responded. His arm around me held me tighter; then he sat up and raised me up with him so he could look me in the eyes. "Jae, I'm yours, okay? I need to figure this mess out, but I will come back to you, to us. No matter what."

He kissed me gently on the mouth, his lips brushing mine. His words were said in shadows. We lay down again, and I closed my eyes, falling asleep in his arms.

When I woke again, it was dawn. Brad was gone. He had disappeared into the night without my noticing. I had let him slip through. In my head, I repeated his words from the night before, but they didn't hold the same power in the weak morning light. I was too tired, and I was alone. Brad had a family, and I would not have his full attention or commitment. For better or worse, I recognized that I would have to accept the status quo for the time being if I wanted him in my life. I sighed and resigned myself to the day and to whatever our relationship was.

Part II

2016

CHAPTER TWELVE

I'm getting married!" my little sister screamed, and I had to hold the phone away from my ear.

"Congratulations, Saf!" I was genuinely happy for her. In fact, I was surprised it hadn't happened sooner, but she had wanted the full experience of her twenties before settling down. She was now twenty-nine and ready.

"And you're going to be my maid of honor!" she screamed again.

"Aren't you supposed to ask me first?" I laughed, teasing her.

"Right! As if you're going to say no," she said gleefully, and I could imagine her rolling her eyes on the other end of the phone.

"Well, okay. Since you asked me so nicely, I am honored to be your maid of honor."

Although I found her soon-to-be husband a little overbearing, he was completely besotted with Saffie, and I hoped they would live happily ever after together.

Saffie's upcoming nuptials, though, made me examine my own life at age thirty-four and lack of happily-ever-after.

The seven-year anniversary from when Brad first stepped

into my office was soon approaching. During those years, time had moved either too fast or too heartbreakingly slow. My days, weeks, and months were measured by when I could spend time with him again. My existence had become a waiting game. I knew we were having an affair, but the word was so tawdry. I felt as if he were my only true friend, my only confidant, my soulmate. I never made demands or issued ultimatums. Our relationship, whatever it was, was less than I ever would have accepted from anyone else. But whenever I was with anyone else, Brad was all I wanted.

How does one fall into such a relationship? More specifically, how did *I* let myself become the other woman? Both law-firm life and Brad were all-consuming, gobbling up my time and leaving me no other outlet. Although I had some random dates here and there, and my mother sought to set me up with her friends' sons, no one compared to Brad and the intensity between us. My female friendships suffered as well because whom could I tell? My closest friend remained Maya, who was safely several hundred miles away in San Francisco. Between work and Brad, I had nothing left over for anyone else. I tried to break it off. Once in a while I would attempt online dating and was always disappointed. I read books with titles like *Will He Really Leave Her for Me*. But I felt that all those women were delusional and that *my* relationship was different, deeper. I thought of going to a therapist, but I couldn't even admit my secret to a stranger. Instead, I isolated myself from everyone. In the end, I was lonely, and I let the loneliness lead me back to Brad.

Brad did make an effort for me. He kept his word and always came back to me. So even after yet another year of our relationship, I never demanded that he leave his wife, since I knew it would be akin to asking him to leave his daughter. While I fiercely love my stepfather and he's always been my "dad," I would still give anything to have even just one memory of my biological father, and I couldn't take Ivy's father away from her. But what *was* I expecting from Brad?

Once I asked, "Do you feel guilty afterward?"

His response was, "I feel guilty leaving you."

He didn't answer my real question. Maybe I was already asking too much. I was asking him to feel normal about our relationship. It could never be normal. I could not tell my few friends or family. We hid it from our colleagues, barely talking to each other at work. At the office, I felt nervous around Jeff and Mindy, and I found myself drifting away from others because my secret was too big and too shameful. And maybe in being secret, it was the most intimate and intense relationship I had known. My earlier dating experience told me that after a year, the lustful phase ends and true colors come out, in some cases, within six months. It had been six years going on seven, and I craved Brad more with each passing day. Though rationally I knew it was wrong, I couldn't give him up. By that point, I had invested so much of my time and my heart in our relationship, that if Brad wasn't who I had built him up to be, then I would have to admit to myself that I was ruining my life for nothing.

Though I had never been the type of girl who dreamed of her wedding day, I also hadn't dreamed of being the type who slept with someone else's husband. As I stood up at my sister's wedding, did I really want a scarlet *A* to be burning inside me? The answer was no. I knew that we needed to move our relationship in either one direction or the other. But I was terrified of interrupting the status quo and at the possibility of losing Brad forever.

***

My first duty as maid of honor was to go wedding-dress shopping with my sister. I was running a little late for the appointment and I felt especially sheepish, as Brad had been over the night before and I was tired. When I stepped into the Monique Lhuillier boutique, my sister, mom, Aunt Ingrid (my mom's sister and Saffie's godmother), and cousin, Eva, were waiting for me. So I girded myself when my aunt greeted me snidely, saying, "Glad you could make it."

Saffie, ever the perfect hostess, rescued me. "Hey, Jae. I'm so happy you're here," she said, and gave me a hug. "We've just been looking at gowns. No try-ons yet. Let's get you some champagne." She released me and looked around for a salesperson. My mom came over and squeezed my shoulders. "Hi, honey," and with pride in her voice, defended me to her sister, "Jae's busy these days. You know she just made partner."

Before I could even get my apologies out, the usual family drama had begun.

Ingrid was always in competition with and clearly jealous of our mom, the younger sister. And because she lacked what my mom had in looks, handsome husband, and money, Ingrid then extended this competitiveness to her children. Saffie had learned early on how to put Eva in her place, while I just tried to avoid them altogether.

The saleswoman came over and proffered me a glass of champagne before leading us to the main floor. Saffie hooked her arm into mine and clinked my glass, whispering, "Giddy up," and I stifled a laugh and said, "Cin cin."

The five-year age gap that had felt like a generation gap when we were kids had seemed to close when Saffie reached her late twenties. And while we were very different people, she had begun to value my advice again. "I know fashion isn't your thing," she had confided in me, "but I don't trust Ingrid or Eva. I just invited them for Mom's sake."

At one point when my mom got up to show a dress to Saffie in the dressing room, leaving me alone with my aunt and cousin, Eva turned to me, her eyes wide with fake concern, and said, "It must be hard for you that your younger sister is getting married."

"Why would it be hard?" I asked casually, but stared at her, daring whatever was going to come out of her mouth next.

"Well, you know." She shrugged. "'Cause you're not."

"Oh. I never thought about that." It was true, since I hadn't thought about it in the way Eva was implying. "So, no, it's not hard. I'm happy for her." I gave Eva a quick smile and then took a sip of my champagne, determined not to rise to her bait.

Not satisfied with my response, Aunt Ingrid chimed in, "Are you bringing a date to the wedding?" If my mother and aunt had anything in common, it was their interest in my single status.

"Um, again, I haven't really thought about it. It's a year away." I took another sip of my champagne and avoided her eyes by scanning the room, hoping my mother and sister would return soon. I should have been more prepared for these questions, or at least used to lying—my thoughts were not on whom I would bring, but on whom I could never bring.

Feeling my temples start to pound, I jumped up, pulling out a pale blue bridesmaid dress on a rack nearby, and said, "This is pretty." I had no feelings about the dress but needed to change the conversation while we waited.

Eva touched the floaty material under the Empire waist. "Hmm, this is nice."

But Aunt Ingrid wasn't so easily distracted. "So, Jae, honey, are you dating anyone?" The *honey* oozed faux sweetness.

"No one serious," I said, growing hot under her questioning and scrambling for a subject change.

Luckily, this was when Saffie came sashaying out in a new dress, and she must have heard the exchange on her approach.

"Oh, come on, you two. Jae barely has time for this nonsense 'cause she works so much."

"Congratulations, then," Eva said, turning to me, but didn't seem impressed. "Guess you're married to the firm."

I was probably more embarrassed that my younger sister felt the need to stick up for me than frustrated by my relatives' nosy questions. Saffie told me later, "Eva's a cow. She's just jealous of you."

But the truth was that with every dress Saffie tried on, Eva was right—I *was* a little envious. Not because I dreamed of a similar big wedding day, but because of how uncomplicated it was for Saffie, how straightforward her relationship had been with her fiancé, and how they were committing to each other for life. At night when Saffie went to bed, her husband would be right next to her until morning. They would fight over mundane things like the remote control or what was for dinner or whether to get a dog. They would buy a sofa together, plan their vacations together, and always be each other's guaranteed plus one for events.

I felt a headache coming on, and it wasn't from the champagne.

When Saffie next came out in a surprisingly subtle lace mermaid dress with a tulle bottom that still highlighted her tall figure and curves, my mom cried, "That's the one!"

Saffie turned around on the pedestal, a huge smile on her face and said, "Jae, what do you think?"

I nodded my approval with a smile, feeling tears in my eyes. Yes, I was happy for my sister, and, yes, I was a little sad for myself.

***

The next couple of days, I wrestled with my emotions. I didn't have to want to get married for Brad to make a commitment to me, and only me. And while I knew he loved me, it was no longer enough. Ivy was in first grade, and over the last few years, Brad had broached the subject of divorce with Kathryn. But every time he brought it up, she would promise things would change.

During the course of their seven-year marriage, Kathryn's compulsive spending returned, and she refused to get a job even though they agreed she would once Ivy was in school. She would claim she was "depressed" and blame Brad, taking out her anger on him by either giving him the silent treatment or incessantly screaming at him about all the ways he had ruined her life. Sometimes when she was supposed to pick up Ivy from school or other activities, Kathryn was nowhere to be found. When Brad would call her out on her behavior, she would threaten to take Ivy away from him and even once threatened to take her own life. She refused to see a therapist for her erratic behavior and mood swings. So Brad hired a nanny, hoping that by having more time to herself, Kathryn would feel less stressed, and *he* started going to therapy instead.

Though Brad tried not to talk too much about Kathryn to me, she was obviously manipulating him. And if I was honest with myself, I was starting to resent not her but *him* for putting up with all that nonsense for so long.

Brad had stayed over on Monday night, and I had told him about wedding-dress shopping.

"Your aunt and cousin sound fun," he said dryly.

"Yes. They're quite the comedy duo," I quipped. "Hopefully, my maid-of-honor status means I'll be sitting far, far away from them during dinner."

"That's good. They sound like they could make anyone lose their appetite," Brad joked, but it sounded forced.

I couldn't think of a comeback, and unsure of what to say next, I merely responded, "Hmm."

And when Brad didn't say anything more, I knew it was time to change the subject from my sister's wedding.

Later, after Brad went home, I lay in my bed and ruminated. I missed him. I always missed him terribly when he left. I wanted to spend the night next to his body and wake up with him. We could never truly spend time together in LA; it was usually dark bars or my place. There were too many eyes, too many constraints, and other priorities. As other women in my situation before must have done, I refused to think our relationship was wrong and justified it by telling myself that we were simply in an impossible situation.

I vowed to think of someplace—somewhere we could be together for at least a few days and have an honest conversation about our future. That night Brad had shown me a new sketch of a man standing alone on the beach at the edge of the ocean. As part of our rituals, whenever he showed me a new sketch or photograph, he'd ask me to write a description for him. So I wrote:

His feet on the warm, soft sand triggers a memory of a woman's body. All he can think about is that woman who haunts his dreams. Barefoot, he wades into the water, hoping the waves will crash over him, drowning out how much he wants to be with her at that moment.

And I knew where we could go.

CHAPTER THIRTEEN

The next time Brad came over, while we were lying on my sofa, I ventured, "I think we should take a trip."

"Where to?" Brad had been lightly stroking my hair and paused. "It would have to be a business trip. I'd have to expense it," he said, his voice tight.

I understood. We could not simply take a trip together. There needed to be a reason.

"My family's place in Lake Tahoe," I said. "It's private and right on the water."

Brad didn't say anything right away, but I could see him working through it, considering the possibility. "I was thinking more of a hotel. For a business trip, it looks better."

Yes, the icky awful truth we carefully danced around—his wife would want to know where he was staying.

"It was just an idea," I said, knowing I was breaking the unwritten rules of our relationship.

But then Brad's arm tightened around me. "Tell me more about your family's lake house."

"What do you want to know?"

"How soon can we go?"

***

I didn't ask him why he suddenly agreed, and he didn't offer a reason. Instead, we spent the next couple days on the logistics.

It seemed best to go when my parents were on their annual two-week European vacation. Saffie rarely used the house, and now that she was in the midst of wedding preparations, I knew she wouldn't be leaving Los Angeles unless it was for a bachelorette party. We timed it for a three-day weekend so that we wouldn't have to both ask for vacation time. Since we planned on driving, we even debated taking two cars. Our paranoia stretched that far. In the end, we settled on one.

It was a seven-hour drive. Brad drove us out of LA, and then we planned on switching on the second leg. As I fiddled with my iPhone and connected it to the radio, I asked tentatively, "What did you say at home?"

"Fishing weekend with old high school friends. Might be potential clients." He took his eyes off the road for a second to look at me.

I nodded but didn't betray any emotion. I was done with this half-life with Brad, but I needed to be patient for the next two days. Although we were finally taking a trip together, unless I forced the issue, the place we were going wouldn't turn our relationship into anything other than what it already was behind the closed doors of my bungalow.

The lake house was secluded on private property surrounded by woods. The other houses weren't visible behind the walls of trees, so we would be free from the prying eyes of neighbors. I was a little nervous that the trip might be too much time together. I worried that it would only make me want him more, while he might get scared off and want me less. Still, part of me was cautiously hopeful that maybe, just maybe, this was the push he needed to leave his wife.

I'm sure I wore my anxiety on my face because when Brad glanced over at me, he said, "It will be okay," and reached over to squeeze my hand. Although his face didn't give anything away, we were strangely quiet on the ride. Brad drove intensely with his eyes straight ahead, the car moving over the speed limit, reckless yet competent. The radio was on, and I made a mocking remark about a pop song. He didn't get it, and I had to explain my joke. The fatalist in me said it was a sign that our relationship would never survive outside the bounds of my bungalow and Levenfield.

We only stopped for gas once and didn't stop for food. This trip was a new level of deceit, making us both uncomfortable. When we did talk, it was limited to work or items in the news, until he asked me to tell him about the house again.

In my best real estate agent voice, I said, "It's a four-bedroom home right on the lakefront. There's a large lawn that stretches down to a private beach. It's quiet, and the most exciting activity is watching the sunset."

Once we were on the road with trees stretching for miles, I kept my eyes open for the little tin mailbox that would signal the private road to the house. Soon it appeared, and I turned down the dirt road that would lead to our reclusive days ahead.

I didn't visit the lake house that frequently; but whenever I did, I always became nostalgic, remembering riding up as a child with my parents and watching the house come into view, excited to go swimming or out on my dad's boat. Over the summer, my grandparents would be there, too, and my grandpa would play card games with us while my grandma would be baking something sweet in the kitchen. I hoped this weekend would not taint those innocent childhood memories.

I drove slowly, keeping my eyes on the lookout for any wayward branches. It wasn't until we pulled up to the house that one of us spoke.

"We're here," I said, stating the obvious.

"You look beautiful."

"What?" I turned to Brad, who was smiling, his eyes bright.

He paused before repeating, "I said, you look beautiful."

The happiness in his eyes and his compliment melted my worry. I loved him, and we were going to spend the weekend together.

"Let me show you the water," I said, finally able to smile.

I got out of the car and led Brad around to the back of the house. I always considered the back to be the "front" since I spent so much time outside playing on the lawn as a child, then later as a teenager dragging out a lounge chair and devouring novels in quiet bliss. The lawn was peppered with large trees that provided shade, and there was a stone path that led to the dock and water.

"Wow! This is incredible," he commented as we rounded the corner and the lake came into view.

"Isn't it?"

Brad walked down to the edge of the lawn right before the beach. He stood with his feet apart, his hands on his hips, surveying the water. I admired his form and made a mental picture to tuck away safely in my memories.

After surveying the huge expanse of lake, he finally turned around and made his way to where I was standing. I couldn't stop smiling. He was smiling too.

"This is such a great place," he said, approaching me.

"I know." I beamed at him.

When he reached me, he put his arms around me and kissed me. This was what I wanted.

"Thank you," he said.

We returned to the actual front of the house. Brad had already taken our bags out of the trunk. I unlocked the front door and he carried in our luggage and set it in the hallway. I took him on a quick tour of the house, and then we drove into town for some groceries. Brad and I had never really done anything "domestic" together, and at the store we were suddenly self-conscious around each other, our natural rhythm slightly out of sync, asking questions such as "which brand do you like better" or each grabbing the cart at the same time. We picked up some items to make no-fuss meals and stocked up on snacks, like tortilla chips and the fixings for sangria. Our awkward carefulness made me wonder if Brad and Kathryn had perfected a seamless routine while shopping and reminded me that Brad and I were simply playing house. I shoved those feelings down but couldn't help looking over my shoulder.

While we carried our groceries to the car, I idly noticed Brad's hand and the absence of a wedding ring. He still never wore a wedding band, and I wondered whether he even owned one. In all the time we spent together, I'd never asked him about it, and the store parking lot wasn't the place to pursue that line of questioning. The less I knew, the less culpable I could feel. It was always filed away with all my other questions to be asked at a later date—or never.

Back at the house, Brad carried the shopping bags inside, and I unloaded them into the refrigerator and pantry. After we put the items away, I stood at the sink and washed the fruit for our sangria later. Brad came up behind me and said, "I'm so glad we're here."

Even after all these years of knowing him, I still found that his breath on my neck warmed my whole being, and I could feel the blood rushing to my core. He rested his hands on my waist and began kissing my neck. I still loved the way his lips felt on my skin. To feel like this was worth the wasted years of my dating youth. I turned around and began kissing him as we worked our way to the bedroom. Once on the bed, we couldn't take off each other's clothing fast enough—kissing the entire time while pulling away at our clothes, trying to get to the other's skin. There was no foreplay, just full body-to-body contact. I wanted to be one person with him forever. I never wanted to move.

As we lay there afterward, I sighed with relief. I didn't have to count the minutes until he would leave me. We were free. There were no rushed moments. No guilty returns. No other constraints. We could be with each other uninterrupted for the next few days. Even with this luxury of time, our bodies did not want to part until finally our growling stomachs forced us reluctantly out of bed.

After a shower, where we still let each other's hands explore the other's body, and a change into fresh clothes, we headed into the kitchen. "Are you ready for my famous sangria?" Brad asked while juggling some oranges and clumsily dropping one.

I laughed. "Yes, and let's break open those chips, too, while I cook."

I found a pitcher for Brad, who went to work. Once he finished his sangria-making, he headed out to the garage to find the necessary outdoor furniture so we could eat outside.

While he fixed our drinks, I had been chopping vegetables for our quesadillas. I had originally planned to make enchiladas, but all that rolling and then baking seemed like too much work, and we were too hungry. *Brad will just have to wait to appreciate my culinary skills,* I mused. Then I remembered that this was probably the only chance I'd have to cook for him unless something finally changed that weekend. I looked sadly out the window at Brad, who was fumbling with the outdoor furniture. Rather than a table and chairs, he had dragged out a couple of lounge chairs that were giving him a hard time. His graceless fight with them made me laugh. I had a lifetime to be lonely; I needed to enjoy this little time we had.

While I was plating the last quesadilla, Brad came back into the house. "Can I help with anything?" he asked.

I directed him to the drawer with the utensils.

In a mock-insulted voice, he said, "You haven't even touched my sangria!"

"Ha, ha. Glasses are in the cabinet above," I said happily.

We brought our drinks and food outside. He had pulled out a small table and placed it between the loungers. The late-afternoon light hinted at the sunset that was only a couple hours away. We chatted about an artist whose biography he was reading and stayed away from any topic that might remind him of "home." When we finished eating, I brought our plates inside. When I came back outside, Brad had removed the table that was between us and pulled the loungers closer, so they were right next to each other. He lay there, looking handsome and relaxed. I just wanted to stand there and admire him for as long as possible. I could never stop looking at him. I was afraid if I did, he would disappear.

But I couldn't linger there forever, because my other instinct was to always be close to him. When I sat back down in my lounger, Brad turned toward me, smiling, and handed me my glass. As I settled in, he reached out for my hand. We stayed that way until the sun finally dipped behind the lake and disappeared. When it was completely gone, Brad squeezed my hand. Maybe he was worried I'd disappear too.

We stayed sitting in the dark and stared up at the night sky littered with stars. It had been a while since I had experienced such darkness and so many stars—there was too much smog and light pollution in LA.

"C'mere," Brad said, inviting me over to his lounger. "I'm cold."

I laughed as I climbed onto his chair. Even though the night was slightly cool, I felt warm wrapped up in his arms. I could have stayed like that for eternity. And we almost did, since the next thing I knew, I was waking up. I could feel Brad's breathing, the rise and fall of his chest, and knew he was still asleep. I tried to stay still so as not to wake him, but within minutes he was also awake.

"What?" he said groggily, not quite realizing his surroundings. "Oh. I must've fallen asleep." He relaxed back into the chair.

"Me too. Should we go inside?"

"No. Let's stay out here a little longer."

He told me about the dream he had. He said he must have been staring at the lake and sky for too long, because in his dream he was just floating on the water.

"Just you?" I asked.

"Yes. It was strange. I wanted to swim. I had to get somewhere. But instead, I just continued floating. There was nothing around, and so I just let the water take me."

"I can't decide if that sounds ominous or peaceful."

"I don't know. Or I couldn't make up my mind to swim, I guess." He shrugged and then hugged me.

The meaning of the dream was obvious to me: Brad was floating between me and Kathryn. He had been drifting for too long, and it was time for him to decide whether to swim against or with the current. I swallowed as I wondered if this was my opening to bring up "the talk." But when he said, "Maybe we should go inside. You're starting to shiver," I lost my courage and decided to float along with him a little while longer.

We brought the glasses inside, and I loaded them into the dishwasher. I turned around to see him watching me and smiling.

"What?" I asked.

"Nothing." He shook his head, still smiling.

I put my hands on my hips and cocked my head, mimicking his expression. He laughed and reached out for my hand to draw me closer. He then smoothed a stray hair away from my forehead and said, "I'm just happy. That's all."

He kissed me and then dramatically and jokingly swept me up and carried me off to the bedroom once again. When he dropped me on the bed, I laughed and pulled him toward me. I was happy too. The night was sweet. Nothing rushed. Nothing forbidden. But instead familiar, as if we belonged together.

CHAPTER FOURTEEN

We spent two easy days in this manner—meandering around the woods, swimming in the lake, or dozing in the warm shade. We never turned on the radio or television, so there were no reminders of the outside world. We made love, we made dinner, and we relished no other existence than our own.

On our last evening as I was preparing dinner, I wanted to ask Brad his preference on wine. When I called his name, he didn't answer. I had heard the front door close earlier, so I went outside. I didn't see him, but I heard his voice speaking quietly nearby.

"Brad?" I tried again.

I could hear his shoes crunching on the gravel of the driveway. Then I heard his voice much more clearly. "I have to go. Love you too."

The words pierced my body like a knife, tearing my heart. I froze. *"I love you too." "I love you too."* My mind repeated his words.

When he came into view, his eyes met mine. He slid his

phone into his pocket and started walking back to the house. His eyes looked guilty. But I did not know whom they were guilty toward. He approached me. "I'm sorry, Jae," he said. His lips brushed my cheek. "I'm sorry."

I found my voice. "Sorry for whom?"

"I'm sorry to you." He wrapped his arms around me and held me tight. I was sorry for me too. I stood limply in his arms. I couldn't bring myself to hug him back. Although I knew it all too well, those words spelled it out loud and clear—I was nothing but the other woman. Brad had never made a promise to me. The next morning, when we would get in the car, he would be driving home. Our weekend was nothing but a vacation for him, I thought bitterly, a quick reprieve from family life, whereas this weekend *was* my life.

I wanted to shake off my depressing thoughts and not let our time together end on a sour note. The honest conversation I'd been waiting for was never going to materialize. I could have confronted him, but what was the point? I was going to lose.

"Jae, I'm sorry," Brad kept saying, brushing my hair with his hand. "I have to call home. I can't just not talk to her." He paused and added, "I need to check on Ivy." I could hear the defensiveness starting to creep into his voice, and I didn't want to hear any more. I didn't want to hear him justify himself, and his wife.

"No. I understand. You don't have to say anything." I pulled away, downplaying my feelings, just like I had for the last several years. "Of course you have to call." Even if it was just a phone call, Kathryn had shown up again and asserted that Brad was hers.

I looked up into his eyes, and they looked lost, as if he wanted to say something more but couldn't. I loved him and wanted to erase that look from his eyes, but I resisted and took a steadying breath instead. Hearing his *"I love you"* to Kathryn hadn't just hurt; it had torn my heart apart. There was no answer, so I turned away and headed back into the house.

I returned to the kitchen. The water was boiling on the stove. Overflowing with pasta, it spilled from the pot, hissed and steamed, and then evaporated. That's when the tears began to fill my eyes and overflow. Large streaming tears. I couldn't finish making dinner, so I turned off the burner and walked out the back door. I walked past the lawn, down to the shore, and collapsed at the edge of the water. I pulled my knees up to my chest, pulling myself as tightly as I could into a ball, hoping to squeeze myself so taut that the empty feeling inside would disappear. Or better yet, I would disappear.

Brad gave me a couple minutes to myself. Soon, though, I heard his footsteps approaching gingerly. He sat down next to me, not saying anything for a few moments, both of us looking out upon the water. Finally, he made a move to put his arm around my shoulders. "Jae," he pleaded.

"No." What was the point of discussing anything? I let him hold me but continued to stare straight ahead. "We have to go home tomorrow," I said quietly.

"Yes, we do," he muttered. His arm fell for a second. Then he regrouped and held me tighter. "Jae?"

I couldn't respond. Brad was going home to Kathryn, and I was going to my empty bungalow, and we were never going to be together. I fought the rising hysteria in my mind that screamed how I had wasted so much time and energy on someone I never had a future with.

Brad didn't say anything else, but just held me. I was so depleted that I let myself lean into him. We didn't move or speak for what seemed like forever. We did not eat dinner. We stayed sitting there until the sun sank into the water, leaving us in the dark. As soon as it disappeared, I started to cry again. Rather than the large fat tears in the kitchen, these were quiet and steady, and I let them run their course. Brad held my face and gently wiped them away with his thumb. I finally looked up at him. I hated him; I hated myself; I hated this situation. But I still let him kiss me, and I returned his kiss, urgent and desperate. As we made out in the sand, I figured it would be our last night, forever. Brad disengaged himself long enough to pull me up, and with our arms around each other we walked back to the house.

We went straight to the bedroom, and I sat carefully on the edge of the bed. I pulled Brad toward me, and we had the most incredible sex we had ever had. Even though we were both ready, we took our time, savoring each second, running our hands over each other's skin, memorizing every inch of each other's body. When it was over, we still did not speak. Rather than pull away, Brad continued to lie on top of me, keeping each inch of our bodies in the closest contact that was possible. We fell asleep like this, until I woke up in the middle of the night to Brad's kisses, once again awakening my desire and letting him find his way inside me.

As soon as the first hint of daylight peeked through the shades, it was over. It had to be over. While Brad was still asleep, I crawled out of bed, grabbed a blanket off the sofa in the living room, and walked down to the shore. Even though it was summer, it was still a bit chilly in the dawn air. I wrapped the blanket around my shoulders and sat down. I looked over the water at the early-morning light. I knew what I had to do that day. As soon as we returned to Los Angeles, I had to make a phone call. I could no longer be in such close proximity to Brad. I could not go into the office every day and see him. I could not even be in the same city as him, and then not see him. I had to put up a boundary, and it had to be physical. It was time to leave Los Angeles.

***

After the long and painful car ride home, I was resolute about my solution and kept my plans from Brad. There was no reason to include him in my decision—whether he let me go or begged me to stay, I was too heartbroken to handle either response.

When he dropped me off, he leaned in and merely kissed me on the cheek. "I'll see you tomorrow," he said. It was brief; after all, we were back on home turf. I grabbed my bag from the trunk. He watched me open the front door and then waved off. After I'd watched him drive away, I went inside and started planning my new life.

That night I went to work updating my résumé and started researching law firms in San Francisco. I had considered returning to Boston or somewhere on the East Coast, but I would have to take another bar exam in a new state, which could delay the job hunt when I was ready to move immediately. My best bet for a quick move was San Francisco. I had Maya there, and I would also have her circle of friends. My friendship with Matt had dropped down to a mere acquaintance level, and he was happily in another relationship, though we still kept in sporadic contact. Once I finished my résumé, it was only ten o'clock, but I surprisingly fell asleep right away.

The next morning at work, Brad and I passed each other in the hallway, and I felt a small tug on my heart. We nodded hello, careful not to let our eyes betray any emotion. By the time I returned to my desk, he had sent an email inviting me out for coffee.

Instead of responding to his email, I closed the door to my office, pulled my phone out of my purse, and called Maya.

"Jae, what's up?" she said when she answered. "Are you at work?"

"Hey. Yeah, I'm at work. You?"

"I'm on my way. Just leaving Peet's."

"Do you have time to talk?"

"Of course," she said warily, perhaps sensing something in my tone. "But do I need to sit down?"

"I don't know. You tell me." I took a deep breath. "I'm thinking of moving to San Francisco."

"You're kidding!" I heard a shuffling noise on her end. "Damn! I just spilled coffee on myself. Maybe I should've sat down." She laughed.

"Sorry about that." I laughed back. "So, what do you think?"

"That's great! When? Where? How? Were you offered a job?"

"The *when* would be as soon as possible. I'm just tired of LA, you know?" She didn't know, but I also couldn't tell her the truth. "I put together a résumé last night and want to start looking."

"Great! I'd love to pass on your résumé at my firm." She paused; her tone cautious again. "But why now? You just made partner. Is something going on?"

I swallowed, and inwardly berated myself for not thinking this through before calling. "What do you mean?" I asked, trying to sound innocent.

"Law firms are going to wonder why you're leaving the second you made partner. It could come across as suspicious or disloyal."

Ah, the practicalities of the job. I had thought of this. But I had to weigh the continued emotional toll with Brad versus the career I had built but could practice in another city.

"Yeah, I know. But maybe they'll just think I want to move to San Francisco?"

"I guess. But you have to have a reason. They're going to ask."

"Tell them I have family up there," I offered, then sighed. "I just need a change."

Not missing a beat, Maya asked, "Is it a guy?"

"No," I said quickly. "You know I'm not dating anyone. And maybe that's why I need a change. No decent guys in LA."

"Unfortunately, the situation isn't much better here. And, anyway, I introduced you to the one decent guy in San Francisco, and you blew him off."

"I know. I know. Matt was great. But with our hours, I didn't want to fail at another long-distance relationship," I lied, knowing she still hadn't fully forgiven me for Matt.

"Okay, let me ask around and see if we're hiring. You know," she added, conspiratorially, "I get a signing bonus if you join our firm."

"Yes, I know." Not realizing I'd been holding my breath, I let out a big sigh and suddenly felt light-headed. "Thank you, thank you, thank you. You're the best, Maya! I'll forward you my résumé tonight."

When we hung up, there was another email from Brad.

Are you mad at me?

That was unlike him, so I called him. "I'm not mad. I have a lot to do. I was out of the office for three days," I said pointedly before he could say anything, demonstrating that, yes, I was mad.

"Come on, Jae." Brad sighed. "I need to talk to you. How about at five?"

"We'll see."

Brad accepted my response, and I figured I could always come up with another excuse later in the day. Besides, even if we met for coffee, it didn't matter anymore. Steps were in place. Soon there would be hundreds of miles between us. I spent the morning researching San Francisco's neighborhoods online and daydreaming about where I would live. I couldn't wait to move to an apartment that had no memories of Brad.

Around four o'clock, he emailed me to make sure I was still free for coffee. I punted again and said I couldn't.

I really need to talk to you, he wrote back. I'll wait until you're ready to leave.

I felt my resolve weakening. Maybe this was it? Maybe the weekend had made up his mind? But I had already made up mine. I left the office a little before five so I could avoid him and not be tempted. I felt like a jerk. I was being a jerk. It hurt me to do so, but I thought back to all the times he ignored me early on or the several-week silences I'd endured over the years. Our non-relationship was going to go out with a whimper. But I didn't want to see him until I knew for sure that I was moving to San Francisco.

***

When I arrived at work the next day, Brad came into my office and cornered me for lunch. Since he wasn't giving up, I decided to get it over with and met him in the lobby at noon. Neither of us was that hungry, so we went to a Starbucks. We ordered our coffees. Brad paid, and then we sat across from each other at a tiny wooden table. Once seated, I cut to the chase. "What do you want to talk to me about?"

"I guess I just wanted to see how you were. You know? After the weekend." He slowly spun his paper coffee cup around, not yet taking a sip.

"That doesn't answer my question. You told me yesterday you had something to say to me."

I knew Brad well enough to know there was something on his mind, but he wasn't able to get it out. But I couldn't sympathize or make anything easy for him. I loved him; he had broken my heart, and I wanted him to be uncomfortable. In my mind, I wanted to be the better person, but my heart wanted his to break too. I didn't unleash any of my own hurt or anger, but I knew it showed behind my eyes as we sat there.

"I wanted to say I'm sorry. I'm sorry about the way things are." He paused again. "Jae, you are beautiful, smart, sexy, funny. You are so many things; I don't even know how to express it all." I wondered if this was the moment. Now that I was moving, was I going to hear the words I had wanted to hear from the beginning? So I kept silent and waited.

"I wish I had met you in another time and place. I wish things weren't how they are right now." He stopped there, then continued, his voice growing more uneven. "And I feel guilty even saying that. I am a father, and I can't change that. Kathryn is . . . ," he said, stumbling over her name, "having some health problems right now. She isn't going to give me a divorce, and I love my daughter." He stopped, and I noticed his hand shaking. I knew he was going to get emotional, and I did not want this to happen, not here, not sitting in the middle of the day in a crowded Starbucks. I put my hand over his, both our hands holding his coffee cup on the table.

"It's okay, Brad. You don't have to say any more." He looked up from the table into my eyes.

Brad stammered, "But—"

"No. Whatever else you want to say," I said, "I don't want to hear it."

Brad remained still, his eyes bloodshot and watery. We continued to hold hands on the table for anybody to see. What did it matter? It wasn't like we had anything to hide anymore, now that my departure from LA was imminent. Everything else would have to remain unsaid. Brad was telling me he'd made his choice, and that choice was not me.

After a couple more seconds, I let go of his hand. Even

though we'd been sitting there for less than ten minutes, I stood up silently and grabbed my coffee.

"Wait," Brad said, and reached for my hand again.

I pulled it away, shook my head, and then turned and left. I had no more words.

I did not hear from him the rest of the afternoon. When I walked past his door to leave for the day, I noticed it was open; his computer was on, but his jacket was gone. I had a feeling he never came back.

Brad didn't come in the next day either. Normally I let those days bother me, but not that day—I had other business to attend to. Even though I was waiting on Maya's firm, I also contacted a recruiter. Unfortunately, the recruiter said the same thing as Maya—it would be difficult to change firms as a new junior partner unless I had a large book of clients willing to come with me or some specialized practice of law to offer, and I didn't. I was a transactional corporate attorney, and my clients worked with my team, not just me. Wanting to move to San Francisco because I loved the city and had friends there wasn't a reason for a law firm to grant an interview. I called Maya and brainstormed.

"You need a business reason," Maya repeated. "How about you want to become more involved in high tech?"

I had no interest in the tech industry, but I didn't have any better ideas. "That could work."

"Or why not just wait until next year? What's the hurry?" she pressed. If I couldn't convince Maya of my desire to relocate to San Francisco, how was I going to do it in an interview?

"The *hurry* is that I'm ready now."

"You know I want you here, but it doesn't seem like the best career move. You've been there seven years already, so what's another year?"

Because the last seven years had been pure agony. Because I

was thirty-four and wasn't getting any younger. I had made my decision, and I needed to act on it. But I couldn't say any of this to Maya, as she was my best hope for a quick escape out of Los Angeles. And considering her strong reaction seven years ago when I first told her about my one-night stand with a colleague, how would she feel that I had kept this secret from her for so long? I couldn't risk it. *Maybe one day I will tell her,* I thought, *but not today.*

"You're right," I said. "It's just that now that it's in my head, I want to follow through with it."

Maya emailed me with an update that afternoon to let me know that she had given my résumé and talked me up to the head of her department. She said that he was busy with a deal that week, so the earliest response would be next week. I was grateful for her help, but I did corporate work and Maya's department was real estate. I didn't want to question her decision to pass along my résumé within her department rather than to the hiring partner of her firm. Every firm has its politics, and I assumed she knew best. But I was curious and asked her about it on the phone later that night.

"I know." She sighed. "I mentioned it to our hiring partner who's also the head of our corporate group here. I told him I had a friend who wanted to move up here to get involved in technology deals, and he didn't seem that interested. But he's a newish partner trying to establish himself, and there's a bit of a power play going on between the corporate and real estate departments right now. So it could just be that since it's me passing on your résumé, he's not interested."

"Got it. But if he's corporate and you gave my résumé to the head of real estate instead, isn't that going to have the same effect? If there's a problem between the two departments, why would the head of corporate want to hire someone suggested by the head of the real estate group?" I asked, more than a little worried.

"Yeah, about that. I told Stan you were interested in the real estate side of things, as you've been involved in both the corporate and real estate aspects of deals. It says so on your résumé. And like I said, Stan doesn't really like this new corporate attorney."

She didn't have to say anything more. I understood. I would be walking into a political minefield—that was hardly news in the world of law. But it was better than the emotional minefield I was currently walking in.

"Thanks, Maya. Fingers crossed I get an interview."

CHAPTER FIFTEEN

Perhaps because it was a referral, things moved faster than I expected. Maya's firm, Gilchrist & Jenkins, scheduled me for an interview a week after Maya had handed over my résumé. The head of their real estate group would be in town from New York that week and wanted to interview me in person. The recruiter hadn't managed yet to secure me any interviews, which meant everything was riding on the Gilchrist one. I flew up to San Francisco a day early to prepare. I stayed at a nearby hotel in the Financial District, and Maya came over after work. We spent the evening prepping for the next day, just like we did in law school before a big exam. Maya asked me questions and gave me tips on everyone who would be interviewing me.

"And remember." She looked at me seriously. "You want to help grow the real estate department."

At nine o'clock on Friday morning, I was in my black suit and ready to begin my marathon interview schedule starting with Stan, the head of the real estate department, followed by interviews with two more partners, and then an interview lunch with both Maya and Mark Dresner, the head partner of the corporate group in that office—the hiring partner who didn't want to hire me.

At lunchtime, my last interviewer brought me to Mark's office. Mark stood up when we entered his office, but rather than walk around his desk to greet me, he simply leaned over it to shake my hand.

"Hello, Jasmine. It's a pleasure to meet you."

As we shook hands, I made sure to return his confident eye contact and plastered on a bright smile, secretly knowing that it wasn't a pleasure for him and that I had to make it so; but I also worried that my unnatural cheerfulness would put him more on alert. I had already researched him online and had memorized his background. His photo on the website was the standard nonoffensive headshot of a reasonably attractive attorney, but in person he was incredibly handsome. He was tall and looked like he logged time at the gym. He had brown hair and brown eyes that looked friendly, ready to deliver a joke.

"Have a seat." He gestured to the chair on the other side of his desk. "While we're waiting for Maya, why don't you tell me about yourself?"

It was such an open-ended question, the type I hate in most interviews because they tend to let you ramble on until the interviewer actually thinks of something to say.

"Sure. I went to undergrad at Boston and law school at Harvard. Since graduating law school, I've been practicing corporate law for the last seven years at Levenfield. . . ."

Mark waved his hand, dismissing my answer before I finished. "Yes, of course. I can see all that from your résumé. What brings you to San Francisco?"

Before I could answer, Maya knocked on the door. "Sorry I'm late. I got tied up on a conference call."

Mark stood up. "No worries. Our reservation is at One Market at noon. We have plenty of time to get there."

As we walked over, we made small talk, and Mark seemed to have forgotten his earlier question from the office. Though Maya had said they weren't close, there was an air of polite professional good humor between them, and I let myself relax. Only when we were seated at the restaurant and placed our orders did Mark remember his question. "So, Jasmine, you were telling me why you wanted to move to San Francisco."

"Besides good friends, of course." I gestured to Maya as I mentally geared up for Mark's questions. "Professionally, I've been involved in some technology deals the last couple of years, and I would love to expand my practice in that area. So the Bay Area seemed a natural choice. Also, I've worked at a large firm my entire career, which has been fantastic, but at a large firm it's easy to become pigeonholed, and there's not always room for crossovers in various departments. I'm hoping that in a smaller office, I'll be able to work on several aspects of deals, rather than focusing on only one part."

During the other interviews that day, I was able to keep my cool, but at lunch I had to concentrate to keep my knees from shaking under the table, knowing this was the one that might count the most.

"So are you looking to join the real estate group?" Mark tilted his head, eyes steady on mine. "Or the corporate group?"

"My intention is to join a transactional group that is growing and help with that growth, which I understand is in the real estate department. But I'm happy to go where I'm needed."

I directed my answers to Mark and Maya. Maya and I had rehearsed various questions and scenarios the night before, and I half expected her to mouth our prepared answers as I spoke. Maya had decided that Mark, being a new partner at Gilchrist, was, therefore, insecure. Since I was only a year behind him, it was best for me to come across as a team player and not a gunner for his job. Maya had rolled her eyes as she warned me.

"So you want to trade sunny Los Angeles for foggy San Francisco?" Mark said. It was hard to tell whether this was his dry humor or disbelief.

"I grew up in LA and have spent most of my adult life there. I'm ready for a change." I gave a small shrug. "And I'm not much of a sun worshipper anyway."

Mark politely laughed and said, "I went to law school there."

I knew that from studying his profile. I also knew he had worked at a firm in Los Angeles for a few years before transferring to San Francisco. I was about to ask him what brought him to San Francisco and Gilchrist, when he said, "One of my law school friends ended up at Levenfield. Do you know Brad Summers?"

My heart was in my throat, and I didn't know how I was going to finish my lunch or keep my voice steady. "Yes, I know Brad. He works in the real estate department. In fact, we've worked together." *And he is the sole reason I'm leaving Los Angeles.* I could feel my palms begin to sweat.

I wondered how close they were. Were they just acquaintances from school? Or were they best friends? Someone Brad would confide in? Perhaps Mark had a reason to distrust me after all.

"Oh yeah?" Mark said. "He's a good guy. I haven't spoken to him in a while. Law is a small world."

That it was. I abruptly changed the subject by launching a barrage of questions about Mark and his practice and life at Gilchrist, basically anything to stop him from asking me more questions. I hoped I wasn't bombing the interview by appearing too eager. But I would do anything to avoid talking about Levenfield, Los Angeles, and, most importantly, Brad.

***

Since it was a Friday, Maya planned to leave work at exactly five o'clock so we could hit up a happy hour and then go out to dinner. To kill time, I wandered around the Financial District for a bit, and then parked myself at a coffee shop with a book. With time to wait, I also checked my BlackBerry to see what I was missing at work. Apparently, someone at work was missing me. There was an email from Brad sent early that morning.

> Hi. How are you?

Then later in the morning: Are you in the office today?

Then at lunch: Are you at home? Is everything okay?

It was strange, since he had pretty much ignored me since our Starbucks outing. Though I wanted to give him the same treatment he'd given me, with idle time and idle fingers, I found myself emailing him.

> Out of the office today. Will be back Monday.

He must have been sitting at his computer, because he shot back: Are you at home?

Me: No, I'm in San Francisco for the weekend.

Brad: What's in San Francisco?

Me: Friends. See you Monday.

I spied Maya through the window, her eyes scanning Peet's, looking for me. I waved, and she headed in. I slid the BlackBerry back into my purse.

"Hey, you. Ready for that well-deserved drink?" Maya said, standing over my table.

"Dying." I tucked my book into my purse, and we left the coffee bar for a nearby wine bar.

Over drinks, we dissected each of my interviews that day. Other than my interview with Mark, I felt pretty confident about the experience. Maya was curious about my impressions of each of her colleagues. Chatting with her reminded me how much I missed having friends at work. Most of the attorneys I started with at my firm had left for greener pastures, and I felt a bit isolated in my department. In fact, I felt a bit isolated in general, as I drifted away from my colleagues and casual office gossiping for fear of giving anything away that would make me the topic of such gossip. Also, our corporate department consisted mostly of men, with only a handful of women partners, giving it a definite boys' club atmosphere. Even though I had succeeded in making partner, it didn't give me the feeling of being part of a team. Or maybe that was an excuse I used to convince myself that leaving would be good for my career.

***

While I didn't know if I had the job yet, if I got it, I wanted the transition to San Francisco to be as quick as possible. So on Saturday, I researched apartment listings and visited various neighborhoods to get a sense of costs and available rentals. I thought Los Angeles was expensive, but San Francisco was even more so with limited housing and the tech industry booming there. Maya had long ago moved out of her rental house in Noe Valley to a condominium in an area that was filled with high-rises. It was convenient to downtown and transportation, but it felt a bit soulless; and being in one of the sunnier microclimates, it didn't feel like much of a change from Los Angeles. Instead, I fell instantly in love with Cole Valley, mostly because it was filled with Victorian and Edwardian homes, large mature trees, and everyone wore warm dark clothes and, thus, it felt worlds away from LA in every way.

That night we met some of Maya's friends for dinner at a vegetarian restaurant, chosen in my honor. Matt was there without his girlfriend, and though that ship had sailed a long time ago, we still shared an easy banter. Wearing an argyle sweater vest, he still had that slightly rumpled English-professor style I remembered. His hair was cut a little shorter than when we first met, and I noticed some subtle crinkles around his eyes when he laughed. And since he was taken, I felt like I could admire his attractiveness without any pressure. For the first time in years, Brad was far away both geographically and from my thoughts. As I looked around the table, the ease of slipping into a brand-new Brad-free life seemed entirely possible.

***

Once I returned to Los Angeles, I began sorting things and cleaning out my bungalow. It gave me a way to burn off my nervous energy as I anxiously waited for an offer from Gilchrist. Much to my mother's surprise and delight, I had spent the last seven years decorating my home into a comfortable nest—splurging on luxury linens and towels. I had also hired a maid service—as if keeping it spotless would make Brad want to stay. It hadn't. The only evidence of him in my home was a collection of vintage Paris postcards that he had bought for me over the years. It was the first thing I packed away.

Maya had warned me that it might take up to a month before I received an offer, so I prepped myself for the waiting game and resisted the urge to call her every hour asking if she'd heard anything. It all came together quickly, though. A week later, my cell phone rang—when I saw the number, I immediately got up and closed my office door.

"So what do you think about joining our real estate department?" Stan's confident voice boomed on my cell phone.

My mouth went dry, and I suddenly felt lightheaded. *Was it really this easy,* I thought as I said, "I think that sounds fantastic!"

Stan briefly described the details in the forthcoming offer letter, and then said, "We're excited for you to join our department. With your experience in corporate, you'll bring a unique perspective to our group. We'll send over the letter today. Once you've had a chance to read it, let me know if you have any questions, and we'll discuss."

While I hadn't yet formally accepted the job, the letter was a mere technicality because I was prepared to take whatever terms got me out of Los Angeles. It was official. I was leaving LA. But I couldn't quite get those tucked-away Paris postcards out of my mind.

***

That night I met my parents and sister for dinner and shared the news. Both my parents were confused about why I wanted to move to San Francisco.

"I can understand wanting to get involved in the technology sector, but why switch from corporate to real estate?" My father eyed me questioningly—as if I had always been the daughter he didn't worry about, and he now needed to worry.

"But what about Saffie's wedding?" my mother interrupted before I could answer him, working the guilt-trip angle.

"I'm so sorry." I turned to my sister. "I know I'm maid of honor, and so whatever you need, I'll do."

"I know, Jae. It's not like you're missing the wedding." She good-naturedly rolled her eyes at our mother before turning back to me. "And you could seriously use an adventure. I'm excited for you!" She leaned over to give me a half hug and whispered in my ear, "And, honestly, it's not like you're that great at the girlie stuff."

"Thanks, Saf. I think," I said, giving a little laugh at her comment. "I will obviously be there for your wedding. And, anyway, San Francisco isn't that far away." Though it was just far enough for my purposes.

***

A few days later, I found myself in Levenfield's managing partner's office, giving my resignation and two weeks' notice. When I walked out of his office, I felt free. Things seemed to go smoothly as I wrapped up some projects and handed off various files. It was easy to avoid Brad over the next few days, since I was truly preoccupied, rather than trying to find ways to forget him; and he had pretty much left me alone since my return from San Francisco.

I had only given my immediate team notice of my departure, but as my office became noticeably cleaner, it probably became clear to those who passed it that something was going on. On a Wednesday afternoon, I saw Brad walk by and look into my office. We locked eyes. My heart beat faster; I had temporarily forgotten the rush I got whenever I saw him. I had hoped my heart would catch up with my mind and move on, but one look at him, and I knew how much I would miss him.

I was not alone in feeling something pass in our stolen glance. An email appeared.

He wrote: How are you? Haven't talked in a while. Been swamped.

I sighed. *Really? This is why we haven't talked?* I thought. Both of us knew the real reasons, but we would pretend it was something else. And I was so tired of pretending. Every therapist and self-help guru out there would have told me to ignore him. But if I could have ignored him, I never would have been in my situation in the first place.

I emailed back: I'm fine. Been swamped too. How are you?

Brad wrote: Deal closing soon. Coffee?

Is he for real? I thought, considering our last coffee outing. And I wasn't going to fall that easy, but I would fall a little. I could risk it, since I was moving and would soon never see him again. Also, I felt entitled to some closure after seven years.

I typed: Only if we can go at 5.

Okay was his swift reply.

Brad was already standing outside our building at five o'clock, and my heart did a leap at the sight of him.

"Hey," he said as I approached. "I was thinking I could go for something stronger than coffee."

"Of course you did," I said dryly.

Brad looked confused at my tone.

"A drink is fine." I shrugged.

We went to the hotel bar where we'd had our first drink together and had frequented over the years, due both to its proximity to the office as well as its dark vastness where others' eyes would gloss past us. It seemed fitting that it should be where we would have our last drink together too. I swallowed down my emotions as we sat in one of the more private corners. I ordered a glass of champagne. As soon as our drinks arrived, Brad clinked his beer against my glass. "To your new job. Congratulations."

"Thank you." I was surprised not so much that the grapevine had reached him, but that he seemed genuinely happy for me. Maybe he, too, was relieved this was all over. "When did you hear?"

"Last week," he said.

I didn't respond as I wondered why he had waited so long to say anything.

He filled my silence. "Congratulations. That's really great. You should get out of this place."

By *place,* I didn't know if he meant Levenfield, Los Angeles, or our hopeless relationship. I didn't ask him to clarify, since I was too surprised at his relief. I wanted him upset. I wanted him to miss me. I wanted him to care that he wouldn't see me ever again.

"You seem really happy for me to leave."

"Of course I am," he said, smiling. "Your department is awful, and you're better off. You're going to a much better firm."

I couldn't believe I had ever loved this man. I was crushed at his nonchalance, but he was giving me the exact closure I needed—*I hated him.*

"I'm looking for a new job too," Brad said.

"Really?" *This is the oddest conversation,* I thought.

"I sent my résumé out on Monday."

"You're kidding? I had no idea you were thinking of leaving. When did this happen?"

"Last week." The gold flecks in Brad's eyes twinkled.

"Where are you looking?"

"San Francisco."

My heart stopped. "You're joking, right?"

"Nope. I worked on my résumé this weekend, found a recruiter, and sent it out."

I stared at him, sure that my mouth was hanging wide open. Brad grinned like the Cheshire cat. I wanted to hurt him.

"Why?" I cried. "Why would you do that?" I leaned back in my seat, still gaping at him.

His grin disappeared. "What do you mean? I thought you'd be happy."

I was confused. Did he seriously believe that? Who was this

crazy person? I leaned forward, put my elbows on the table, and rested my forehead in my hands. I needed to hold my head to stop it from exploding.

"No, no, no, no, no," I said to the tablecloth. I lifted my eyes to look at Brad. "Did you ever think that maybe I was moving to San Francisco to get away from you?"

Brad eyes widened in surprise and then hurt. He was silent for a second and then said, "No."

He looked down at his beer, and then his voice turned cold. "Well, I actually have a job lead, and it's good." He took a swig of beer. "San Francisco is a big place. So if you don't want to see me, you don't have to."

"Do you want to see me?"

"Of course I do."

In order to avoid looking at him and to give me time to think of what to say, I finished off my glass of champagne and motioned to our server for another. When it arrived, I felt brave enough to ask, "Does your wife want to move to San Francisco?"

All these years and I still had a hard time saying her name.

"No. She thinks it's full of hippies." He snorted, and I wasn't sure if he was disgusted or amused. *How charming,* I thought bitterly.

Brad continued. "I think she just doesn't want to leave LA. But she'd be willing to, I guess, if it's for my career."

He wouldn't get a divorce, but he would relocate his family to be with me? I felt sick.

"But you're moving there because of me," I said flatly.

Brad was quiet for a second. After all, I wasn't as pleased as he was with his news. "Well, yes," he started, then continued. "But also I've been wanting to challenge myself professionally. So I researched the market, and it seems there are a lot of opportunities right now in the Bay Area."

Bullshit. Right when I was leaving him, suddenly he was able to pack up and move to another city? I wanted to kill him. Or at least pour the rest of my drink over him. Instead, I downed my second glass of champagne before responding. "So now, sending your résumé to San Francisco *doesn't* have to do with me?"

"Yes and no." He was starting to shift in his seat. "I mean, as I said, that's where the jobs are."

"It was *my* plan to move to San Francisco, and now you've ruined it," I sputtered, the alcohol affecting me.

"What? What are you talking about?"

"I was all excited to move to San Francisco and get a fresh start, without *you*. Now all I can imagine is you and your wife moving there. And now my dream of moving is all tarnished." I was tipsy and felt like a drama queen, not making much sense.

"Well, I certainly didn't make this decision to *tarnish* your dreams." Brad took the last swig of his beer and motioned to the server for another. "And maybe you shouldn't imagine so much." His tone was bitter.

I didn't know whether his response was biting toward me or his wife. The only thing I knew was that this night was ending badly. I weighed my options. I could stay and maybe get some real answers from him and the closure I desperately wanted. However, I knew my emotions were so heated that I would probably end up yelling at him or crying or both. I couldn't sit there a minute longer. I took two twenties out of my purse and put them on the table. "Here. This is my share. I'm leaving."

I pushed back my chair, and Brad reached over and grabbed my wrist. "Wait! Why?"

"Because I'm upset."

"Stop. There's no reason to leave. Stay with me while I finish my beer." He paused. "And let me explain."

But I couldn't. I shook my head. "No, I have to go now." I could feel the hot tears beginning to well behind my eyes, and I had to get out before I caused a scene. I grabbed my purse and rushed out. Luckily, there was a cab outside the hotel, and I climbed straight in. I rested my head against the seat, willing back the tears until I was home. My cell phone was ringing in my purse. I didn't answer. Then I could feel my BlackBerry vibrating, but I didn't reach for it. *Just get me home.* I had my money ready in my hand and as soon as the cab stopped in front of my place, I handed it all to the driver, ran into my house, and collapsed onto the sofa.

Moments later, my doorbell rang. My eyes were already wet and puffy. I wanted to be left alone, but I got up and answered it.

There stood Brad.

"God!" I shouted. "What do you want?"

"Can I come in?" he asked tentatively, his head down, his eyes looking up at me imploringly.

I had avoided a scene at the bar and now saw one playing out before my neighbors. I had no choice but to let him in. Without saying anything, I turned around and lay back on the sofa.

He closed the front door and walked over to me. "Can I sit down?"

In response, I moved my feet and scooted up into a semi-seated position, wrapping my arms around my knees. Brad sat at the edge of the cushion on the opposite side.

"Jae, I'm sorry my news upset you."

"Uh-huh," I said, pulling my knees closer to my chest, as if I could physically protect my heart.

"You don't think I was upset when I found out you were moving? That it was awful to hear it from others at work? Were you even going to tell me?" He paused. "I have good memories of San Francisco. I thought maybe you did, too, and it was a sign."

I looked at him, not understanding. So he continued. "If I moved to San Francisco, Kathryn and I also discussed the possibility of my commuting until the end of Ivy's school year," he said, a trace of guilt in his voice.

"Between LA and San Francisco?"

He nodded, watching my expression to see if I understood. I did.

"That's only a temporary solution," I sighed.

"It's something." Brad's voice had a pleading edge.

"It's not enough."

Brad dropped his head in defeat. "I know." We sat quietly for a few minutes. "I wish you had told me, but I understand." Then he looked at me, anguish in his eyes. "You have no idea how much I'm going to miss you."

I wanted to say, *You should've thought of that the past seven years.* But my anger had already turned to sadness, and now resignation. "It's for the best."

Brad nodded, then swallowed. "I can't imagine not having you in my life, but you deserve to be happy."

I looked at this man whom I had loved for so long and moved closer to him. I put my hand on his cheek, touching the light stubble and burning this image into my mind. And though it was wrong, it had been for so long it didn't matter, so I kissed him. Brad returned my kiss with the same urgency. Though we both knew it was over, our bodies weren't ready to say goodbye.

That night, Brad slept over. In the morning, I woke before he did. His back was turned to me, and I studied it, memorizing each faint freckle on his skin. I wanted to touch him but didn't want to wake him. Only a few more days and I'd be gone. I'd be free. I know I should have regretted my relationship with him, but watching his sleeping form, I decided I would regret nothing. I loved him. But now it was time to move on. Brad must have sensed me watching him, as he started to stir. He shifted so he was lying on his back and saw that I was awake.

"Good morning," I said.

"Good morning," he said, his voice heavy with sleep. "What time is it?"

"Five thirty."

"It's early."

"Yes."

He made a motion with his arm, inviting me to curl up with him. We lay there in the half-light, not speaking, not wanting to break the spell. When the sun came in stronger, we had to make a motion to move.

"I need to go," Brad said apologetically.

"I know," I said.

Brad turned to look at me. "I love you."

"I know. I love you too."

The problem was he didn't love me enough to leave his wife. Or maybe he thought I didn't love him enough to ask him to. I preferred not knowing the truth.

CHAPTER SIXTEEN

On my last day, my department threw me a goodbye "happy hour" at a nearby wine bar. Everyone from corporate showed up, as well as some other colleagues I'd worked with over the years. Brad had emailed me earlier saying he would try to make it. I said he didn't have to.

"We're going to miss you, Jae," said Mitch, the head of my department.

"Thanks, Mitch." Mr. Potato Head, the partner who I had thought tortured me as an associate, had become my biggest supporter for partnership. When I had given him my notice, he was floored. "*San Francisco?* Why there? And why real estate?" My voice faltered, and my skin prickled as I explained my flimsy reasoning in his office. He then merely shook his head and said, "If that's what you want to do." And we left it at that.

"You were the hardest-working associate. A rising star." He shook his head once again. "I thought you'd still be here when I retired."

It made me uncomfortable, since not too long ago he had congratulated me on making partner. And when I spotted

Mindy, in the corner, I felt even worse, since she had been passed over for partner that year and was bitter. Plus, she was now even more bitter that I had gotten it and was leaving. (Jeff had paid off his law school loans and left long ago for a cushy in-house job.)

In retrospect, I had been the perfect associate. I had kept my head down and didn't involve myself in office gossip or politics. Since I didn't have a personal life and had alienated my friends, I could put my full focus on my job and would work long hours. Everyone must have thought I was a gunner, and it was obvious I would make partner. But not so obvious I would leave right after. And for a real estate position? I had spent all those years trying to stay out of the gossip mill, but I'm sure I was the main topic that week.

As I looked around the party, I briefly wondered if I was making a huge mistake. But then each time I nervously scanned the room to make sure it was still Brad-free, I knew I had made the right decision.

***

I had a two-week break between my last day at Levenfield and my first day at Gilchrist. During that time, I shuttled between Los Angeles and San Francisco, helping Saffie with her wedding preparations, finishing my packing, finalizing my new apartment, and making appointments for phone, internet, and cable before the big move.

That first week, Maya let me stay with her as I toured potential apartments. I could have just done a corporate rental until I found a place, but I wanted to get settled in San Francisco as soon as possible. Although Maya and I had toured other neighborhoods during my visit, it soon became clear that the easiest option, transportation-wise, was to live close to downtown. Also, the most ready-to-rent places were in Maya's neighborhood with its never-ending, new high-rise developments. It hurt me to give up my little bungalow and trade it for a soulless box, but it seemed the most practical choice, even if it dampened my move a bit.

On Monday, only the second day of my stay, Maya came home from work to find me lying on her sofa. "Are you okay?" she asked, dropping her laptop bag on the floor and shrugging off her jacket.

"Yeah, I'm just exhausted. The apartment hunt, you know?"

"It shouldn't have you that tired. Most of the places are around the block."

I laughed. "True. I think it's just from trying to coordinate all these appointments. And maybe I'm coming down with something."

I hadn't felt like myself for a couple days. I kept thinking I was getting the flu, but then it never manifested. I finally decided it was simply a case of nerves. I wasn't always the best with change—even good change.

"Or PMS?" Maya suggested.

"Maybe." I was on the Pill and I was due, but sometimes when I was stressed, my cycle overrode it. When I took the bar exam, my period completely stopped. I figured it was probably the same thing.

"Or pregnant?"

"Ha! Very funny. I should be so lucky." I had perfected my lonely single girl rant to hide the truth for years.

"Maybe you'll be lucky here?" Maya walked over to the sofa and sat at the other end. She cocked her head and gave me a look. "You know Matt and his girlfriend just broke up."

"Didn't we have this conversation already? Like five years ago or so?" I gave a small laugh, trying to hide my uncomfortableness.

She smirked and gave me a friendly poke on the shoulder. "Don't they say timing is everything?"

"Let me first sort out my housing situation and start work. Then you can meddle in my love life."

"So you don't want me to see if he's free tonight to meet us for drinks?"

"No. In fact, a drink doesn't sound too good right now. Is it okay if we take it easy tonight? My stomach hasn't been feeling the greatest."

"Sure thing." Maya got up from the sofa. "But you should be out there. Your boobs are looking great."

"What?" I shook my head and then looked down at my chest.

She was right. My B cups were straining at my bra even though I had barely been eating. *It could just be stress and prolonged PMS,* I thought. *Or it could be something else.* And until I could take a test, Maya's joke wasn't so funny anymore.

The next morning, I waited until Maya was out the door; then I ran down to the nearby Walgreens and bought a pregnancy test. *It could all be nothing,* I reassured myself. But better to be sure. When I got back to her place, my hands were shaking so much I could barely open the packaging. *It's nothing; it's nothing; it's nothing,* I kept repeating to myself. But rather than wait out the three agonizing minutes the test was going to take, I went to the kitchen and filled up a kettle with water for tea. Right when I was turning on the burner, Maya burst through the door.

"Hey," she said, rushing toward the kitchen table. "Forgot something." When what she was looking for wasn't on the table, she went into her bedroom. "Ah!" I heard her say, grabbing something that sounded like paper and putting it in her bag. I heard her footsteps pause for a second, then start again.

"Hey, Jae?" she called from the hallway.

"Yeah?"

"Why is there a pregnancy test on my bathroom counter?"

I turned around in horror. Maya was now standing at the end of the hallway looking at me expectantly.

"Uh . . ."

"I think you should take a look at it."

I didn't have to because the look on her face confirmed my worst fears. "Positive?"

She nodded.

I hurried past her and went into the bathroom to see the test. There was a blue plus sign staring back at me. No faint lines or any question. Maya was behind me and put her hand on my shoulder. "I'm sorry, I hate to do this, but I have a meeting at ten. I need to go. Do you want to meet for lunch to talk?"

I shook my head. "No, it's okay. This might just be a fluke. I'll call my doctor today."

"Okay," she said, but I could see the worry, and confusion, in her eyes. "I'll see you tonight. I'll try to call this afternoon."

"Go. Don't be late."

"Right. We'll talk tonight." She squeezed my shoulder and ran out the door.

I took a deep breath. *It can't be,* I thought. I went back to the kitchen, downed two big glasses of water, then headed back to the bathroom to take the second test in the package. When the second one came out positive, too, I then convinced myself it was the brand. But after three brands of pregnancy tests, and eight tests later, I was still pregnant. I called my doctor, who recommended I schedule a blood test and buy some prenatal vitamins as a precaution.

In the meantime, I racked my brain. It just couldn't be true. I was on the Pill. Granted, our relationship was steady, but sporadic. Sometimes going months without sex. I tended to take my pill at night. And if I forgot, I took it in the morning. And if I still forgot, I would take two the next day. So maybe I wasn't the most consistent, but I didn't have a consistent love life either. But I had been on the Pill since I was eighteen and had never had a pregnancy scare.

I thought about Brad's story about his wife and how she said she was on the Pill. I suddenly felt very, very bad for her. I was a thirty-four-year-old partner at a large law firm, and I accidentally got pregnant; she was a college student on vacation with her boyfriend. Shit happens.

Shit.

I grabbed my purse and made a third trip to Walgreens, this time for prenatal vitamins.

***

"When was your last period?" Maya asked later at her place that night.

We were sitting on her sofa drinking herbal tea. I wished it were something stronger.

"A little over a month ago," I said.

"And you're on the Pill?" she asked, her eyes wide in shock or disbelief.

"Yeah. But I've been stressed, and I thought it was a fluke."

"A fluke?" She made a tsking sound that would normally annoy me, but I was too scared to be annoyed. "I didn't realize you were dating anyone."

"I'm not."

"I meant were."

"I wasn't." I tightened my grip on my mug and inwardly squirmed.

Maya leaned forward and peered at me. "A one-night stand?" She sounded surprised.

I sighed and evaded her question. "Something like that."

She then leaned back and studied me from this new vantage point. "Okay. I mean, *do you know* who the father is?"

I nodded.

"And? Who is he?"

This was yet another moment for me to come clean to her about Brad, but my move and my career were in a vulnerable place; I had already burned bridges at my last firm, and Maya was my only alliance at my new one. I still couldn't risk the truth.

"He's nobody, and I'll never see him again."

"You're not going to tell me who he is?" Maya looked confused.

I shook my head no, and gave her a pleading look to stop this line of questioning.

"Fine. I'll get it out of you later." She relented. "Anyway, you're not going to tell him?"

I shook my head again.

Maya stared at me. "*O-kay*. So what *are* your plans? Are you keeping it? Are you still moving up here?"

These were the questions I had been asking myself all afternoon, my thoughts spinning out of control. I had never considered children, but it was also not something I'd had to think about before. I had accepted the status quo with Brad for so long, knowing deep down that it precluded my creating my own family. But maybe I had been the one with commitment issues, too afraid of the responsibility of a real relationship. I was thirty-four. My adult dating life had not been the greatest—in fact, it had been almost nonexistent. And I felt like if I said no to this baby, I'd be forever shutting the door on the possibility of motherhood.

"Yes and yes," I said, finally meeting Maya's eyes.

It wouldn't be the obvious answer to my friends or my family. And I didn't think Maya even wanted to know. I felt like a bad friend. She helped me get this new job, and now I'd be out on maternity leave. Suddenly I couldn't stop questioning my move to San Francisco. I had already quit my old firm. I was moving away from my family when I needed them the most. I was starting a new job with morning sickness and would be taking maternity leave and raising a child alone.

"You're going to be a single mom? How are you going to do that? Have you thought this through?" Maya sounded upset. "The only person you know up here is me. And, frankly, I don't know anything about babies. I would give this some careful thought, Jae."

"I know. But I just found out today. There hasn't been much time to even absorb the fact that I'm pregnant." It appeared my life path was not meant to be normal. And now that this baby—my baby—was growing inside me, I couldn't bear the thought of not keeping it. It was mine.

"Huh. So you're having a baby," she said, her tone shocked.

"So I am," I said, and took a sip of my tea. I was having my and Brad's baby.

***

Over the next couple days, my thoughts continued to spiral as I debated whether to tell Brad. We had just cut ties. I could move to San Francisco, and he would never know I was pregnant. But at some point, there would be a child who would want to know who their father was. All dirty secrets come out in the wash. I had thought I'd made a clean break, but this was the most complicated situation I'd ever gotten myself into. For once, I had to do the right thing. Even though it was the last thing I wanted to do, I had to let Brad know.

When I got back to Los Angeles, I emailed Brad on his personal email account.

I'm moving this Saturday. I need to talk to you.

It was only Monday, but when I didn't hear anything from him for over twenty-four hours, I emailed his work account.

Hi Brad,
I am moving on Saturday and tying up loose ends. I really need to talk to you before I leave. Please call me.
—Jae

By Wednesday morning, I was stressed out by his silence. I texted his phone, I really need to talk to you. It's a very important matter.

I worried that maybe his wife saw his phone. Maybe she deleted my message. Some rational part of the old Jae floated above this mess of bordering-on-hysteria Jae. *If he's not calling you back, he doesn't want to know.* Or maybe he was out of town? Even so, he would check his emails and texts. Perhaps he was ignoring me just like I ignored him before moving. But I said it was "important." The entire duration of our relationship, I had never uttered the phrase "we need to talk" or said something was "important." I would have thought he'd respond.

I called his work number. I got voice mail and said, "Brad—This really is important. Please call me ASAP."

When I still hadn't heard back, Thursday morning I parked across the street from the office when I thought he'd be arriving and waited. Brad had the same schedule every morning because he dropped his daughter off at school, and so I figured I would catch him going into work. Rational Jae shook her head at me in disapproval. *You have been reduced to stalking your ex-lover.*

While I was looking at the building, I heard a rap at my window. "Jae?"

I jumped a mile. *Oh god.* "Mindy?"

She made a motion for me to let down the window.

"What are you doing here?" she asked, cocking her head. "Don't tell me you miss us already?" Whether intentional or not, her statements always had a bitchy edge to them.

"I'm picking up my check for vacation time." The firm paid out any unused vacation days, and since I had rarely taken a vacation, this amount was quite sizable.

"Lucky you." She cocked her head. "Why don't you come in with me?"

"Um, okay." My anxiety-ridden brain couldn't think fast enough to make up a reason why I needed to continue sitting in the car.

Just before we reached the front doors of the building, an SUV pulled up. A tall woman with long blond hair, wearing aviator sunglasses and a fitted sundress that highlighted both her willowy limbs and a very pronounced baby bump, jumped out, screaming obscenities. A look passed between Mindy and me as we slowed down to watch the spectacle.

The driver's-side door opened, and I nearly passed out. The driver was Brad.

"Can you just calm down for a second?" his frustrated voice said as he got out of the car.

"Wow," said Mindy, and I just nodded, unable to speak.

One would think Kathryn's face would have been burned into my brain from the few photos I'd seen of her, but I had never seen her looking like she was soon to give birth. With my own new pregnancy, I registered that she must have been in her third trimester.

"Just give me the fucking keys already," she shouted.

"I'm not giving you the keys until you calm down," Brad repeated.

Kathryn came around to his side of the SUV and pushed him. "Don't you tell me to calm down!" she screamed and made a grab for the keys.

Brad put his hands up in the air. He lowered his voice, and though we couldn't hear his exact words, they appeared to be something along the lines of, "Don't make a scene." My eyes had watched his mouth long enough to lip read. He then looked toward the office and saw us standing there. I could feel a pain in my heart when he looked at me. I saw fear in his eyes, because where Brad had thought his wife was already making a scene, he saw a potentially bigger one being played out. I thought I heard him say, "Here," and he handed his wife the keys. She got into the SUV and barely let him clear the car before she peeled out into traffic without another word.

"Show's over," Mindy said, shrugging and turning toward the building, and I followed her inside.

Brad's wife was pregnant. She had been pregnant when we went to Tahoe. She had been pregnant when he was busy impregnating me. I thought I was going to pass out or vomit on the floor. Perhaps both.

As we waited at the elevators, Brad joined us. From the corner of my eye, I could see his jaw was clenched, his body almost rigid.

"Rough morning?" Mindy asked him.

"You could say that," he said, not making eye contact with either of us.

I couldn't say anything. Not good morning. Nothing. I was too shocked to carry on the charade. Although I avoided looking at him, I could feel the tension pulsating from him.

"Hello, Jae. What are you doing here?" Brad said, his tone distant and stilted.

I had lost my voice, but Mindy spoke for me. "She's picking up her vacation check."

"How nice for you," Brad said.

I said something like an "uh-huh" and continued avoiding eye contact.

As a group of us all piled into the elevator, I took a far corner from Brad and then tried to sneak a peek at him from behind the safety of others. Brad, though, was looking up at the floor numbers. My stomach churning, I turned my gaze to the numbers above us too. At least I was getting off on another floor.

Thankfully, accounting was before Brad's floor. As I scurried through the open doors, Mindy called out, "Don't forget to come up and say hi to everyone!"

Yeah, right. I numbly walked down to the accounting office where they were surprised to see me, but at least they had my check ready, so I felt less like a stalker and more like a woman with a purpose. After accounting, I left as quickly and discreetly as possible. I was done with this building, with this life. In the car, I checked my phone for messages and had a new email—from Brad.

Finally!

I opened it up.

> Jae—
> I got your messages, but as you saw this morning, I've been having a difficult time lately. I can't talk to you right now. Just email me whatever it is you want to say, and I promise to read it.
> Regards, Brad

Regards??? His words seared through me. He had been ignoring me after all, after seven years, and clearly seven years of lies not just to his wife but to me as well. He was growing a family with Kathryn, and never had any intention of being with me—ever.

I wanted to go back inside and punch him. What the fuck type of email was this? Anger was making me shake so much, I couldn't drive. I now knew for certain I wanted nothing more to do with him.

"Fuck you, Brad Summers!" I shouted, and banged on the steering wheel. I looked up at the building. "Fuck you!!!"

I had never in all the years of our relationship acted like a crazy woman. But all of a sudden, I felt a kinship with Kathryn. I bet she knew he was cheating on her. And now she was pregnant. Of course she was pissed at him. I'd probably be deranged with anger and acting like a lunatic too. That scene that morning—Brad was not the victim.

I was so angry, I was tempted to go to his house. Tell Kathryn about the affair. Tell her I was pregnant. If it was so easy for Brad to believe I was a scary ex-lover, then I would show him how easy it would be for me to become one. Although I was tempted, the rational part of me knew these revenge fantasies were simply selfish. How would Kathryn, pregnant and vulnerable, feel with her husband's ex-lover on her steps? All this time I had accepted Brad's version of her. But in that moment, I thought that maybe Brad, and not Kathryn, had been the crazy one all along. She was the one married to an asshole. I was lucky. I was free. With those thoughts, I turned on the car and drove away.

On my last day in Los Angeles, when I closed my bungalow door behind me, I was shutting the door on the past. And as the cab backed out of my driveway to take me to the airport, all I could think was good riddance to Brad Summers.

CHAPTER SEVENTEEN

"Good morning, Jasmine. Welcome to Gilchrist." Mark greeted me in the lobby at nine o'clock on my first day.

"Good morning." I stood up and shook his hand. "I'm excited to be here."

Mark was tall, built, and had brown hair and warm brown eyes, and outwardly seemed friendly. But as we shook hands, I sensed a professional wariness from him. I had gotten the same vibe during our interview. Even though he was young, he was the head corporate partner in this office. And when he said, "And we're happy to have you here in our real estate department," I wondered if he felt my interest in real estate was simply to get hired and perhaps worm my way into his department. I had never had any issue with office politics at Levenfield, so I was confident that once Mark got to know me, his reservations would disappear.

Mark showed me around the office space, which consisted of only one floor. "We're a small office now, but we have a lot going on and will probably be branching out into two floors as soon as we hire more lawyers."

"That's wonderful!" I said in my best cheerleader voice. "I look forward to helping build this office."

Mark nodded and continued with the tour. I realized I probably sounded overeager, but it was my first day and I needed this move to work. Also, my morning sickness kept threatening to take over, and I was overcompensating.

I managed to survive until Mark was able to show me my office. Once there, Doris, the head of Human Resources, came by with a stack of paperwork for me to fill out, which kept me busy all morning. Maya and Stan had a client meeting that morning, after which they took me to lunch at Boulevard, a restaurant nearby.

After we ordered and our server took our menus, Stan leaned back into his seat and asked me, "How's your first day going?"

"It's good. So far just paperwork. Then some phone and server training this afternoon."

"Glad to hear it. And I may have to sit in on some of that phone training. I'm still trying to figure out the darn thing." He chuckled at his own joke.

Even though Stan was friendly, our lunch wasn't the most comfortable. The only thing I could stomach was some soup. The other strange thing was Maya. I had always seen her in personal situations where she was in command, but, sitting next to Stan, she emitted a new anxious energy. Her eyes were wide, her laughter was unnatural, and every word was extremely deferential. Whenever Stan said something that was meant to be funny, she let out a high-pitched laugh that I had never heard before. This Maya made me scared of what I was walking into. I wondered if her nervousness meant that their meeting hadn't gone well that morning, though Stan didn't seem too bothered as he calmly ate his salad and made bad jokes.

Later that afternoon, in between my training sessions, I

walked over to Maya's office. I found her squinting at her computer and clicking through furiously. "Hey, there," I said as I stepped inside.

She turned toward me and smiled. "Hey, how's it going?"

"Good." I sat down on the chair in front of her desk. "So what are you up to? How was your meeting earlier?"

"It was good." She shrugged and then looked over at her computer and started scrolling through her emails.

"Glad to hear it. I was worried, since you seemed a little stressed out at lunch."

Maya turned back to me, her brow furrowed. "What do you mean?"

"I don't know. You seemed nervous, so I thought maybe the meeting went badly or something."

"I wasn't nervous. Why would you think that?" Her voice got a little high pitched, the same tone I had never heard before until that afternoon.

"Whoa! Sorry." I put out my hands. I had clearly touched a nerve. "Maybe I'm projecting because *I* was nervous." Okay, so work-Maya was not the same person as friend-Maya. It was a little disconcerting, but it was a different environment and it was only my first day. "I should probably get back to my office. Doris will be waiting."

"Yeah, whatever you do here, there's one rule: Don't piss off Doris."

"Got it," I said while thinking—I thought the one rule was *Be careful with Mark.* It was only my first day, and there seemed to be a lot of rules.

Maya and I had planned on having dinner together, and since I didn't have any projects yet and my orientation was over, I was ready to leave by five o'clock. I called Maya, who put me on speakerphone. "I see your phone training paid off."

"*Ha ha*. Apparently. So, hey, what time are you leaving?"

"Hmm . . . Give me ten minutes so I can finish something up and get my stuff together." She sighed. "I'm going to have to do some work after dinner, so I need to pack my computer."

"Okay. Take your time."

While I waited for Maya, I looked out my new office window. I had a view of the water and could see for miles. It was only my first day, but I'd had a sinking feeling in my stomach all throughout it. Maybe I was projecting my nerves onto Maya, and since she was the one instrumental in getting me hired, I needed to pretend to be positive. Also, she was my only friend in San Francisco.

"Ready?" Maya stood outside my door, startling me out of my anxious thoughts.

"Sure."

We took the Muni home together and then went to a small restaurant in our neighborhood that served what it called "California comfort food." Once we had ordered, a burger for her and a pasta dish for me, we both rested back in the small booth we were seated in.

"So what do you think?" she asked. "How was your first day?"

"I guess it was good. Mark gave me a tour this morning and introduced me to everyone who was in their offices."

Maya raised an eyebrow. "How was Mark?"

"He was fine. Nice. We didn't become BFFs, but give us time." I grinned.

"What about your secretary, Tracy? She's a piece of work, huh?" Maya leaned forward, crossing her arms on the table.

Though I agreed with her assessment of Tracy, I was uncomfortable with this sort of discussion on only my first day. "She seemed nice."

But Maya went on, naming everyone in the office and

asking my opinions on them and sharing her own. She reminded me of Mindy, and I guess looking back, Maya was a bit of a gossip in law school. But she finally had a friend at work, and so what was a little dirt dishing? I really didn't have anything to add, and I didn't want to know too much about everyone just yet. Thankfully, since it was a small office, the topic of others was soon exhausted.

"So when are you planning to tell work you're pregnant?"

"Oh god. I don't know." I shook my head. "Any advice?"

"Uh, I don't know the protocol on this, but I would wait till you're about to give birth," she said wryly. "I mean, one of the female partners in the New York office got pregnant during a big project, and Stan told her that it was very irresponsible of her. Even though he was just joking"—she did finger quotes around the word—"if you tell him too soon, he might be too scared to pull you onto projects, knowing you'll be leaving soon." She took a quick sip of water, and continued. "Also, I'm not sure how this will affect my signing bonus."

"That was my concern on projects." I carefully sidestepped the issue of her signing bonus, feeling bad but also starting to get a little annoyed. "One of my millions of concerns."

"So when are you going to tell me who the father is?" She leaned in farther, conspiratorially.

"I'm not." I gave her a look, and she rolled her eyes, still not believing that I would forever withhold his name from her.

"Oh, c'mon . . . ," she cajoled.

But I shook my head.

"Well then, can you tell me if you've changed your mind about not letting him know you're pregnant?"

"I haven't. I mean, he doesn't want anything to do with me, so I can only assume he wants nothing to do with his child."

I wasn't even two months pregnant yet, and I wasn't going

to tell anyone until after my first trimester. My condition wasn't obvious yet, but because of my small frame, I felt super pregnant already.

"So what's the story?" Maya asked. "You're up here now. I'm assuming the father is in LA. People are going to ask. What are you going to tell them?"

I shrugged. "It's nobody's business. I could just say sperm donor."

"I guess you could." Maya laughed as she considered this. "So sperm donor? Is that the secret?"

The secret that had weighed on me for seven years wanted to come out. I was tired. The relationship was over, so what could it hurt?

I sighed. "I was in a relationship, but it was rocky. Very on and off again. I didn't tell anyone because it was never consistent."

"Huh. So you were in a relationship," Maya said slowly, digesting this news I had kept from her. "Did you love him?"

"Yes."

"Did he love you?"

"Yes."

"So why was it so rocky?" She stared at me.

"I don't know." I avoided her eyes. "His life was complicated. I work a lot. A lot of things. But we ended it for good, and he's been an asshole ever since. So I don't want him involved."

"Was he married?"

This is why it's not even worth it to relieve the pressure of a secret. Because you have to tell more lies to cover it up again. "No. What a weird question."

"Not that weird. You slept with a married guy before, and that would make sense why it was 'complicated.'" Maya did air quotes again, and I wondered if she knew I was lying.

"Well, not to my knowledge." I played with my water glass,

fiercely wishing it were a wine glass, and changed the subject. "Anyway, I'm meeting Stan at ten tomorrow to talk about projects. I'm a little nervous."

"Don't worry about it. He'll probably give you something that's corporate-related to ease you into things. And I can help out with any real estate questions you have."

"Thanks." Breaking my office politics rule, I said, "Between you and me, I don't think Mark likes me."

"He's just protecting his turf. I wouldn't worry about it." She pointed her fork at my stomach. "You have bigger problems to worry about."

***

My meeting with Stan didn't go quite as I expected. Maya had promised me that they needed all the help they could get in their office and I'd have more than enough work and clients. But when Stan's first question to me was about what projects I could expect down the pipeline, I felt a cold bead of sweat drip down my spine as I quickly assessed that Maya had told him I was coming with a book of clients. Even though many of my long-standing clients said they were disappointed that I was leaving Levenfield, they assured me that if they had any real estate projects in Northern California, they would get in touch. If I had stayed in corporate, maybe some of them would have thought of following me, but that wasn't the case. I improvised some hopeful projects and tried to keep a poker face as I processed that my friend was a double agent, working both sides. True, she had talked me up to Stan, but by lying about my book of business; and if I were hired, she would benefit with a signing bonus. If she was going to be so duplicitous, I wished she had at least warned me at dinner the night before.

"Okay, Jasmine." I had told Stan several times to call me Jae, but interestingly "Stan" didn't believe in nicknames. "Let's start you off big. We've been pretty swamped, and Maya's been focused on this Casey building. I'm going to ask you to help on this new project. Our client Soto Technologies is looking to build new facilities in the area, possibly Mountain View. They want us to advise them on some areas they're interested in, so we need to do research on building codes, what they can and can't do there, tax benefits of various locations, etc. Have one of the associates help with the research. We'll have a conference call with the client and introduce you. And then we'll put together a presentation for them."

"Okay," I said while writing down as much as I could. I had worked closely enough with our real estate department to get some of the basics down and what they did, but I was still going to need help. So I figured I would talk it over with Maya to make sure I knew what was expected of me.

Maya must have sensed that my meeting with Stan was over because she dropped by my office on her way back from the kitchen.

"You're back," she said as she walked in with a cup of coffee. The smell made me a little nauseated. She closed the door and sat in one of the chairs. "How'd it go?"

"Good. I think." Although I wanted to confront her about what she had told Stan, it was not the time. "But I'm definitely going to need your advice to get started."

"What are you working on?"

"The Soto Technologies' offices." I looked down at my notes. "I'm supposed to research the best areas to build and put together a presentation. I'm not totally sure how to begin."

I looked back up and saw that Maya's face had fallen. "He gave you Soto?" She sounded upset.

"I'm working on it, yes." Now I was panicking. "Why? What's wrong with Soto?"

Maya shook her head, snapping out of her state. "Nothing. It's a great project. It's just that Stan promised it to me."

"Oh." I had been concerned about Mark, but now it was Maya's ego that needed soothing before she became too worried about my presence at Gilchrist. "I don't think he's excluding you. He specifically said you were swamped right now and could use the help."

"I am swamped. But that's 'cause I'm working my ass off to clear my plate for the Soto project," she huffed.

"This is just the preliminaries," I said. "If he said you're going to be working on it, you probably are. If you weren't, then he wouldn't have bothered mentioning you were busy right now. Right?"

"Yeah," Maya said, but I could tell she wasn't convinced.

"So hurry up and finish whatever else you're working on so we can work on this together," I said, as if there were no question. "In the meantime, how would you start?"

Maya outlined the steps I should take and suggested I ask Rachel, a fifth-year associate, to help out. "I would normally say use a more junior associate, but Rachel's done this stuff before, so that will be helpful to you."

After Maya left my office, I felt awful. I wondered if she was back at her desk regretting her decision to help me get hired at Gilchrist. I would have gladly traded the Soto project with her to save our friendship, but it wasn't my call to make on only my second day. Considering first the weird vibes from Mark, and then Maya, I tried to quiet the unsteady feeling in my gut by rationalizing that my hormones were making me paranoid. Whom else could I succeed in alienating in San Francisco?

As I was wondering this, an email from Matt popped up on my screen.

Want any help unpacking this weekend?

I thought that was pretty generous. Maya hadn't offered, and I wasn't going to ask her *now*, since it was probably best for her to work over the weekend. Normally, I would do everything myself, but I had been so tired that I would take any helping hand.

I wrote back, That would be amazing, yes. Thank you and I owe you!

I had enough personal items unpacked to get me into work during the week, but my dishes and other items that would make life easier were still packed away. So we set up a time for him to come over Saturday morning.

That afternoon I met Rachel, who physically reminded me of Saffie (all long limbs and long light blond hair), but a much grumpier version. Rachel was an associate in the corporate department, but she also did a fair amount of real estate work. Because it was a small branch office, there was a lot of overlap between the real estate, corporate, and intellectual property groups.

Rachel seemed to understand, better than I did, what was expected of her on the project. I was grateful for that, but there was something unnerving about her.

"I can't wait to work with you," she said eagerly. Yet in the next breath, with an air of superiority she asked, "But are you sure about this deadline? This Friday is tight. I have a lot on my plate, and if you want me to give it my full attention, then I need more warning."

It was only my second day, and I didn't know her workload.

From this exchange, I couldn't tell if she actually wanted to do the work or not. In short, Rachel was an enigma.

"Stan told me he wants it by the end of the week. But that's not feasible?" I asked.

"Oh! *Stan* needs it by Friday?" she said, her demeanor and tone suddenly agreeable. "Oh, okay. I'm on it."

Apparently, *Stan* was the magic word. "Let me know if you have any questions," I said.

She simply nodded in response.

"And if you can fit it into your schedule," I continued, "I'd love to take you to lunch this week."

I wasn't sure *love* was the right word, but I figured I should reach out to the associates and get to know everyone in the office sooner rather than later.

"Will do!" Rachel waved at me and turned back to her computer. I was dismissed.

Maya had assured me that because they were a smaller outpost, they were much more laid-back than the other offices. I had interpreted *laid-back* as friendly, but I was beginning to feel a bit intimidated.

The rest of the week, I worked mainly with Rachel and Stan, and tried to ignore my unsettled feelings—not to mention my morning sickness that tended to extend into the afternoons as well. Maya didn't have time to go out to lunch or meet after work since she was busy finishing her projects, hopefully to work with me. At my other firm, I kept to myself out of choice; but at Gilchrist, I was mostly left alone. For the first time in a working environment, I felt a little lonely.

CHAPTER EIGHTEEN

"I'm stopping at Starbucks for some coffee. Do you want anything?" Matt called me from his car on his way over that Saturday morning.

I hadn't seen Matt since our dinner the weekend after my interview, but we had restarted our email correspondence after I accepted my new job. When we'd last hung out together, he had a girlfriend, but as Maya had informed me while apartment hunting, he was single again. And while I still found him attractive, my pregnancy had put another snare in everything. I had planned to move on from Brad and date again, but I was no longer a desirable candidate. Matt and I seemed destined to be only friends.

"Thanks, but I'm fine," I said, already opening one of the boxes in my kitchen. I had signed a year lease on a one-bedroom, one-bathroom apartment in a high-rise building in the SOMA district, close to downtown and near Maya's place.

"Are you sure? Nothing like a little caffeine to help with unpacking." I could feel him smiling on the phone.

"True, but I don't drink caffeine." *Because I'm pregnant.* But I couldn't say that.

"Really? I knew you were vegetarian, but no caffeine either? What about alcohol?"

"It's too early in the day to start thinking about alcohol," I joked, because, no, I also could not drink alcohol. *Because I'm pregnant.* I still couldn't wrap my head around it.

So started the morning.

Matt helped me move boxes into zones in my apartment. While I unpacked and put away items, he broke down the boxes and carried them out to the building's recycling room. It took all day, and while unpacking, my morning sickness reared its ugly head. Though I was trying to hide it, Matt came back from the recycling room while I was in the bathroom.

"Jae?" He knocked on the bathroom door. "Are you okay?"

"Yes, I'll be out in a sec." I suppressed a groan.

Now I was lying to Matt. Maybe he was the next person I was on my way to alienating.

He looked concerned when I opened the door. "Uh, were you throwing up in there?"

"Yeah." I shrugged and then walked past him to finish unpacking the rest of the boxes in the bedroom. Other than my books, we were almost finished.

"Are you sick?" Matt followed me.

"No."

"Hung over?"

"No." I sat on the floor and started pulling out the last of the bedroom items.

Matt sat next to me.

"Pregnant?"

"Ha!" I said, but not with much vigor, and avoided his eyes.

Matt put his hand on the box to stop me from unpacking it. "No, really. Are you pregnant?"

"Please. How can I be pregnant? I'm not dating anyone." I continued to evade his eyes.

"Well, you were just throwing up. And you're not sick or hung over. And you don't drink caffeine, which is strange because you drank a ton of coffee last time you visited. And you're avoiding the question."

"I'm not avoiding it."

"Look at me."

I reluctantly gazed up at him and saw the concern in his green eyes.

"Yes or no, Jae. Are. You. Pregnant?"

I cast my eyes down. "No."

"No? Can you look me in the eye and say that?"

"No."

"No, you're not pregnant? Or no, you can't look me in the eye?"

"I can't look you in the eye." Even though I glanced up to see his expression.

He knew.

Without warning, I started crying. I was tired. Tired of lying all the time. Tired of secrets. This was not how my new life was supposed to start.

"Oh, Jae. Come here." He held me and rubbed my back. I felt like the biggest baby, but also suddenly relieved.

After he let me cry it out for a couple minutes, I pulled back, wiping my tears with my sleeve, and said, "Sorry about that. Hormones. Also, I haven't told anyone yet. It's very early days."

"I understand. My sister's pregnant, and I guessed early on. I knew she didn't want to tell anyone. But I see her almost every weekend, and there're some signs."

"So that's how you guessed?"

"Well, that and in your bathroom I saw some prenatal vitamins." He put his hands up in an *I'm innocent* gesture. "I wasn't snooping. I was just putting the towels in there and saw them in the closet."

"Oh. That's pretty damning evidence."

"So what's the story?"

"No story."

"O-kay." Matt raised one of his eyebrows, but didn't press. "How far along are you?"

"Not even two months. It's early 'early' days."

"And the father?"

"The father isn't involved."

Matt's eyes narrowed, and his tone grew cold. "He doesn't want anything to do with it? Are you serious?"

"It's not that simple."

"Does Maya know him?"

"No." *But she badgers me about it at every opportunity,* I thought. "The only reason she found out I'm pregnant is because I took the test at her place when I was apartment hunting."

Matt sat back and studied me. "So you quit your job, moved, and found out you're pregnant?"

"Yep."

"How are you planning to do this?"

"I don't know. I've only known for a couple of weeks. I just know that I want to have this baby," I said, and leaned against the foot of my bed, instinctively placing my hand on my stomach.

Matt looked at me for a beat, and then put his arm around my shoulders. "If this is what you want to do, then go for it. It'll be hard. But you're a smart woman, you have a great job, and most importantly, you can afford a nanny."

I laughed, even though it wasn't funny. Matt continued. "And I'll introduce you to my sister. She and my brother-in-law both work at Google. They have one kid already, and she'll get you hooked up. Doctors, nannies, the stroller scene."

I put my head on his shoulder. "Thanks, Matt."

"You're welcome." Matt gave my shoulder a squeeze. "Are you sure you don't want to tell me the details?"

"Yes. I especially don't want to tell you the details."

For helping me, I treated Matt to dinner that night. We avoided the topic of my pregnancy, and instead talked about the places I should visit now that I was unpacked. He promised to show me around when I was ready. As we chatted, the knot in my shoulders finally began to loosen, and for the first time since I had moved, I felt as if I had something to look forward to.

***

As promised, Matt put me in touch with his sister, Suzanne. Since she worked outside the city during the week, we made plans to meet for tea over the coming weekend. That Saturday, I navigated my way to Noe Valley where she lived. We met at a cozy tea shop where we ordered pots of decaffeinated tea and bonded over our morning sickness.

"It's much less this time around, but I remember how it was with Erin." She shuddered as she finished pouring each of our teacups.

Suzanne was small and blond, and shared Matt's green eyes.

After the second cup of tea, she got down to business. "Matt told me the father isn't involved."

"That's correct." I took a sip of my tea, not wanting to elaborate on the subject.

"He's in LA?"

"Mm-hmm," I said noncommittally.

"I don't mean to scare you, but it's a lot. Even with Derrick and me, it was hard. Thank god we have a nanny and family in the area to help." She paused, then asked hopefully, "Do you have family nearby?"

"Nope. I'm kinda screwed." I put down my tea. "I haven't even told my family yet. The timing of everything couldn't be worse. I had quit my job already and accepted a new one, so the train for San Francisco was leaving the station. Jobless and pregnant would've been worse."

Suzanne nodded and immediately launched into telling me all the best doctors, hospitals, schools, baby stores, websites and blogs, how to get a nanny, and how to get into the mommies-who-work groups. All the details made my head spin. "I don't know what your relationship with your mother is, but I'm thinking you'll want her up here. You'll want someone those first few weeks, if not months."

Although her tone and demeanor were businesslike, I could detect the sympathy behind her eyes. And I wondered, too, how I would do it.

***

That night I met Maya for dinner in our neighborhood. As soon as we sat down, Maya said, "I need a drink. Is it okay if I have a drink?"

"Of course. Why wouldn't it be?"

She gestured to my midsection. "That just means you get to drink for me," I said lightly while picking up my menu and diverting her attention. "So what's good here?"

Once we ordered, we talked about work. Or mostly Maya talked about work. She complained about her client and an attorney she was working with in the Dallas office. I had noticed that everyone Maya worked with was "an idiot," and, according to her, the worst kind of idiot—the arrogant kind. I'd had my fair share of unreasonable demands at Levenfield, but I didn't let them get to me the way she seemed to.

"So I noticed you went to lunch with Henry this week," she said.

"Yes. He's a quiet guy, but pretty nice."

In the intellectual property department, there were two other youngish partners, Henry and Denise. Henry looked like a gangly teenager and as if he had fallen into partnership (which he admitted to me he had, after working with some steady clients—a biomedical firm and an electronics company) rather than it being a studied career move. Maya had warned me that Denise could be a drama queen and that it was best to stay out of her way. However, I noticed Maya spent long chat sessions in Denise's office, and it made me wonder why she didn't heed her own advice.

"He is, but be careful. Denise was talking about you."

"What do you mean?"

"She was wondering why you're spending time with Henry and not getting to know her."

"You warned me to stay away." My eyes widened in surprise.

"Now I'm warning you not to stay away too much. Just drop by her office to say hello." Maya finished off her wine. "By the way, she heard you throwing up in the bathroom."

"Oh god." I put my face in my palms and sighed before looking up again. "I only just got here, and already people are talking about me?"

"It's a small office. You're the new person, so people are curious. Don't worry about it." She motioned to the server for another glass of wine. It seemed lately that the more Maya told me not to worry, the more worried I became. "But maybe don't hang out with Henry. He's not viewed very well by the others."

"How come?"

"He's kind of an idiot."

Since I was quickly learning that Maya felt 90 percent of the people around her were idiots, I took her statement with a grain of salt.

"Okay, but if Denise is so interested in me, she could also invite me out to lunch or something."

"I know. Just trust me, though; don't get on her bad side."

"I could use a drink right now," I groaned.

She handed me her glass. "You can have a sip, right?"

"Yes and thank you." I took a sip of her red wine. "Oh, that is *delicious*," I said, handing the glass back to her. "I can't decide what I miss more: caffeine or alcohol."

"I don't think a glass will kill you."

I shrugged. "Probably not, but better safe than sorry."

"So any progress with the father?" Maya asked.

"Nope. We had a clean break."

"Are you ever going to tell me who it is?"

"Nope. Since I'm not telling him, I feel I shouldn't tell anyone else."

Maya eyed me in a way that made me uncomfortable, then finally said, "Fine. So have you told your parents?"

"Not yet." I swallowed anxiously. "Can we not talk about it? I'm getting too freaked out about it already. I met Matt's sister, Suzanne, and she gave me an overview of what life is going to look like. And it's not pretty."

"Well, it was your choice," she muttered, roughly tearing off a piece of bread from the basket.

Every time we talked about my pregnancy, her attitude grated on me. "Getting pregnant wasn't my choice. But now that I am, I'm choosing to keep it." I wanted to add, *So lay off.*

Instead, I figured it was time to shift the conversation away from me, so I asked, "What's up with you?"

"Just work."

"Are you dating anyone?" I asked, even though I knew the answer.

Maya laughed so hard she almost spit out her food. "Are you kidding? I can't remember the last date I went out on."

"Maybe now is the time? And then I can live vicariously through you, since I'm a lost cause."

She shook her head. "There's no time, you know? When I get home, I'm tired. And dating just takes . . . so . . . much . . . energy." She dragged out each word in a wearied voice.

I took a sympathetic look at my friend, but she didn't look tired or frazzled. So my assessment was simply that Maya had given up on men and was married to the firm.

But then something niggled at the back of my mind. "So how come you and Matt never dated?"

"He's great but not my type. We met at some law event when we were associates and then just kind of kept up our friendship. You need someone to hang out with at those things."

"Uh-huh," I said. "And what makes him not your type?"

"I don't know. There was never a spark," she answered, still tearing away at the bread in the basket. "When I first met him, he had a girlfriend. She was super possessive, and I don't think she liked him hanging out with me. And when they broke up, we just continued being friends." She shrugged and changed the subject. "So, tell me, how is the Soto project going?"

***

That night when I got home, I went straight to bed but didn't fall asleep right away as my conversation with Maya replayed in my head. I used to love hanging out with Maya, but lately our interactions left me exhausted. In law school, we had been roommates and best friends. And while I still considered her my best friend, our friendship had been long-distance now for several years, sometimes going for long stretches without contact. We no longer knew the daily ins and outs of each other's days. In retrospect, I realized Maya never really dated anyone in law school or in San Francisco, at least, not that I knew of. I think she had been interested in some guys, but it never really went anywhere. She was being extremely judgmental about my pregnancy, but how could she understand when she'd never even had a relationship?

Whether it was pregnancy hormones or paranoia, something didn't seem to sit right when it came to Matt. Maya loved talking about him, and as one who was all too familiar with secret desires, I began to wonder if she harbored a small crush on him. Though I wasn't in any condition to date, I began to question if my growing friendship with Matt would further complicate my friendship with Maya.

And while I was trying to be appreciative of Maya's efforts to give me the "inside scoop" about Gilchrist's office politics, it was starting to stress me out. She didn't assist me with any areas of law, but instead was constantly telling me whom to talk to and whom not to talk to, who was important and who wasn't. Even though I knew that she thought she was helping me, I would have preferred to form my own opinions of others. Her "friendly" advice was only making an already difficult situation worse.

CHAPTER NINETEEN

The next weekend, Matt took me sightseeing as promised. He drove us on Saturday morning to the top of Twin Peaks where I saw the city stretched across the horizon. The buildings seemed to glow white in the soft morning light. It was smaller than Los Angeles, and I liked San Francisco's urban compactness better than LA's suburban sprawl. And even though everything still felt uneasy and tenuous with work and Maya, and I wasn't sure yet how I was going to balance single motherhood with my career, in that moment looking out over the city, I felt I wouldn't be moving back to Southern California.

Over brunch in the Presidio, after taking my first bite of omelet, I said, "Thanks again for showing me the view this morning and this brunch. It's great to finally explore the city outside of my neighborhood, and Maya's been swamped at work."

"Maya's always swamped at work." Matt smirked.

"Yeah, golden handcuffs and all. We should call her and see if she wants a break," I said, but more out of a sense of friend duty than actually desiring her company. And now with my suspicion that she had harbored a crush on Matt in the past, I was reluctant to share with her how much we were hanging out.

"Let's not," Matt said, pouring syrup on his waffles. "She's on the other side of the city, and by the time she makes it over here, we'll be finishing up." He looked up at me and smiled, seemingly unbothered by our failure to include her in our outing.

I wasn't going to argue. I still hadn't gotten over my weird vibe with her the weekend before, and I was enjoying having an uncomplicated time with Matt.

"Are you busy this afternoon?" Matt asked.

I shook my head. "Nope. You?"

He shook his head no. "Do you want to walk around after brunch? We can go down to Crissy Field or maybe hit Lands End Trail?"

"Sure." I smiled at him, not wanting to end what was my first truly fun outing since I had moved almost a month ago.

After brunch, we left Matt's car parked in the Presidio as we walked down a couple trails, then strolled along the water and sat on one of the many benches when I was feeling tired. During one of these breaks, I leaned my head back and looked at the sky. "I've read articles that say you get a second wind during the second trimester. God, I hope that's true," I said.

"You're doing great." Matt squeezed my knee. "Have you told anyone yet?"

"Nope. It's pretty easy to hide when you're a few hundred miles from interested parties." I was still debating when to tell my family about my pregnancy. And while it was probably my imagination, I felt like I was already starting to show and took to wearing A-line dresses and loose sweaters at work.

"Still not talking to the father?" he asked.

"Still not talking." I turned to face Matt. "And can we not talk about it? I prefer to keep my head in the sand for as long as possible."

"That's going to get harder to do, you know." He held my gaze, concern in his eyes.

"I do."

"In that case, just one more thing and then I'll drop it," he said, his voice serious. "If you ever need anything, someone to take you to the doctor or anything, really, just call me, okay?"

"Thanks, Matt. I appreciate that." I smiled at him. "Okay, I'm ready to keep walking. But you know the farther we go, the more we need to walk back."

"I'll let you decide."

"I'm pregnant, not an invalid."

"So we keep walking."

Matt stood up first and then chivalrously offered his hand to help me up. We continued along the water for a while, sharing old law school stories and then talking about our families, with no more mention of my pregnancy.

We worked our way back to the Presidio and his car by way of the Palace of Fine Arts. We wandered around with the other locals and tourists and paused to admire the lagoon. Matt stood just a little too close to me. His hand touched the back of my hand. I wasn't entirely sure if he meant to take it and then lost his nerve, but the proximity of him and the view brought back memories of Brad and the last time I was there. I remembered how much I hated and loved him, and how at the time I thought that there was hope for us. I was so naive then. If that trip had never happened, perhaps the pull wouldn't have been there. Maybe I wouldn't have wasted all those years on him. *Damn it*—I was lonely with and without him. But his actions had spoken louder than his words. With that thought, I started to cry.

As the tears filled my eyes, I kept trying to blink them back to hide them from Matt.

Matt turned to me. "So, Jae, I was thinking. . . ."

I looked away.

"Are you crying?" He put his hand on my shoulder and gave it a light squeeze.

"No." But I was unable to stop the tears from escaping. "I'm sorry. It's . . . It's hormones," I stammered. "So, um, w-what were you thinking?"

"Oh, Jae, never mind. Come here." Matt wrapped his arms around me, and this made me cry even harder. I buried my face in his sweater, not worrying if tears got on it. It felt so good to have someone next to me. All the emotions I'd been hiding from everyone started spilling out.

"How could he do this to me?" I said, my voice muffled by his sweater.

"Say again?"

I pulled back. "How could he do this to me? After everything. I'm so stupid."

Matt kept his arm around my shoulder as I stared out at the lagoon, my hands balled into fists.

"Do you want to talk about it?" Matt asked.

"No. I just want to curse his name."

Matt laughed politely. "Are you sure? I'll do whatever you want. I'm a good listener. I'm also a good curser."

I laughed, and with the back of my hand wiped away the tears that were still leaking out of my eyes.

"Guys suck, Jae. What can I say? I apologize on behalf of my people."

"You don't suck."

"I'm sure some woman out there still curses my name. But I never got anyone pregnant and abandoned them. Or not that I know of."

I felt like I was leading Matt on with his thinking that someone had abandoned me. But in a way, Brad had. Brad abandoned me right at the point where I actually needed him. I wanted to tell Matt everything. But I knew I was a guilty party—a pregnant mistress to a man whose wife was also pregnant—and I wasn't ready yet to lose one of my few friends in San Francisco.

"Hey, let's get back to the car, okay?" Matt said gently.

"Why? You don't want to stand here with a crying woman?" I said, trying to lighten the mood.

"Ha ha. No, don't worry. I'm not trying to ditch you quite yet." Matt smiled at me.

True to his word, we went to his place in Cole Valley. Matt's flat was in an Edwardian-style building. It was the first time I had been there, and I appreciated its cozy vibe with dark navy paint on the walls and his broken-in brown leather sofa. His furniture had character, not like it had merely been purchased out of an IKEA catalog. There were photographs displayed of family and friends, people who could vouch for him. I had never been to Brad's house, but I always imagined it decorated in Kathryn's taste, whatever that was, without any indication that Brad lived there too. But, *enough*, I was done thinking about him.

"How about some hot chocolate?" Matt asked, after he hung up our jackets.

"Sure, thanks. It's suddenly so cold out."

"Microclimates," Matt said. "I dubbed Cole Valley, 'Cold Valley.'"

"Nice one," I said as I perused his shelves, looking at the various books and comparing them to those I'd read while he headed off to make our drinks.

Calling out from the kitchen, Matt asked, "Any plans tonight? You and Maya doing anything?"

"No. I had dinner with her last weekend."

"Would you be up for a movie tonight?"

"Sure." It did feel a little weird hanging out with Matt all day, and now on a Saturday night, without Maya. But she was working, and I had no desire to be alone in my apartment.

"I've been wanting to see the latest *James Bond*, and it's finally available."

"*James Bond* sounds fantastic." There was nothing nostalgic or romantic about 007—nothing to turn me into an emotional basket case again that day.

"Great!" he said, walking out of the kitchen and holding two mugs, sporting a big smile.

Both nestled with our hot chocolate, we watched the movie on his sofa with our feet up on his coffee table. I kept telling him I didn't mind if he had a beer, but he insisted he was fine. I wished I had gotten my act together seven years ago and accepted his offer to visit me in Los Angeles—perhaps my life could have been completely different and uncomplicated. Matt's friendship was comforting, and as we sat together, I couldn't help but wonder what he was like as a boyfriend. He was probably the type to remember anniversaries and birthdays, who always got along with his girlfriend's family, and because she liked cinnamon in her coffee, he always kept a bottle on his kitchen counter. I also briefly wondered if our spending time together meant he was still romantically interested in me; but since I was pregnant, I quickly extinguished that thought.

We finished the movie around eight o'clock. It was still early, but for a platonic, nonalcoholic Saturday, I figured it was time to call it a night.

"So what's the Muni line around here? Is it the N?"

"Yeah, the N comes through, why?"

"I'm trying to figure out the best way to get home." I started typing my address into my phone to find the best route.

"One, I will drive you home. And two, the night is young.

You're really ready to go home?" He looked at me, his eyes wide with his question.

I shrugged. "Yes, exactly—the night is still young. I don't want to stop you from going out to the clubs."

"I think I stopped going to the clubs ten years ago, so don't worry about that."

I laughed. "Really? A single guy like you? I would think you'd be getting ready for your next hot date," I teased him.

"Oh, so this date isn't hot enough?" His mouth twitched with a smile.

"Well, if a single pregnant thirty-something lawyer is your idea of a hot date, you might want to up your standards."

"I think my standards are pretty high." Matt took my hand and squeezed it. Suddenly, I realized he wasn't joking.

My face must have given away my confusion, because after a pause, Matt moved closer to me, still holding my hand. He looked straight into my eyes as if to make sure I understood exactly what he was saying. "Listen, Jae. I know the timing isn't great. But our timing never has been. I was attracted to you when we first met, but I respected that you weren't into the long-distance thing. But you're here now. We're both single. I think this is as good as our timing is going to get."

I didn't know what to say. I didn't pull away, but I did cast my eyes down toward my stomach to remind him of where our timing was wrong.

"I don't care," he said in a serious tone. "You're not with the father. He's not involved, right?"

"Right," I said, still feeling cautious.

"Then the question is, What do you think? Should we try this?"

I wanted to try it. I had felt so alone, and this was the anchor I needed. *But . . .*

"What if it doesn't work?" I said. "I wouldn't want to risk losing your friendship."

"If it doesn't work, then we go back to being friends."

I nodded. "And if it does work, *how* does it work?" I again gestured to my baby bump.

"Then we figure it out. But you never know what can happen unless you try. I like you, and I think you like me." He gently caressed the top of my hand with his thumb. "I'm a good guy."

I nodded. "You got me there," I said quietly, my eyes cast downward, my hand feeling warm in his. I hadn't properly dated with the promise of a real relationship in years. "But that's precisely why I'm nervous. You *are* a good guy, and I don't want you to have to deal with my mess."

Matt lifted my chin with his other hand so I'd look at him. "Hey, now." His eyes were earnest. "I'm sitting here telling you I like you, I want to date you, and I'm quite aware of your situation. The only holdup is you. So?"

"Sorry. I, uh . . . ," I started, trying to gather my thoughts and delaying. "I just didn't see this coming."

I did like him. And if it hadn't been for Brad, I would have said yes to Matt years ago.

"Yes or no, Jae?"

I laughed nervously and said, "You're pretty persistent when you want an answer." He kept his gaze on me, and I looked into his green eyes and saw a man who was kind, reliable, and kept his promises. "Okay, yes. We'll try this."

Just as I wasn't prepared for Matt's question, I especially was not prepared for his kiss. It was sweet, but forceful, and tasted of chocolate. When we pulled apart, I started laughing. Probably the worst reaction, but it was more like hysterical laughter.

"I'm so sorry," I said, trying to control myself. "I just had no idea any of this was coming."

Matt smiled. "I don't know about that, but I'm going to assume you're happy?"

"Yes, I am." I grinned back. "So, uh, we're dating. Huh? Now what?"

"Hmm . . . I'm a little out of practice myself. But I think we do this thing called making out and then I drive you home before curfew."

"Yes, if I remember correctly, that sounds about right."

Matt kissed me again, confidently, and I tried to relax. This was another twist my life was about to take, and I hoped that this time I was making the right decision.

CHAPTER TWENTY

A couple weeks later, Maya walked into my office unannounced and closed the door behind her. She sat down on one of my chairs. "Busy?" she asked.

"What's up?" Expecting the latest office gossip, I turned away from my computer to face her.

"So, Matt's got a new girlfriend," she said. I was that day's gossip.

I couldn't read if she was merely intrigued or upset by the news, so I simply nodded and waited to hear the rest.

"I emailed him to see what he was up to this weekend, and he said he was busy with his girlfriend."

My heart thumped a little. "Oh?"

"Don't you want to know who she is? I mean, how has he kept this from us?"

I wasn't entirely sure if she truly didn't know or was playing me for a gotcha moment.

"I have an *idea* of who it might be," I said cautiously, carefully watching her expression.

"You're kidding! Who?" Folding her hands under her chin, she propped her elbows on my desk and leaned forward.

I cleared my throat nervously. "Me."

She squinted and stared at me for a second. Then said, "No, come on."

"No, really. It's me. We've been dating for a couple weeks now."

I tried to interpret the look on her face. It was frozen. There was no smile, no congratulations. Was she hurt? Angry? I was afraid to say more, until she spoke first.

"Why didn't you tell me?" she asked, her voice cold as she leaned away from my desk and into her chair, crossing her arms.

"I'm sorry. I should have," I said, cringing a little but also feeling a creeping defensiveness. "But it's so recent that I don't really believe it myself."

"When have you guys been hanging out?"

"On the weekends and sometimes after work."

The look on her face was stony. *"On the weekends? After work?"* she parroted. "Is that why *we* haven't hung out?"

"I've invited you out, but you're always working. Matt's been filling in."

"It's not a bad thing to be working," she said, her tone clipped. "In fact, you should probably be spending more time at the office. It might be good for you. You still have to prove yourself, you know." Her eyes challenged mine.

"Oh?" Now I was surprised. "Has someone mentioned I'm not working enough?"

She shrugged. "It's been noted."

So I didn't tell her about Matt, and she didn't tell me I was failing at my new job. *Touché.*

"Who's been noting it?" I asked, not totally sure if I believed her and if she was simply saying it out of spite.

She shrugged again and stood up, while ignoring my question. "So Matt's okay with the pregnancy stuff?"

"That's what he says. We'll see." I tried to soften my tone even though I'd been hurt. My silence had hurt her too. "Maya, it's still new. Who knows if we'll even last the next couple weeks?"

Of course, as soon as I said that, I regretted it. She'd probably repeat it back to Matt. In all the years I had known Maya and her penchant for gossip, I had naively assumed I wouldn't be a target. Right there I knew, if someone is telling you others' secrets, they're probably telling others yours too.

***

That afternoon, passing by the kitchen, I heard some whispers and thought I heard my name. Intrigued, I slowed my pace to overhear and make out the voices.

"No, I think she's bulimic. I've heard her throwing up in the bathroom. And she's been looking puffy lately. That's a sign." I recognized Maya's voice.

"That would make sense. I was wondering if she was an alcoholic or something." I recognized that voice as Denise's.

Okay, maybe I hadn't heard my name, I thought, and entered the kitchen. I noticed Henry was also in there using the microwave but had his back to them.

"Hey," I said as I walked past them to grab a mug out of the cupboard for some tea.

They immediately stopped their conversation. "Oh, hey, Jasmine," Denise said.

"Hey, Jae," Maya mumbled, looking down at the floor.

"What are you two talking about?" I pulled a mug from the cupboard.

Denise said airily, "Oh, nothing. I was talking about this case I'm working on."

Placing my mug under the hot-water spigot on the cooler, I said with a smirk, "Is it the bulimic one? Or the alcoholic?"

"Oh that. Sorry. That's a friend of mine." She immediately turned back to Maya. "Okay, then. I should get back to work. See you guys."

Before I could turn to Maya and ask, "What was that about?" Maya also said hurriedly, "Yeah, me too. See ya." And disappeared.

As I stood there, confused, the microwave beeped, and Henry took out his food. He then turned around toward me and said, "Don't mind them. They say terrible stuff about me too." And shook his head.

"R-right," I stammered, in shock. "Thanks."

Henry shrugged in response and then left with his dish.

So, I *had* heard my name. *They had been talking about me.* Even though Henry had confirmed it for me, I needed to hear the truth from the source.

Maya's office door was closed. I asked her secretary if she was in there, and she nodded. I knocked.

Maya said cautiously, "Yes?"

I opened the door and closed it behind me, the maneuver she had done to me earlier that day. "What was that about in the kitchen?"

"Hey, Jae, I can't talk long. I need to return this call."

I sat down anyway across from her desk. "Maya, were you two talking about me?"

She narrowed her eyes at me. "Is pregnancy making you paranoid now?"

"Well, you were talking about someone who was either bulimic or alcoholic, and completely shut me out when I walked in."

Maya's eyes flickered, trying to decide how to handle it. Finally, she sighed. "Okay, yes, we were talking about you. Denise and others have heard you throwing up in the bathroom, and there're rumors going around that you're an alcoholic or bulimic or something. It's a small office. People talk."

My mind reeled. "But you didn't defend me. I heard you say I was bulimic."

She rolled her eyes and said in an exasperated manner, "Well, maybe if you *told* everyone you were pregnant I wouldn't have to say that you're bulimic. Would you rather I had said you're an alcoholic?"

"Are you serious? *You're* the one who told me not to tell Stan because otherwise he wouldn't give me work. And why would you say anything at all?"

Maya leaned back in her chair and folded her arms. "Yes, maybe I should be more like you? Maybe I should keep secrets from my friends?" She shook her head. "Sorry, I was just trying to help." But her tone was spiteful. It wasn't worth trying to explain my predicament. I sympathized with her, but I also felt that if she was my friend, she would have understood.

I stood up. "If someone was talking about you, one, I would've defended you. And two, I would've told you so you could've defended yourself."

And I left. When I got back to my office, I tried my hardest not to close my door and start crying. With the mistakes I'd made and secrets I kept, I had driven my only female friend to turn on me.

***

That night, Matt came over. Maya was right in that I was keeping Matt a secret from her, because even though we were new, our relationship had moved into hyperdrive, and we had established coupledom. We spent all of our free time together, and he usually slept at my place on weeknights because it was closer to our offices. On our second official date, we had sex. It wasn't as electric as between Brad and me, but Matt's touch was gentle and he made me feel beautiful, quelling my anxieties. And in my mental, emotional, and physical condition, it was comforting to have that sort of quiet energy in bed.

Over our bowls of buttered noodles, my latest pregnancy craving, he asked, "What's wrong?"

"Nothing." I shook my head and focused on my dinner.

"Oh come on, Jae. Don't be that girl."

I laughed sadly. "What if I told you it was just mean-girl drama?"

"It always is," he said dramatically, teasing me out of my bad mood.

He was Maya's friend, and I wasn't sure if I wanted to get between them. But considering he also hadn't told her about us, I wondered if he shared the same concerns.

"It's to do with Maya," I said cautiously. "She knows about us."

"Well, that's not terrible. She was going to find out at some point. How did it happen?"

I told him how she had come into my office, and that I told her I was the mysterious woman he had been hanging out with, and her angry reaction.

"Maya likes to know everything and everybody's business," Matt said, shaking his head. "Yeah, I'm sure she was a little pissed, but she'll get over it." He shrugged and took another forkful of noodles.

"I'm not so sure . . . ," I said, and then laid out the details of what I'd heard in the kitchen and her response to my confrontation.

I watched as Matt's expression changed from shock to outrage to red-hot anger. *Exactly,* I thought.

"What can I do? I work with her." I shrugged helplessly. "But I have to admit, I don't think I can be friends with her anymore."

"You shouldn't be!" Matt spat angrily. "That's not a friend. That's what they call a *frenemy*."

"So there's a technical term for it." I was so glad Matt had a sister and not brothers.

"I want to go over there right now and tell her off. If she were a guy, I'd punch her. That's slander!" I could see a vein pulsing in his temple as he got more riled up.

"It's fine." Now I was the one trying to calm him down. "Thank you, but I don't need you to defend my honor. And I'm sorry I told you because I know you're friends."

"Not anymore, *clearly*. And if you haven't noticed, I've been keeping my distance."

"I have noticed, but I thought that's because we've been dating and there are only so many hours in the day."

"Partly, but that's not all. The truth is things have been a little strange between us since I learned she had a crush on me," he said, confirming my earlier suspicion. "I never really saw it, but my last girlfriend definitely did and pointed it out. She didn't feel threatened by her, but it was uncomfortable. And then when we broke up, I think Maya thought that we might move our friendship to a different level." He groaned and looked up at the ceiling. "Maya took me out for drinks to cheer me up. But when she sat too close to me, kept touching my knee, and weirdly flicking her hair, I realized that she was trying to come on to me. I avoided it with a lot of talk of not being ready to date and stuff, and we never discussed it again. But now . . ." He then looked back at me and gestured between us.

"I see." This contradicted Maya's version of events when I had asked her why she and Matt never dated. "Still, it's such a low move."

"Well, also, you moved up here pregnant, and so she's worried you won't stay out the year and she won't get her signing bonus.

And," he said, pausing for dramatic effect, "not to be vain, but you're now dating the guy she had an unrequited crush on."

I stared at Matt for a second, absorbing it all. "Wow, you're right. I suspected the crush thing, but I didn't think about the signing bonus. I thought she was just mad it would make her look bad by recruiting someone who is going to take maternity leave."

"Either way, none of those are things a friend would think."

Which meant that since the day I told her I was pregnant, my friendship with Maya had been broken.

***

Adding to my dismal work drama, that week there was an email that a new senior associate would be starting soon in the corporate department. Her name was Adeline Turner, and she was transferring from Gilchrist's Chicago office to work on an acquisition deal with Mark. Since my issues with Maya, I had been trying to approach Mark, hoping I could eventually move away from real estate back into corporate law (unfortunately, also confirming his earlier suspicions of me). But now that a new corporate associate was being transferred from the Chicago office, my hopes of moving back to corporate were dashed.

Since I was new, Stan had been giving me a lot of work on the Soto Technologies matter. Maya was still full-time on another project but was looped in on team meetings. And even though she had a limited role up to that point, she would still be at the client presentation. At our last team meeting, before the official presentation, Maya took a sudden last-minute interest in my work product.

"Now, Jae, did you cross-check title on all these?" she asked, acting as if she were my superior. And before I could answer, she then turned to Stan. "Actually, I'll see if Rachel has done that." And she wrote it down on the legal pad in front of her.

"No need to check with Rachel," I said. "We've already verified titles."

"If you're sure," she said, staring at me. "Then did you talk to any environmental lawyers regarding these sites? I vaguely recall that Mountain View one having some easement issue." She turned to Stan again. "Would you like me to double-check on that?"

"There is no easement issue at the site," Stan answered her. "We've done our due diligence on all of these, which is why we're recommending them to Soto."

Maya nodded, slightly chagrined. But when Stan called the meeting over, and we gathered our files from the conference table, she flashed me a look that said, *Beware.*

Since Maya was the one who had given my résumé to him in the first place, I wondered what Stan thought of her undermining me. During the meeting, I could tell in his shrewd blue eyes that he knew there was discontent among the troops. Although he had been asking me if I had any leads from my old clients or had been drumming up any business lately, the sad truth was that I had nothing yet. I was just trying to get through one day at a time.

On the morning of the Soto Technologies presentation, Stan had flown in from New York for it. I had done similar presentations at Levenfield, but this was my first real estate one and the first impression I was going to make on the client and Gilchrist. Though Maya had offered to "help," her only useful advice so far had been her suggestion to use Rachel on the project. Granted, every time I had a higher-level question, I was reluctant to ask for Maya's help, and in the few instances when I did, Maya would give me a vague answer. I had hoped Rachel could sit in on the presentation, but it was for partners only—Stan, Maya, and me.

After some brief pre-meeting introductions and niceties, we settled down to business.

"Based upon land availability, building codes, and tax concerns, we focused primarily on Mountain View," I began.

I outlined each of the pros and cons of various Silicon Valley locations, which was no easy feat because Maya constantly interrupted me: "Are you sure that's the correct tax rate, Jae? I don't remember it being that high." "Did you consider any options farther south?" "Actually, I wouldn't recommend that site because that zoning board can be difficult."

I noticed confusion in the client's eyes as he looked between Maya and me. Every time Maya challenged my research, I could feel my nausea rising. Normally, I wouldn't have a problem shutting down someone who was undermining me in front of a client. But that was before I was pregnant. Now I was battling not just a case of nerves, but also a debilitating bout of morning sickness. Though I tried to power through and address each of Maya's questions, all of a sudden I could feel my hands go clammy. Sweat broke out on my forehead, and I needed to make it out to the bathroom.

"I'm sorry," I said as I rushed out just in time, not quite making it to the restroom, but at least to my office, where I promptly threw up in my wastebasket.

My secretary, Tracy, heard me and stood in my doorway. "Jasmine? Are you okay?"

"Yes," I said weakly. "Something I ate. Nothing to worry about."

But her eyes looked worried. I went to the restroom, and when I looked at myself in the mirror, I noticed my skin had taken on a green tinge. I splashed some cold water on my forehead and cheeks. Tracy came in with a bottle of water.

"Here," she said.

"Thanks." I took the bottle from her. "Can you please check how it's going in the conference room? Let them know I may have a touch of flu."

I knew I should pull myself together and try to make it back to the meeting, but I was feeling extremely weak and felt sure that another wave of nausea was going to hit. *How will I ever recover from this?*

CHAPTER TWENTY-ONE

Stan had emailed me after the presentation on Friday to let me know that everything had gone smoothly after I left and not to worry about anything. He flew back to New York that night, and even though it was the weekend, I stayed at home the entire time to cover my "flu" story.

As soon as I was back in the office Monday morning, he called me.

"How are you feeling?" he asked with measured concern.

"Much better, thank you," I said, then immediately went into grovel mode. "Stan, again I am so sorry about Friday. It hit me suddenly during the presentation; otherwise I would've let you know I was sick."

"I'm glad to hear you're better. That was very unfortunate, but sometimes these things happen." He cleared his throat before continuing. "But, also unfortunately, first impressions count for a lot in this business. Going forward, since Maya stepped in and is more experienced in this area, I am going to have her take the lead on this matter."

"I understand." I did. And maybe my work tension with

Maya could be resolved too. Now that she finally had her coveted project, perhaps she would call a truce and we could start over.

"You'll still be working on it, but take direction from Maya."

After I hung up with Stan, I walked over to Maya's office, preparing my apology to her. I knocked on her door. "Hey there," I said, keeping my tone conciliatory as I stepped into her office. "I'm so sorry about Friday. I'm mortified."

She swung away from her computer. "Yeah? You should be. How are you feeling?"

I half expected, or hoped, she would apologize for her role at the meeting, but from her tone, I could tell it wasn't going to happen.

"Better, thanks." Even though she hadn't invited me to, I sat on one of her chairs. "I talked to Stan. He told me you're taking the lead with this client."

"Yes, well, I should've taken the lead on it in the first place. If you had told people you were pregnant, it would've gone to me. *Flu* . . ." She shook her head, clearly disgusted.

"Come on, Maya. You said not to tell anyone at work. You know what I'm dealing with."

"Actually, I don't." She glared at me. "And you don't seem to want to fill me in. I guess you have Matt now to confide in."

I sighed and looked up at her framed law school diploma, the school where we became best friends—a friendship that had quickly been unraveling since I moved to San Francisco. Maya was still angry with me. I didn't know if it was my secret about my pregnancy, my performance at work, or that I was dating Matt. Before I could ask, Denise was at Maya's door.

"Oh, hey, guys," she said. "Are you busy, Maya?"

"Nope. Jae was just leaving."

Just like that, I was dismissed.

***

"I should be done by seven. It's just a networking event," I said on the phone to Matt as I turned off my computer for the day.

"Okay, text me when you're about to leave, and I'll pick you up for dinner."

After the disastrous presentation, I had decided that I needed to get serious about bringing in business. I had already updated my LinkedIn profile, and when I left Levenfield, I had contacted my old clients to let them know I was moving to a new firm, but *nada*. So I contacted some old law school acquaintances who were in-house counsel and let them know I was now at Gilchrist, and to let me know if they or anyone they knew needed real estate counsel in the Bay Area. I also researched if there were any local bar associations and signed up for those, figuring it might help me keep my sanity if I met other attorneys outside of Gilchrist.

That week I had found a networking event for women attorneys. I thought that adding networking and new business development to my time sheets might impress Stan and show him I was trying. At my old firm, I was valued for my work product, negotiating skills, and keeping clients happy; but after the Soto meeting, I felt I was starting at ground zero to prove myself as an attorney all over again. And if I didn't bring in any new business, I knew I ran the risk of exposing that perhaps I wasn't capable of rainmaking either.

After dropping my phone in my purse and closing my office door for the night, I headed to the elevators where I ran into Maya and Denise.

"Hey. Heading home?" I asked, forcing myself to be polite.

"Yup," said Maya. She gave me the once-over. "No computer bag?"

"Not tonight. You?" I said, noticing the absence of hers.

"Nope." She shook her head. "First time in a long time."

I inwardly rolled my eyes at this stupid pissing match. As if a computer bag by your side made you the better lawyer. Kind of like those conversations when we were associates and "complained" that we billed over two hundred hours that month or had to stay in the office until two o'clock in the morning all week. At a normal job this would probably be cause for complaint; but in a law firm, I always found it to be a passive form of bragging, since everyone was trying to bill more than the next person.

As we walked out of the elevator into the front lobby, I said, "Have a good night."

"You too," Denise and Maya said cheerfully, and I assumed they were happy to be leaving at a reasonable hour.

We exited the building together and started heading in the same direction, walking beside each other, and then continued to awkwardly do so for the next couple blocks. I felt looks pass between Maya and Denise; but for the life of me, I couldn't think of any small talk. Obviously, they were going someplace together, for a drink or something, since neither dropped off at any of the Muni station stops; I told myself I didn't care because I couldn't have a real drink anyway.

So I was surprised when we stopped in front of the same building, and all paused at the entrance—me to check the address and them no doubt to wonder what I was doing there.

I looked sideways at them. "Are you going to this women's event too?" I asked, breaking the tense silence.

"Yes," said Denise. "You?"

"Yes."

"How funny!" she said, and laughed. Not even a nervous laugh, but a genuine one.

I didn't think it was that funny. Maya didn't say anything and avoided my eyes. I could forgive Denise for not thinking of inviting me, but I couldn't forgive Maya. Even though I no longer wanted to go inside, I plastered on a fake smile and said, "Very. Shall we?" I opened the door, and together the three of us went inside to network, all the while keeping a wide berth between us.

***

Over dinner with Matt at a nearby restaurant, I recounted walking to the event with Maya and Denise.

"They didn't even think to include me," I said, exasperated. "I don't know what to do. Now that a new attorney is starting in corporate, I have no hope of moving into that department. And I'm never going to progress at Gilchrist in real estate with Maya there, unless I can build my own client list."

"Have you thought about just leaving altogether?"

"Of course, but it's barely been two months, and that raises questions. I don't want to be a firm hopper. And being pregnant makes it difficult because no one wants to hire someone who's going to go on maternity leave."

"Can you stick it out until maternity leave? Then you could go in-house and say you want something with more life-work balance," he suggested, casually popping a fry into his mouth and making it sound like the easiest solution.

"Of course that might mean less money, and less money to pay for childcare," I countered.

In my mental state, I couldn't absorb his reasonable-sounding advice. The event had been a nonstarter, whether it was because I was tense going in or was too preoccupied avoiding Maya, and I no longer felt hopeful for any new client or in-house opportunities.

Suddenly, my heart started to race, and my breathing became shallow.

"Hey." Matt grabbed my hand on the table and held it. "We'll figure it out."

"Thank you." I squeezed his hand back. "I know, and I shouldn't stress."

But our relationship was another source of stress. Though I was nearing my second trimester, I was only vaguely showing, and the baby still seemed theoretical. Once I really started showing, would Matt still be interested in me? When the reality of single motherhood hit, would he be able to handle it? Thanks to growing up with the kindness of my own stepfather, I wanted to believe, yes; but I was wary. What little trust I had in friendship or lovers had been sorely tested, and no one could be completely counted on. For now, I just had to try to stay in the moment and not get too overwhelmed by the future.

Part III

CHAPTER TWENTY-TWO

Hi, Jae. How's life these days? Hope you're doing well.

Brad's email stared at me from my laptop screen.

I was still at home, as I had a doctor's appointment scheduled before work that morning. Matt was in the bathroom after having spent the night, and when I heard the shower turn off, I quickly closed my laptop.

I hadn't heard from Brad in months. *And then he writes me an email out of the blue? As if nothing ever happened?* I wanted to respond, but I wasn't going to. He cut me off. And now I was carrying his child and had decided not to tell him. I wasn't about to reopen the lines of communication. He was dead to me.

***

In the car on the way to my appointment, Matt asked, "Are you nervous? You seem pretty quiet."

"A little." But really I was still fuming over Brad's email.

"Are you sure you don't want me to park and come to the appointment with you?"

"Thanks, but it's not necessary. It's just a routine appointment," I said. "I'll take a cab or Uber to work afterward. No reason for us both to be late today."

I snuck a quick glance at Matt. Each day, as we became closer as a couple, I became more nervous. While he never put pressure on me regarding the father of my baby, I wondered if at some point I would have to confess to him about my affair with Brad. I knew he assumed it was an ex-boyfriend who jilted me, which in some ways was a version of the truth. I was so grateful for Matt's acceptance of my situation, but I had to push down the lump of sadness in my throat that the actual father of my child wasn't the one taking me to my appointment.

At the hospital, looking over my chart, my doctor said, "Your blood pressure is higher than I'd like it. Are you under a lot of stress?"

"I'm a lawyer. What do you think?" I gave her a small smile.

"You need to be doing something different," the doctor said. "Less work, more sleep, and learn to relax. High blood pressure can cause many complications during pregnancy." She must have registered the worried look on my face, because she followed it with, "For now we'll keep an eye on it. Many women in this situation go on to have a healthy baby. Regardless, it's something to manage earlier rather than later."

I nodded. "Got it." But between work stress and facing single motherhood in a city where I had no social network, the doctor's orders seemed far-fetched.

"Okay, then let's get a look at this baby," she said, putting down the chart and grabbing the bottle of gel to rub on my belly for my ultrasound.

When she turned on the machine and moved the wand over

my stomach, I felt a flip in my heart as the image came into view. At my first ultrasound to confirm my pregnancy, the image was blurry, and so I took my doctor's word that what she was pointing to was my baby. Now I could make out an actual shape and the head of my child.

"Ah, everything looks like it should," the doctor said, her eyes on the screen. She then looked back at me and grinned. "Do you want to know the sex?"

As I walked outside her office with the sonogram photo of my daughter tucked safely into my bag, under the entrance canopy to the building, I spotted a mother holding her newborn baby and felt tears welling up in my eyes. It was strange that I'd never really thought about children or having my own before, which was probably why I wasted so much time on Brad. Maybe if I wanted marriage and children and the white-picket-fence scenario, I would have moved on much earlier. Now here I was, blubbering at the mere sight of a mother and child. The pregnancy to this point hadn't seemed real. But after seeing my developing baby on the screen and my doctor's stern warning about high blood pressure and the fear of it possibly threatening my baby's life, things were coming into focus. I needed to get my act together. Brad and his stupid email that morning were not important. The only important person was the one growing inside of me.

***

When I got to work, Maya came into my office.

"I need to talk to you. Are you busy?" she asked.

"No. Have a seat." I gestured to one of the chairs across from my desk, wondering what news had merited her visit. Maybe she was going to apologize? Maybe our friendship could get back on track? After my visit with the doctor, I was ready to let go of all grudges and move forward.

She closed the door behind her and took a seat.

"I'm leaving," she said. "I accepted an in-house job with Soto Technologies."

I sat there mutely, not sure how to respond.

"Jae?" Maya snapped her fingers.

"Um, *wow*." I tried to gather my thoughts. "Congratulations?" I said cautiously.

"Thanks." She ignored my unsure expression. "I just gave Stan my notice this morning. My last day is next Friday. I would've liked to have given a full two weeks, but they need me to start right away."

"That's . . . That's great," I stammered, trying to get over my surprise. "How did it happen?"

"It *is* great. I'm ready to get out of firm life, and I need a change. And I have you to thank." I gave her a confused look. "After you screwed up the presentation, their CEO called me and said they would like to hire me in-house to oversee the construction of their new facilities."

"That's really impressive. Good for you." In a conciliatory tone, I continued. "Hey, I know things have been weird between us, and I blame myself for that. But you know I'll work really hard for you here, and you can count on me."

Maya shook her head. "I'm not going to use Gilchrist. I can manage most of it on my own. Also, you'll be on maternity leave in the middle of this project, and there are no other real estate attorneys in this office. If I need outside counsel, I'm going to have to use another firm."

Oh! So, she wasn't here to apologize but to deliver the death blow to our failing friendship.

"I see," I managed. "What about your other clients? Is there anything I can help with? Do you need to transition their matters to me?"

She shook her head no again. "I'm recommending them to others in the firm. I worked hard building those relationships and, like I said, you'll be on maternity leave and would have to transition them to someone else all over again. It's easier to hand them over to someone who can manage the relationship on a long-term basis."

I was speechless. Once Maya left, I would not have a single client matter to work on. Not only was she ending our friendship; she was also purposely trying to end my career at Gilchrist.

When I didn't say anything, Maya rolled her eyes and sighed heavily. "Do you have any questions?"

I had a million questions, none of which were work related.

"I'm sorry," I said, unsure if I had been such a terrible friend to deserve her rancor to this extent.

"That's not a question," she huffed. "Anyway, my last day is Friday. So if you do think of something, let me know." She stood up and left.

I was trying not to stress according to the doctor's orders, but my mind reeled with Maya's news.

I took a deep breath, got up, and closed my office door to process everything.

I would have no work.

But I would also have no Maya.

That was something to seriously consider. With our friendship officially over, all the energy I had spent trying to manage Maya could go toward getting new clients. In the most positive light, it could be an opportunity to build my own practice, I told myself. Or maybe, *just maybe*, I thought, I could return to corporate law. There was only one way to find out where I really stood.

I immediately got up again and headed to Mark's office.

Before I had a chance to knock, he noticed me in his doorway.

"Hi, Jae," he said, sitting behind his desk. "Can I help you with something?"

I took that as an invitation and walked in, sitting down on a chair on the opposite side of his desk. "Actually, I'm here to see if I can help *you* with anything. With Maya leaving, if you have any real estate questions, please let me know," I said, feeling my hands quietly trembling with nerves and emotion from my encounter with Maya. I clasped them in my lap to keep still. "And since Maya will not be using outside counsel for this Soto project, my plate isn't that full right now. So I'm also happy to help out with any corporate projects."

He nodded. "Did you know Maya was going to go to Soto?"

"No," I said, and wondered whether he had been listening to me at all.

Mark folded his hands into a steeple and tapped his chin. "Huh. I thought you two were friends."

"We are." I wasn't about to let loose my frenemy drama on Mark. "But it happened pretty quickly, and I guess Soto doesn't want to spend money on outside counsel."

He then broke with his typical reserved facade and said, "I'm surprised she's leaving you here high and dry."

I felt Mark was still making up his mind about me, and I wasn't sure if it was a test. So I just nodded neutrally in response.

"Thanks for coming by, and I'll let you know if we can use any help. We have a new deal brewing, but the client is pretty particular on who he wants on the team. As you may know, a senior associate from the Chicago office is moving here to work solely on this project. So I guess we'll see how her workload goes and go from there."

While he wasn't unfriendly, I walked away with the feeling

that Mark was still wary of me. At Levenfield, I had never felt the competitive streak that seemed to permeate the small offices of Gilchrist, since everyone had more work than they could handle and they were grateful for any assistance. Or maybe I hadn't been involved in Levenfield's office politics because I was so distracted by Brad and too busy navigating my double life. But this was a different firm, and I had already experienced how possessively everyone guarded their projects. It seemed my only option was to hustle for new business.

When I returned to my office and opened up my email, there was another message from Brad.

> Are you mad at me?

Mad?!

It took all my strength not to scream *Are you fucking kidding me?* and smash my computer to the floor in a Hulk-like rage. *Mad* didn't even encompass everything I was feeling—toward Brad, toward Maya, toward Mark—in that moment. I closed my eyes and tried to take deep breaths to calm down, but instead found myself taking in huge gulps of air. Remembering my doctor's advice to manage my stress, which seemed an impossible task, I deleted Brad's email and then stayed hidden in my office until five o'clock. My hustle would have to wait another day.

***

That night I woke up bleeding. I tried not to panic, as I had read that bleeding happened in one out of four pregnancies and everything could still be fine. I didn't know whether to call Matt. It was a little after two o'clock, and he lived on the other side of the city. What could he do? Plus, I was scared to move too much. With a pounding heart and shaky fingers, I called my doctor's emergency answering service. They told me to head to the hospital right away and a doctor would be waiting for me. I called a cab and bundled myself up in a frantic scramble.

As the cab went through the empty streets, to fight my rising fear and calm my racing heart, I tried the same deep breathing techniques I had done earlier that day, counting to four, and still failing—each shuddering breath feeling like a quiet sob. I knew I was losing my baby.

As soon as I arrived, the hospital staff ushered me into a room. A nurse or technician performed an ultrasound. They did not say anything except, "The doctor will be with you shortly." And he was. He patted my knee kindly and said, "I'm Dr. Yang. Let's see what we have here." He knew it was over. I could tell from his eyes that he knew he was going to have to deliver bad news. But I held onto a small hope that maybe the technician's silent opinion was wrong. The doctor studied the screen, while he moved the wand over my belly.

"We're going to have to do a transvaginal ultrasound to get a closer look," he told me.

During this second ultrasound, the doctor and technician remained silent and pointed to the screen while communicating to each other with their eyes. I didn't like what I "heard." So I stared up at the ceiling, feeling the tears prick behind my eyes as I tried to keep my dread at bay. Finally, Dr. Yang said, "We're having a hard time hearing the heartbeat. We want to do a couple more tests."

I nodded. There was no heartbeat, there was no baby.

"Is the father with you?" he asked.

"No," I said as I wiped the tears that were leaking out the sides of my eyes.

"Do you want to call anyone?"

I knew the doctor was carefully trying to tell me I shouldn't be alone at that moment. That someone was going to have to take me home while I processed the bad news. The only person to call was Matt.

"Yes, I'd like to call my boyfriend." I hated to do it, but I followed the doctor's orders, since he was probably right—I shouldn't be alone.

Matt answered the phone in a blurry, then panicked voice and said he would be right there.

The doctor performed a couple more tests that I went through in a haze. Then he said the inevitable.

"I'm sorry. The fetus's heart has stopped beating. This can happen in the first trimester. . . ."

I didn't hear his exact words because I was filling them in with, *"Your baby is gone. Your baby is gone,"* on repeat in my head. He told me to make a follow-up appointment with my doctor, and that if the bleeding continued, I might need a D&C. And I gave a silent prayer that I wouldn't need one because I couldn't wrap my brain around the finality of it all.

As a nurse escorted me out of the examination room into the waiting room, Matt, who was sitting there, stood up as soon as he saw me. I didn't have to say anything because he could read it on my face. "Oh, Jae." He came over and hugged me tightly. "I'm so sorry." I just nodded and let myself cry while he held me.

Matt took me home and stayed with me that night.

In the morning, I was still bleeding, and I called my doctor, who recommended I come in for a D&C procedure. Matt took me to my appointment and also stayed home from work that day. He brought me food. We watched a couple movies. But mostly I slept or pretended to. I couldn't talk about it. The grief was crushing. I would have traded the worries of single motherhood over the grief of loss. And since I hadn't told my family or

Brad, there was no one to reach out to. I wasn't sure if it was a good or bad thing.

The next day, Matt went into work and left me with a stocked fridge and a promise to return that night. Still in bed, I reached for my phone to check my work emails to see if I was missing anything. The only new email I'd received was from Brad.

> Jae, I need to talk to you.

Fuck him. My anger at Brad gave me a respite from my grief. But he was also the reason for it. I wanted to scream at him. I had asked the doctor whether high blood pressure or stress had caused my miscarriage. Probably not wanting to rub more salt into the wound, he said, "It just happens sometimes. Something wasn't developing properly. There could've been a genetic abnormality. I wish I could give you a more concrete answer, but it's nothing you've done."

Yet I couldn't help but think that it was my fault. I remembered from my torts law class that someone is always liable, even if indirectly. I felt a visceral hatred for anyone who caused me stress. But I mostly hated Brad for getting me pregnant in the first place, ignoring me, and then attempting contact after all this time, when I was finally trying—and obviously failing—to make a new life for myself without him.

For the first time ever, I went to sleep wishing I wouldn't wake up. I dreamed I was back at that construction site in front of Levenfield, that the fence gave way, and I was slowly falling into the dark pit and didn't care enough to scream or save myself. I just wanted to cease to exist because the pain was too much and there was no solution. Everything felt empty. The only bright spot was Matt. I had been keeping up an emotional wall with him because I didn't trust that our relationship was real and worried that he would leave me. But the fact that he was taking care of me showed that he was someone to take seriously. I needed to fight my sadness, if not for me, then for him and our relationship.

And because I was weak and tired, I emailed back Brad.

> Fuck you.

Of course, any response was opening up the lines of communication, and so Brad responded immediately.

> Jae—
> Maybe I deserve that, but your email was very hurtful. All I said was I needed to talk to you. I don't wish you anything but the best. I hope you believe that.

I didn't. Because everything had turned out for the worst, and it was easier to blame Brad for it.

FUCK YOU, I typed back, and threw my phone across the room.

I didn't check my email for the rest of the day.

CHAPTER TWENTY-THREE

On Monday morning, the week after my miscarriage, I was back at my desk, physically and emotionally depleted, and I wished I had more work to keep my mind off everything. Instead, despite how depressed I was, I needed to become a rainmaker. So, starting that morning, I sent out emails and made phone calls, contacting partners in the other offices to let them know that with Maya's departure, I would be able to handle any local real estate matters or assist on any current projects. I reached out to as many remaining law school alumni as I could think of. I researched construction companies and their in-house counsels. I scoured the news for any projects coming up and who the outside attorneys were.

I wanted to meet with Mark again that week, but he was busy working with Adeline, the new corporate attorney in the office. While I was on the phone with a partner in the New York office, Adeline had sent me an email asking if I wanted to grab lunch. I thought that was promising, and I planned to respond yes as soon as I was off my call.

And then Brad emailed me on my work account.

> Jasmine—
> I've received an offer to work in San Francisco and am seriously considering it. I would like to ask you a few questions at your convenience.
> Sincerely,
> Brad Summers

My heart stopped. Just then I thought I heard a faint knocking on my door though I wasn't sure if it was my heart trying to beat again.

"Jasmine?"

It was an unfamiliar voice. I tried to compose myself before turning around. The voice kept talking. "Um, I was wondering if you were doing anything for lunch today."

It was the new attorney, Adeline. I had wanted to say, *I'm sorry. I saw your email and meant to reply yes, but the morning flew by*, but then I was trying not to say how my world had just stopped.

"No, I'm not," I responded.

"Well, would you like to grab lunch together?"

Hiding any emotion on my face, I turned around to meet her.

I had seen her around the office. She was average height with wavy highlighted brown hair; and up close, I could see she had green eyes. She kept shifting slightly from side to side as she rambled on a bit, her nervous nature making me more anxious. When I found my voice, I said, "Sorry, I can't today," but to be conciliatory, I added, "Maybe we can do coffee another time?"

She thanked me, backed away slowly, and then rushed out of the room as if she couldn't bear to be there another second. I had never thought of myself as an intimidating person, and I knew I had to make it up to her. After all, I was trying to find allies at work. But the only thing I could focus on at the moment was Brad's email. Was this really happening? And if so, how soon? And how could I find out more without having to communicate with him?

I thought back to our Levenfield clients in LA but couldn't think of any real estate projects tied to San Francisco. I tried to stalk Brad online, but he kept a low profile. We weren't friends on any social media. Other than Levenfield's website and some online networking sites like LinkedIn, he didn't exist. I read a list of Levenfield's clients featured on the website. There were a few technology companies, but nothing I remembered Brad working on. Even so, I researched those companies listed in the Bay Area, but couldn't find anything about imminent real estate developments.

At the end of my research, with nothing coming up, there was a knock at my door.

"Hi," said Rachel.

Shoot. In my turmoil, I had forgotten my quasi-mentor coffee date with her.

Rachel had started in the corporate department at Gilchrist, but then realized after her third year she was more interested in real estate. As a fifth year, she officially remained in the corporate department, but divided her time between the two. Unfortunately for her, with Maya gone, I was the only real estate link at Gilchrist. She had asked me out for coffee to discuss the latest changes in the department and what I thought going ahead.

When I was an associate, I had been nervous around partners. But now that I was a partner, this associate made me nervous.

***

Sitting at a nearby Starbucks, I started in on my partner-mentoring-an-associate speech. "Although I'm sad to see Maya leave, I'm excited to have the chance to build the real estate department in this office and take on my own clients, as well as being the point person in San Francisco for our other offices," I said, maintaining eye contact with Rachel to convey confidence, though I wasn't feeling it.

I took a sip of my tea to study her reactions and give her a chance to ask a question. She didn't. So I continued. "I know you have an interest in real estate, so I'll bring you onto any new projects."

"What sort of projects do you anticipate?" She tilted her head, and I wondered if she was calling my bluff.

"For the moment, I'm focused on client development. So I would like to get started with putting together some pitch decks. Maybe that's something you can help me with in between your corporate work?"

"I'd love that," Rachel said, her face brightened, showing the first hint of enthusiasm.

"Great! Why don't we meet on Friday to talk about it?"

"Okay."

"Is there anything else in particular you wanted to talk about?" She had asked me for the mentoring session, so I wanted to make sure she felt I was fitting the role.

"No, that's all. I don't mind corporate work, but I want to expand my real estate experience. Maybe I shouldn't say this, but my goal is to go in-house one day. And so getting more experience in different departments could help me."

That was candid. Maybe Rachel wasn't all that bad. At the very least, she was honest—a trait that had been missing from most of my recent communications.

"Of course. I'll do my best to make sure you get exposure to different projects." I took the last sip of my tea. "I missed lunch, so I'm going to get a scone or something. Would you like anything?"

Rachel shook her head so violently I thought she'd shake it off. "No, I don't eat that stuff."

"Okay," I said carefully. *It's a scone, not exactly poison.* "Low-carb diet?"

She shrugged. "You know how it is."

Actually, I didn't. Other than being a vegetarian, I wasn't that particular about what I ate or the latest *diet du jour.*

She gave me a quick head-to-toe once-over. "You look like you've lost weight."

Yes, it was baby weight! I wanted to respond, along with, *Thank you for reminding me, Rachel!* Not that I needed reminding, since it lived at the forefront of my thoughts.

"Yes," I said. "I was sick for a couple days. But I'm feeling better."

I stood up quickly with my purse and jacket and headed to the counter. I was ready to return to the office and worry about other problems.

On our way back in, we passed by Adeline's office. I saw her look up briefly, and we made eye contact. Enough for me to see that she registered the Starbucks coffee in Rachel's hand and that we were coming in from outside. Her eyes widened, and I detected some hurt and wanted to explain, *This was already scheduled. I'm sorry I couldn't go to lunch.* I felt bad and made a mental note to reach out to her that week. Although, how would I introduce myself exactly? I was the real estate attorney who had zero work or clients. I needed to figure something out.

I decided to go to the only source I had in the office.

I knocked on Mark's door. "Hi, Mark. Are you busy?"

He looked up at me from his desk. "Just the usual. How can I help you?"

I noticed he didn't say come in, but I came in anyway and sat in the chair across from his desk. "I would like to put together a real estate presentation for business development here. I was wondering if you could tell me how to get that started? I assume there's some template on the system. Or if there's anyone in another office you think I should contact to get the procedures and materials?"

Mark leaned back with his hands folded in a point as he tapped his chin, thinking.

"Hmmm . . . You know, I'm somewhat new here myself and haven't worked with many of the real estate attorneys other than some due diligence, which Maya mostly handled. Let me think about it and get back to you."

"Okay. Thank you."

Mark leaned forward again and turned to his computer while I still sat there. "Is that all?" he asked, seeming confused that I hadn't gotten up yet to leave.

"There's something else." I dreaded this, but maybe he would know something about Brad. "During my tour, you mentioned that Gilchrist was planning to grow this office. Do you know of any immediate plans to hire new attorneys?"

Mark sat there looking at me, his brow wrinkled. I felt stupid.

"Well, we just transferred Adeline over here. So for right now, I can't say that there are any immediate plans," Mark said, somewhat evasively. But I still wondered if he knew something about Brad. "Anyway, I'll make sure to get you in touch with someone on the presentation materials. Probably tomorrow or at least this week."

"Thanks, Mark."

"Of course," he said as his eyes drifted back to his computer screen and he started typing. I stood up and left. Our interaction wasn't a total victory, but it was a step forward.

***

The next day, true to his word, Mark put me in touch with Meghan from the Chicago office, and she walked me through what marketing materials I would need. Of course, she was also very interested in how things were going without Maya.

I let out a small laugh. "I can't lie—without Maya here, it's pretty quiet. And, I'm feeling the pressure of being the sole real estate partner in this office."

"If it's at all reassuring, I wasn't a big fan of Maya. Let's just say, I was glad she was in your office and not mine," she said. "I heard she decided not to use Gilchrist for the new Soto offices. *Wow!* Talk about burning bridges."

"Yes." I cleared my throat. Maya's betrayal still hurt, but I had betrayed her, too, in my own way, and I needed to take the high road now. "Which is why I'm looking to put together some presentations. I need some clients." I gave a hopeless laugh.

"What are you working on now?"

"Just new business development. I have some leads, but in the meantime, I was hoping that the other offices might need some assistance or have some clients based here that I could help with."

"Hmm . . . so you're saying you got nothing?"

"Well . . ."

"It's okay. I actually have some contacts out there. I went to school at Stanford, but marriage brought me out to Chicago," she said, her voice animated and cheerful. "Some of my friends are in-house now, and I can give them a call and make introductions."

Who is this angel? "That would be fantastic! Thank you."

"More wealth for the firm, right?" she laughed. "We're actually stretched a little too thin in this department. We don't have enough senior associates over here. And even though you're a partner, perhaps there's something you could help out with?

Probably won't be very glamorous, though." I could feel her frown on the phone.

"I don't need glamour. Just some client matters to assist with and introductions would be great."

Over the next few weeks, I had meetings over coffee and dinner with some of Meghan's contacts, which weren't as heavy on business as they were on socializing. But it kept me out of my apartment and not as dependent on Matt. Whenever I told him I had a potential client meeting or something, I felt I could see the lines on his forehead relax as he said, "That's great, baby. Have fun, okay?" He knew how depressed I was from the miscarriage, and anything to keep me from brooding was good news. And with each new lead, I felt more like I might actually become a productive member at Gilchrist.

Since I hadn't heard anything from Stan regarding hiring a new real estate partner, and Brad hadn't followed up on his email that I never responded to, I finally let myself relax and focused on moving forward.

CHAPTER TWENTY-FOUR

One morning, waking up with Matt next to me, I checked my email.

> I miss you.

Brad had sent it around two o'clock in the morning. There was no subject line. Just I miss you in the body of the email. Fury ripped through me, as if Brad had interrupted my cozy life by walking into my apartment. I chose to ignore it.

A few days later there was another email.

> I hope you are doing well. I wish you no hard feelings.

I also chose to ignore it.

Then there was an email that was more businesslike.

> Hi Jae—
> I'm going to be in San Francisco on

> business at the end of this week. I would love to meet for coffee or a drink if you're free.
> —Brad

I wasn't free. I was with Matt, and so I deleted his message.

Since Brad wasn't getting a response on my email, he next tried my cell. I was at Peet's before work when my phone rang with a local 415 area code. Thinking it might be work related, I answered.

"Hello, this is Jae Phillips," I said as I carried my tea over to a table to set it down.

"Hi, Jae. It's great to hear your voice."

His voice made me freeze. I looked around the coffee shop as if I were in some horror movie and the caller could see me, but I couldn't see him. I should have hung up the phone, but I was too startled.

"Jae? Are you there?"

He clearly wasn't going to leave me in peace until we spoke. "What do you want, Brad?" I said, making sure he could detect the irritation in my voice.

"I just want to talk to you," he said calmly. "It's been a long time."

"Not long enough."

"You've been ignoring my emails."

"Yes, and I would've ignored this call if I'd known it was you."

I could see the two twenty-something girls at the next table trying to discreetly eavesdrop. Deflecting my irritation from Brad to them, I shot them a look to mind their own business.

"I figured as much, which is why I'm calling from my hotel."

I sighed. "I'm asking again, what do you want?"

"I want to see you."

"Why?"

"Do I need a reason? Because I care about you."

I squeezed the phone, wondering if my anger would crush it.

"People who care about someone don't blow them off like you did to me."

"I know," he admitted, sounding apologetic. "I want to explain. It's been hard these last few months."

"*It's been hard*?" I parroted. "What about me?"

"What about you? You escaped."

"Ha!" I let bitterness punctuate my sentence. "Not unscathed."

"Jae, if you could just meet me, I can explain everything."

"A little too late, Brad. Have a great life." I hit End Call and threw my phone back in my purse.

My hands were shaking. I could feel the eyes of the two girls on me, but when I looked up, they looked away.

Fucking Brad. It had been hard for him? *What about for the woman you impregnated and then ignored and who lost her baby in a miscarriage?* I almost wanted to meet him just so I could tell him everything I'd gone through, and he could witness the depth of my hatred for him.

Brad emailed me as soon as I got to work—I need to talk to you. I didn't respond. There was a text on my phone—I need to talk to you. Followed by another—Please. That was pretty impressive, since Brad rarely texted, probably for fear his wife would pick up his phone. But he was in San Francisco. And just knowing he was in the same city made me feel as if the walls were closing in on me.

Finally that afternoon, my office phone rang. Normally I always answered it, but that day I let my secretary get it. As Tracy could clearly see that I was in my office ignoring my ringing phone, I heard her say, "Let me check if she's in."

She called me on my line. "I have Brad Summers from

Levenfield on the phone." She didn't ask me if I wanted to take it. She was perfunctory that way. I obviously wasn't busy and didn't want to arouse suspicion. Brad was not going to give up, so I said, "Okay." I closed my door and then picked up the receiver, placing it against my ear.

"Hello," I said, my voice clipped.

"Hi, Jae," Brad said, his tone professional, not giving anything away. When I didn't say anything in response, he continued. "I'm sorry to call you at your office, but this is important."

"I understand. I had something important to tell you in LA, but when I tried to reach you, you wouldn't talk to me. So I'm going to do the same. *Stop. Stalking. Me.*"

Ignoring my plea, Brad continued. "I can't say much, but I'm probably going to be moving to the Bay Area in the near future. Kathryn and I are separated."

I didn't believe him and rolled my eyes even though he couldn't see me. If he used Ivy as an excuse not to get a divorce, then was he really going to get one after child number two? "Really? You're moving up here," I said dryly. "What's up here?"

"You." Oh, I wanted to punch him. "And a good job offer. I haven't accepted yet, but I would like to."

Oh god. This was actually happening, and soon. A paranoid thought hit me. *What if the job offer is from Gilchrist?* Was he being hired to replace me?

But first, "So you and Kathryn are separated? And why is that?" I couldn't help but be sarcastic.

"Yes, and I don't want to get into it on the phone. It's a lot. I just really need to talk to you in person. Please, Jae."

Seeing him would actually give me a chance to punch him. That thought was entertaining.

"I know, *Brad*, but I don't really want to talk to you. I have a boyfriend I love and a job I'm happy at in a city I enjoy. And it took moving away from you. So I'm sure you can see why I don't want to talk to you."

Brad was silent for a second at the other end.

"I understand. And I'm sorry that I hurt you. It wasn't my intention. You don't owe me this, but I still think we should talk."

Brad deserved the same treatment he gave me. What could he want to talk about that was of equal importance as "I'm carrying your child"? But my curiosity finally began to overpower my anger. Even though I wanted nothing to do with him, I found myself saying, "Why can't you tell me on the phone?"

"Jae, please?" he said, his voice plaintive.

I let out a deep sigh. "Fine." I did want to learn more about his job offer. "When can you meet? I'm free tonight."

Brad also sighed, as if he had been holding his breath on the other end of the line. "Thank you. I can meet anytime after five. Where should I meet you?"

"There's a Peet's Coffee on Market. . . ."

"Is there somewhere more private than a coffee shop?"

"You know what? Ask the concierge. Just email me the place and I'll be there, okay? I gotta go."

I was shaking when I set down the receiver. I couldn't believe I'd just agreed to meet him in person. But this was it—perhaps it would bring some closure. And if I could convince him not to move to San Francisco, it would be worthwhile.

At 5:30 p.m. I arrived at the spot Brad suggested. I wasn't thrilled—or surprised—that it was a bar, but it was walking distance from my office and quibbling about it would have meant more communication with Brad than necessary. I spotted Brad as soon as I stepped inside. He was already seated at a table with a drink in front of him, something hard and clear. Despite my hatred for him, I felt a familiar shock of electricity course through my body.

"Hello," I said as I set my purse on the chair and began to take off my coat. Brad had started to get up when he saw me, but I put my palm up in a stop gesture to tell him to stay seated.

"Hi, Jae. It's good to see you. You look great." His deep voice vibrated down my spine as he held my gaze.

It had been a few months since I'd seen him, and his hair was a little longer and in need of a cut. But if I was honest with myself, he looked even better than when I last saw him in LA on that horrible day at Levenfield with his pregnant wife.

"Yeah," I said, refusing to respond to his compliment, and sat down.

"Wow. I just haven't seen you in so long. It's good."

Unable to bring myself to make more eye contact, I looked around the bar. One of the servers took that as a sign to come to our table.

"I'll just have a sparkling water, please," I told her.

"Are you sure?" asked Brad. "That's not the Jae I remember."

I looked at him. "I can leave, you know." I turned back to the server. "Sparkling water will be fine. Thanks."

Probably sensing the tension at the table, she looked relieved to turn around and leave us.

"So." I crossed my arms and leaned back in my chair. "What do you want to talk about?"

"A lot of things. But first, how are you?"

I rolled my eyes at him. "I'm fine. But what do you care now? You haven't seemed to care for the past few months."

All of a sudden, Brad's eyes flashed with hurt and anger. "Jae, you left me, remember? You made the call to move to San Francisco and end our relationship."

I wanted to say that we never had a real relationship, so there was nothing to end. I had so many hurt feelings and so much anger that I didn't know where to begin, so I didn't. Brad looked away from me and down at his drink. "So you're in a relationship now. Is it serious?"

"It's none of your business, but, yes, it is."

He nodded, still not looking at me. "Good. I don't want you to be alone." After a few more seconds of silence, Brad said, "I still think about you, you know. A lot."

"Is that the important thing you needed to tell me? Because I've moved on."

Brad winced slightly, and I felt his anger turn to defeat. "I wanted to explain. I know you kept trying to talk to me when you moved, but there was so much happening. And you were leaving LA, and at the time I could only deal with so much. It's not an excuse. I was a complete asshole. But I want you to know how sorry I am."

"That's fine. It's in the past." It wasn't fine and I hadn't forgiven him, but it was over between us. And I figured that the sooner I gave him my blessing, the sooner I could learn about this job offer and convince him to stay put in LA.

Brad's glass was empty, and he motioned to the server. When she arrived, he ordered another drink and turned to me. "Are you sure you don't want something stronger? You're going to need it."

I shook my head no, figuring our conversation was almost finished. Except, "What is this about a job? Are you really moving up here?"

"Yes. My client wants me in the Bay Area, and I need a new start."

"You're really getting a divorce?"

"Yes."

All the years I was with him and he never left Kathryn. Then once we were over, he finally made his decision? "You're right," I said. "I do need something stronger."

When my vodka arrived, I finally asked, "So why divorce now?"

"Kathryn killed her son."

I needed something even stronger than vodka to hear this. "I don't understand."

"When we were in Tahoe, Kathryn called and told me she was having issues with her pregnancy." I shook my head as he said this, and he shrugged remorsefully. "And, I know, I know—I should've told you she was pregnant. I was going to that weekend. It was not exactly a planned pregnancy. Well, *she* had her reasons. . . ." Now Brad shook his head. "Up until that point and all during that weekend, I had thought that I was ready to divorce her. That I would figure something out with Ivy and the baby, if I had you." He looked at me beseechingly. "But when she called, I knew if I handled that moment wrong, she'd never let me have custody of Ivy—out of spite." He paused and took a deep breath. "Long story short, without consulting her doctor, she started taking some so-called antidepressants that she ordered off the internet. She didn't tell anyone, and it caused the baby to have a heart defect. He was stillborn."

At first, all I heard in the beginning of his story was that he was still having sex with Kathryn while he was with me. But when he told me the outcome, all the grief from losing my baby swelled to the surface, and I could feel pinpricks of tears stabbing my eyes.

"I'm so sorry," I said.

Brad's eyes were shiny, and he looked simultaneously grief-stricken and relieved, as if he had shed some of the weight of his sorrows by telling me. Maybe the vodka was hitting him, because he reached over and squeezed my hand. "Thank you," he said. But I snatched my hand away. He held Kathryn responsible for their stillborn child, but I still held him responsible for my miscarriage.

Brad continued. "When I first found out she was pregnant,

I didn't know what to do because I didn't want to hurt you, and I couldn't ask you to keep waiting."

"You never asked me to wait," I said.

Brad looked at me, surprised. While Brad had brought up the subject of divorce to Kathryn, he had never actually asked me to wait. I was the one who had chosen to stay, until I hadn't anymore, and who had made the decision to move to San Francisco without him.

When I didn't clarify, he kept talking. "But when I heard you were moving to San Francisco, it gave me an idea. Kathryn wouldn't want to move, so maybe I could commute? Or buy some time in our relationship? But the way you reacted when I told you that, I knew I had to let you go. It wasn't the answer. I had ruined enough of your life."

"You didn't tell me any of this. Perhaps if you had told me, things would've been different? Instead, you ignored me." My voice caught on the word *ignored*.

Brad ran his hands down his face and looked anguished. "I was hurt. And things were getting out of control with Kathryn, and I couldn't handle any more. It's not an excuse. But if you were leaving my life, then I had to move on. Talking to you was too painful. I'm sorry I couldn't give you closure. I'm trying to now."

"Is that what you thought I wanted? Closure?"

"I'm sorry, Jae. I'm not seeking forgiveness, but I wanted to give you an explanation."

I nodded and then signaled to the server for another vodka soda. "Well, I'm glad I can give you some *closure*," I said, with a hint of bitterness.

"I want to show you something." He pulled out a sketchbook from his laptop bag, opened it to a page, and handed it to me. In the dimness of the candlelight, I could barely see the image. At first all I could make of it was a feeling. The charcoal lines followed each other and tumbled over like hot, heavy tears. Then it came to me, the scene floating before me, growing larger, and I realized what I saw. It was the moment Brad realized his son was dead. My mind and body reeled. I could not form words, and I thought of my own pregnancy, unexpected, but lost and forever mourned.

Brad grabbed my hand again, and this time I let him. "I wanted to share this with you. I needed you to understand."

I could not say anything. Brad just held my hand like a drowning man. And when I looked up at him in my unbalanced state, I remembered his dream in Tahoe where he was just floating in the water. Brad had finally decided to make a choice and swim, but now was drowning as a result.

What a tragedy. When I could finally find my voice, it was simply to say, "I'm sorry."

"I'm sorry too, Jae. I'm so, so sorry."

I pulled my hand away from his.

"I can't," I whispered.

He nodded, gently taking the sketchbook from me and putting it back in his bag. "You're still the only one I show my drawings to."

His emotional state was too big a responsibility. I knew he needed me, but I also knew we would never be together.

I felt my tears starting again and said, "I'm sorry, but I have to go." I grabbed my purse and rushed out of the bar.

I didn't share my own miscarriage story with Brad that night; I still needed to keep it to myself. And we never properly talked about his job offer. It seemed a pointless topic after what he told me about his son.

But the other reason I had to leave was—while neither of us had acted on it, I could almost see the sparks from the electricity humming between us.

CHAPTER TWENTY-FIVE

In the morning, I received another email from Brad.

> We still need to talk about my job offer.

Followed by a text from Matt.

> Good morning, beautiful. Missed you last night. Dinner tonight?

I put the phone back on my nightstand and got up to brush my teeth.

After Brad had revealed his state of affairs with Kathryn and his stillborn son, the question of whether we could both live and work in the same city seemed petty. The bigger issue was—though I was with Matt, I was still drawn to Brad. I tried to tell myself we weren't together, so what did our attraction matter? It mattered because I was with someone good. Someone I never expected or felt I deserved to have after seven years with Brad. Someone who was reliable, honest, and wanted to be with me.

Matt was the one I was destined to be with. He accepted me at my lowest point. He lost a friendship over me. He had been willing to raise another man's child in order to be with me. I had blown him off years ago, while I continued my mistakes with Brad.

All those years, Brad could have divorced Kathryn. Though I had pretended that I didn't doubt his fear of losing his daughter, I still felt that if he was stronger, or smarter, or more in love with me, he would have figured out a way. Yet, he didn't until I was out of the picture.

I finished brushing my teeth and drank a glass of water. Then I retrieved my phone from the bedroom and texted Matt back.

> Missed you too. Dinner tonight sounds wonderful. Love you.

When I got into work that morning, I responded to Brad's email.

> Okay. Tell me about the job offer.

Within seconds, Brad responded.

> When can you meet to talk? I'm still in town until tomorrow.

After the night before, and realizing that I was still attracted to him, I wasn't ready to see him again so soon. I thought of Matt and wrote back.

> I'm in the office right now and have some time to talk. If you're free, give me a call.

My cell rang shortly after.

"Can you meet for coffee? It's best to talk in person about this," Brad explained.

I had wanted him to call my office; to talk to me on the phone, and *not* in person. Why all the secrecy? Why wouldn't he just tell me? But we had already played out the avoidance game, and Brad wasn't letting up.

"Yes. There's a Peet's near my office. What's your schedule?" I said, feeling my heart begin to race.

"I'm free now. I can meet you there in five minutes."

Business for me was still slow, so this was the closest thing to work I had. Reluctantly, I said, "Okay. I'll see you there in five."

I ended the call and took a deep, steadying breath. Why was he in town all day? And what was he doing that he was free to meet whenever? I guessed I was going to find out.

***

When I arrived at Peet's, Brad was already there and standing by the counter. "Thanks for meeting me," he said.

"Of course. It's a slow morning." I shrugged.

Brad seemed to eye me warily, and I chose to ignore it.

"What would you like?" he asked. "It's on me."

"A medium green tea. Thank you."

"And a medium coffee for me," Brad said to the barista. While he handed over his cash, he commented to me, "No coffee?"

A wave of anger hit me. I was about to say that I gave up coffee when I found out I was pregnant, and that after the miscarriage I realized that it made me jittery.

"I gave up coffee," I said, "and I sleep much better now." It was a lame statement. But the other night was too personal, too emotional. In the daylight hours, I just wanted to talk business.

We carried our uncomplicated drinks over to a table in the corner.

"Thank you again, Jae," Brad said as we sat down.

I didn't want to hear his grateful, guilty, over-apologetic spiel, so I cut to the chase. "So what's going on? What's this job offer you want to talk about?"

He explained that his client, an animation company, was acquiring a 3-D technology company and that they were planning to build facilities in the Bay Area. "I've done almost all of their real estate work in Los Angeles, and they want me involved in this new project. It works out timing-wise regarding my divorce, with moving out and all. But I realize the awkwardness of this situation . . . for us."

I nodded, and thought, *This is my chance to dissuade him from moving to San Francisco.*

"Here's the thing," Brad said. "Now is not the time to jeopardize my career. This is my biggest client. I need to go where he wants me. And that is at Gilchrist."

"Gilchrist!?" I almost knocked my tea over. "What do you mean, he wants you at Gilchrist?" *Way to bury the lede, Brad!* I wanted to shout.

Now he was not only moving to San Francisco, *but he was joining my firm!* True, lawyering could be a small world, but it was all too coincidental. I wondered if he had engineered it. My heart pounded, and I could feel my temples begin to throb as well.

"My client really needs me up here, but I won't do it if you tell me not to. I know it's an uncomfortable situation."

"Why *exactly* does he want you at Gilchrist?" I sputtered.

Brad had yet to say the name of his client. "Because they're doing the acquisition deal."

"Who is?"

"You, Mark Dresner, Gilchrist."

"Mark is? So that's the big deal they're working on?"

Brad looked at me curiously. "You didn't know? I know it's confidential, but I wondered if they had you working on it, too, since you do corporate."

"Did corporate. Now I'm in real estate," I said bitterly.

"I can probably get you involved if you want," Brad said.

I didn't want to go into the politics of everything that happened at work, though I was tempted. Brad was familiar. He was once my only confidant. But I still needed to tread lightly—with him and at Gilchrist.

"There've been some changes in the real estate department. Mainly that the other real estate attorney left and took the work with her."

"Ouch." He winced in sympathy.

"Yes. So I may have made a mistake in joining that group." My real mistake was my relationship with Brad, which ultimately caused me to flee Los Angeles and take the quickest job offer. But I suppressed my rising anger and continued. "Unfortunately, all my contacts and expertise are strictly in corporate. I've been trying to network and have been taking on some smaller projects from the other offices. And I thought I could help in the corporate department, but Mark's pretty self-sufficient." I didn't want to say that Mark didn't trust me.

Brad read between the lines. "I could see Mark being protective of his turf. He's a good guy, but sometimes he can be a bit of a control freak. He was like that in law school. Probably why he was top of his class."

"How do you know that?"

"We went to law school together. We were and still are friends."

"How good of friends?" I didn't mention that during my interview, Mark had brought up Brad's name. Ever since that lunch, and despite Maya's reassurances, a small part of me had wondered if Mark's reticence around me was a result of the fact that he somehow knew about my relationship with Brad.

"Enough that I can talk you up to him. Better yet, I can talk you up to the client."

I couldn't believe the sick twist of fate that Brad might be my best chance to resuscitate my flailing career, to set things right at Gilchrist and prove my worth.

I gave him a small nod and sighed. "So what can I help you with regarding Gilchrist?"

"Just let me work with you," Brad said, his eyes looking deeply into mine.

I swallowed. "Did Kathryn ever know . . ."

"No," Brad said emphatically.

"Because coming to work with your . . ." I paused. I wanted to say ex-lover, ex-mistress, but I couldn't seem to form the words. So I sighed again and finally said, "*Me*, could look bad in your divorce."

He shook his head. "No, she didn't know. And anyway, it doesn't matter. She's not too clean in this." He clenched his jaw.

I wanted to talk about Gilchrist, but it was clear that we first really needed to talk more about his divorce.

"A lot of stuff could come out in a custody battle," I started. "I'm assuming you want full custody of Ivy."

"It will be sorted out. Kathryn will be flexible." Brad's eyes flashed, and his jaw tightened.

I narrowed my eyes. "Really? Because that's not usually how this type of thing goes down. Custody is biased toward the mother, you know." I couldn't help but think how deluded Brad was.

"Not to mothers who take sketchy antidepressants ordered online while pregnant and don't tell anyone. Or to mothers who carry on affairs with ex-cons in front of their children."

I felt my mouth fall open, but no words came out.

Brad nodded. "That's right. Kathryn was having an affair—is currently having an affair—with a *criminal.* I don't even care about her affair and that she wants to be with her 'soulmate.' My concern is Ivy. *So*, she's not going to fight too hard because it will be easy to prove that she's put Ivy in danger."

"I don't know what to say." I truly didn't. I couldn't say that I was sorry, since that would be hypocritical. Granted, our affair hadn't put Ivy in danger, but still . . . Pot. Kettle. Black.

I wanted to ask if the baby had been his, but I couldn't risk another emotional conversation like the one from the night before without breaking down. In that moment, I decided that I would never tell Brad about our baby.

Moving forward, we needed everything between us to be professional—and he was counting on me as much as I was counting on him. And judging from Brad's demeanor that morning over coffee, it appeared that we were on the same page. We had worked together before and we would again, and I couldn't fail any more than I already had at Gilchrist. For better or worse, we needed each other.

Shoving down all of my emotions—heartbreak, anger, grief—from the last several years, I took a deep breath and stood up, slinging my purse onto my shoulder.

"Well then, congratulations on your new job. Have a good flight, and I guess I'll see you in the office," I said as calmly as I could, and then turned and walked back to my office before he could say anything more. One more Brad bomb, and I would explode.

***

At dinner that night when Matt asked me how my day was, I

told him all about Brad. Well, maybe not quite "all." I told him that a lawyer I used to work with was coming to work with me and promised to bring me onto his high-profile project.

"It's crazy. Turns out he and Mark went to law school together, and they're good friends," I said, and then took a spoonful of the lentil soup that Matt had made for us.

"That is crazy," Matt commented. "So things are looking up?"

"We'll see."

After just two meetings with Brad, I was already lying by omission to Matt by not telling him the truth about my prior relationship with Brad. But it had to be buried and forgotten. There was nothing to be gained by Matt knowing about my past, as it would only make him nervous and angry, and ruin the peaceful balance we had found in our relationship. But I ate my soup very slowly, my stomach turning, sour with anxiety about my future work relationship with Brad at Gilchrist.

***

"Adeline told me I couldn't work on your presentation because she needs me to work on Project X. She said, and I quote, 'It's all-hands-on-deck time,'" Rachel said, standing in my office doorway. I knew the corporate department was busy, but I didn't know their deal was closing so soon. Did that mean Brad would be joining the office soon too?

"That's fine. The presentation research can wait. Project X is a higher priority right now."

I knew very little about the deal and was embarrassed. I didn't want to tip my hand to Rachel, and, frankly, I needed some breathing room away from her. She unnerved me at a time when my nerves couldn't handle much more. I was more than happy to release her to Adeline.

"But I'm right in the middle of my research," Rachel huffed.

"It's fine," I repeated. "I promise to keep you on this presentation and future ones. Client development is an important skill, but our current clients are our first priority."

Rachel sighed, looking defeated. Her allegiance to me was strange, and while I appreciated the work she had done for me, I secretly hoped she would find a new mentor in Adeline. As soon as she left my office, I let out a long breath I didn't realize I'd been holding.

Since Rachel had claimed to Adeline that she was doing work for me, I wanted to make sure that Adeline knew that Rachel was all hers. Like children with their parents, associates sometimes liked to play one partner against another. Ever since the awkwardness of the missed lunch invite, Adeline and I, being in different departments, had mostly circled around each other. I decided to change that by walking over to her office. At least now I had a reason to approach her, since I still needed to make amends for not having properly welcomed her to the firm.

When I reached her office, I knocked on her door and said jokingly, "I see you're stealing my associate."

Adeline looked up from her desk, and her eyes shot daggers at me. "It's just this week. Things are heating up, and I need more of her time."

I was taken aback by her response. Maybe things on the deal weren't going well? Or maybe she was having problems with Rachel? Anyway, she was new, and I could relate.

"Oh," I said. "No worries. I understand. I was just teasing." I took a step inside her office. "I can do the research myself or find another associate." I paused. "So this deal is closing, huh?"

"Yup. End of this week."

She looked at me as if to say, how dare I step into her office, so I quickly retreated. "Good luck," I said, and left.

That didn't go well at all. It was my own fault for not talking to her earlier. I would have to wait until the ink dried on the acquisition deal before trying to befriend Adeline. I had asked Mark several times if they needed help on it, but to no avail. The only tasks I could do were to continue working on client development and helping out on whatever piecemeal projects the other offices could give me. I couldn't believe I felt this way, but a small part of me was actually looking forward to having Brad join our office, if only to help me restart my sagging career.

CHAPTER TWENTY-SIX

I hadn't heard from Brad since our conversation at Peet's. I wasn't sure if he was going to show up at Gilchrist any minute or if the whole thing had fallen through. But the "Will he or won't he?" question was answered a few weeks later on a Monday morning when Mark popped into my office with Brad.

"Here she is. I know you two know each other from Levenfield, but I thought we'd stop by to say hi. I'm giving Brad the official first-day tour of the office," Mark said cheerfully. "As you know, he'll be working on the Moonstruck-Imogen facilities."

I didn't know, but I could read between the lines—*Brad is working with us; you are not.* I didn't know yet what Brad had said to Mark. Had he put in a good word for me as he had promised to?

While a flight of surprised butterflies swirled inside of me, I stood up and leaned over my desk to shake Brad's hand. "Of course. Welcome, Brad. It's great to see you again." As our palms made contact, a frisson of electricity shot up my arm. His hazel eyes locked onto mine, and from Brad's half-worried look, I knew he felt it too.

"Thanks, Jae. Same here," he said, pulling his hand away slowly.

We stood there staring at each other for what felt like a second too long. I sensed Mark looking between us, sizing something up, before he said smoothly, "We should probably keep moving so we can get Brad settled into his office. We just stopped by to say hello."

"Of course. Enjoy the rest of the tour, and I'll catch up with you later," I said to Brad.

As they left my office, I felt somewhat irritated that Brad hadn't alerted me to his start date; but by then I had long gotten used to Brad's vagueness and omissions, and it wasn't as if I had asked him either. I figured at least I had my answer. I would seek him out later or let him come find me to discuss work projects. After all, as he promised me long ago, *he would always come back to me,* I thought to myself sarcastically.

That afternoon as I was leaving the building to run some errands during a late lunch, I spotted Brad, Mark, and Adeline walking down the street, clearly returning from lunch. My heart sank when I realized that I had not been invited—it told me everything I needed to know. I didn't bother trying to meet with Brad the rest of the day. I was persona non grata.

***

"That's it." I dropped my laptop bag onto the floor with a thud as soon as I walked through my front door. "I have to leave Gilchrist. This isn't working. It's not going to work. I'll collect my paycheck for as long as I can, but I know I'm going to get fired eventually."

Matt had beaten me to my place.

"What do you mean?" he asked as he walked over to me and gave me a hug.

I told him how no one had alerted me that the new real estate partner was starting that day and that I wasn't invited to take him out to lunch.

"That sucks. Didn't you say that he used to work at your old firm?"

"Yes."

"And you got along?"

"Sure." I shrugged.

"Before you start sending out your résumé, why don't you invite him to lunch tomorrow. Find out what the story is with this . . . What's his name again?"

"Brad." I swallowed, his name feeling stuck in my throat.

"If you get a bad vibe from him, then, yeah, it might be time to start thinking of the next step." Matt released me from his arms and gave me a serious look. "Speaking of which, what's the dinner plan tonight?"

We ended up walking to a nearby sushi restaurant that had decent vegetarian rolls and a good wine list—something I was in need of. Matt took the edge off my bad mood by telling me about some funny stories from his day. Then in bed that night, I tried to focus my attention on Matt by having phenomenal sex with him. My relationship with him was real, something I had never had in all my years with Brad.

That night as Matt softly snored next to me, I decided that I needed to make a move up. Brad was my past. And I concluded that Gilchrist was also going to soon be in my past. I would start looking for a new job. Go back to corporate law, perhaps something in-house. With this resolution made, I fell into a contented sleep.

***

The next morning, I ran into Brad in the kitchen. He was standing by the coffee machine and seemed to be contemplating how it worked.

"Good morning," I said as I walked in, ignoring the hammering of my heart.

He seemed to jump a little. "Oh, hey, Jae. Good morning."

"How are you?"

"Perplexed. Not sure how this coffee machine works."

"I haven't used it myself, but I've seen others. Let me try." I walked over to the machine, which allowed one to brew a cup to exact specifications. "Large? Dark roast?" I asked.

"Sure." While I set up his coffee to brew, I had to focus to keep my hands from shaking, acting as if Brad were simply a new colleague. "There. It should start brewing soon."

"Thanks, Jae." Brad stood in front of the machine again while I grabbed a mug from the cabinet and poured hot water into it.

"It's great to have another real estate partner around here," I said. "What do you think so far?" At least this awkward encounter allowed me to bring up the matter of our working together.

Brad turned away from the machine to look at me. "It's only been twenty-four hours, but you know, I think it's a great place to build a practice."

"Oh." I touched his arm. "Looks like your coffee is ready."

Brad looked down at my hand and then at me. "So it is. Thank you."

I removed my hand quickly as if on fire. I hadn't meant to touch him. I had done so out of pure instinct, and I cursed myself. Though I pulled my hand away, once I did, I was dismayed to realize that I wanted it to linger.

I heard someone clear their throat, and I glanced toward the doorway and saw Adeline entering the kitchen. She clearly saw me touch him. I looked back at her, then down at my mug to compose myself.

"Oh, hi, Addie," Brad said. "Ready for the meeting?"

Addie?

"I will be once I have some coffee in me," Adeline answered, slowly walking up to the machine and looking askance at us.

"Here," Brad said. "Take mine. I just brewed it. Extra dark, if that's okay? I can make another cup."

"Oh, that's not necessary. I can wait."

"Are you sure?" Brad held out his cup to her.

"Um, okay. Thanks, extra dark is fine." She took the cup, and after taking a sip, then said to me, "Oh, I'm sorry, Jasmine. Are you also waiting for the coffee machine?" She didn't sound sorry as she stood there, assessing me with her gaze.

"No, I only drink green tea. I was just getting some hot water and chatting with Brad." To avoid her scrutiny, I turned my attention back to Brad. "So what will you be working on?"

"I'll be working with Addie and Mark on some real estate deals for Moonstruck."

Project X, which Mark and Adeline worked on, had been the code name for Moonstruck Animation acquiring a small studio named Imogen. But real estate deals? Why was Adeline, a corporate associate, working on that? And Mark knew about these real estate matters and hadn't told me?

I looked at Adeline and said, "But you're not a real estate attorney. That's so strange that they would have you working on that."

She jutted her chin at me. "Not really. They're my client, and I worked on the Moonstruck and Imogen deal. The whole reason I moved here was because their chief counsel requested that I work more closely with them." Her tone was defensive, and I worried I had struck a nerve. "What about you? What are you working on these days?" My guess was she already knew the answer: absolutely nothing.

"I've got some balls in the air right now," I said. I had clearly made an enemy of Adeline. Or was it Addie? And it was time to leave. I said to Brad, "We should talk. Maybe we can get together for lunch?"

"That sounds great. Today might not work. Depends on our meeting. But sure, let's talk later."

"Okay. It's nice seeing you again. Welcome to the firm."

I could feel hostile vibes coming from Adeline's direction, and I avoided looking at her as I left. Sure, maybe I hadn't been overtly welcoming when she started, and maybe Mark's prejudice toward me had worn off on her. It was far too late to try to redeem myself in her eyes. Like many associates on the cusp of partnership, she was going to jealously guard her billables. Fair enough. But, *Addie*? I hadn't heard anyone call her that before, and even though I introduced myself as Jae, everyone still called me Jasmine. It seemed the result of the prior day's lunch bonding. For some inexplicable reason, the nasal way Brad pronounced her name grated on me. Although Matt's advice about "sussing out the new guy" was sound, I knew I was working with a stacked deck. The sooner I could remove myself from Gilchrist, the better, but what firm would take me with no clients? I headed back to my office, planning to spend the rest of the day working on potential client research and stewing.

Later that morning, after his meeting with Mark and *Addie*, Brad swung by my office.

"Hi, Jae." He stood in my doorway almost tentatively.

"Hey." I waved him in as if holding up the white flag.

"I was hoping we could go to lunch today, but Mark invited me out after the meeting. Any chance you're free to have a drink tonight?"

I wasn't planning on seeing Matt that night, but I knew all too well the dangers of having drinks with Brad. If I was going to try to behave professionally with him every single day, I needed to avoid having a personal relationship with him—and that meant avoiding drinks.

Brad must have sensed my hesitation. He walked closer to my desk and lowered his voice. "It's to discuss work."

"I assumed," I said coolly, tapping my pen against my legal pad. And though I was nervous about going, I did want to discuss work. "What time?"

Brad's face looked relieved. "Is five thirty too early?"

"Five thirty it is. Just swing by when you're ready."

This was different—openly leaving together. I wanted Mark and Adeline to see us, since they had so pointedly left me out of lunch.

But as soon as I spoke, Brad shifted on his feet. "It's a plan," he said, but with a nervous look on his face, taking a few steps backward before he turned and walked out of my office. I tried to push his strange behavior out of my mind.

When 5:15 p.m. rolled around, my office phone rang. "Hey, Jae. I stepped out early to run an errand. Let's meet at the bar. The same one as last time."

I couldn't help but feel that he left earlier on purpose, presumably not to be seen leaving with me. Whether for personal or professional reasons, or maybe old habits die hard; I wasn't sure. But I still wanted to learn whatever I could about his future, and my current, situation at Gilchrist.

Once again suppressing any negative thoughts, I said, "See you soon."

***

When I arrived, it was happy hour and the bar area was crowded. I found Brad sitting at a table in the corner.

"Hope this is okay. It was really loud up there in the front, and I wanted to talk about work." Brad stood up as he said this, almost going in for a hug, then seemed to think better of it and sat back down.

"This is fine." My nerves were a little frayed with this new dynamic, and I tried to hide my emotions as I set my purse on the sofa cushion, took off my coat, and sat next to him. "Have you ordered yet?"

Brad shook his head no and handed me a menu. I didn't bother perusing it; instead, I asked the server for something "cool and crisp," and she came back with a glass of sauvignon blanc.

After we'd both taken a sip of our drinks, Brad said, "Have you spent much time in wine country since moving?"

"Funny you should ask. Matt and I"—I wanted to remind him that there was a Matt and I—"were just up there for the weekend." I smiled pointedly. "Sometimes we'll drive up for the day, have lunch, and visit a winery or two . . . or three."

"Nice. I'm looking forward to exploring it myself," he said in a casual tone, taking a sip of his beer, and not pursuing the topic of Matt.

After seeing Brad last time, and noticing that the gravitational pull I felt toward him was glaringly absent with Matt, I had suggested to Matt that we visit Napa that Saturday, as if I needed to solidify our relationship. As Matt and I sipped our wine while admiring the rolling hills and the changing colors of the vines in the valley, I thought about how, after the excruciating drama and pain of wanting someone who didn't belong to me, it was a relief to be with someone so down-to-earth. *Matt is reliable,* I told myself. *He makes me feel safe. Maybe the edge I feel with Brad is missing, but around Matt, I can relax.*

Matt and I did mundane couples' activities, such as ordering pizza and spending marathon nights watching television. I acquired some long-overdue domestic skills and started cooking for him—something I'd never had a reason to do before. He was kind to me and made thoughtful little gestures, like running an errand that I had forgotten or buying me a new tea he had heard about. And although we both had full bookshelves, I found that I read less in favor of watching movies with him.

Life had become slower. I was slower. Softer. Less ambitious. And maybe a little bit bored. I didn't miss the stressed-out, constantly brokenhearted person I had been in Los Angeles, yet I couldn't help but wonder sometimes whether this new Jae was the person I was meant to be.

"I take it you're already living here?" I asked, trying to shake off the Matt and Brad comparisons in my thoughts. "Or are you commuting?"

"I moved in over the weekend. It happened pretty fast."

"Yes, obviously." I was still a little annoyed that he failed to mention how imminent his relocation to San Francisco was going to be when we first talked about Gilchrist. But this wasn't the time to mention it.

"Not like I had much to move. Just some clothes and personal items. I ordered all new furniture online and am still waiting for most of it."

He told me some more about settling in and described his new apartment in Pacific Heights (luckily on the other side of the city from mine). But growing impatient with what felt like small talk and trying to ignore the way my skin grew hot sitting so near him, I redirected the conversation to work.

"So, what do you think of Gilchrist?" I asked.

"Very different from Levenfield. It's weird, but it's sort of a nice break. It's like being in-house counsel without having to deal with outside counsel. And since it's such a small office, there's none of the petty politics and gossip like at Levenfield."

I may have actually snorted. "How would you think so?"

Brad eyed me critically. "So what's the story with you? Why are you in real estate now? Why didn't you stay in corporate?"

"Do you want the real reason or my professional spin?"

Brad did a small double take before saying, "The real one, of course."

But I couldn't give Brad the truth, as that would be delving into the personal, which I was still trying to avoid. So I kept my answer semi-professional, evading my running away from him at the time. "I thought it'd be good to work with a friend. I was wrong. There was some tension between us that unfortunately carried over to work. And it seemed best that we didn't continue working together."

"What sort of tension?"

How could I say that it started with my pregnancy? I couldn't. Or that Maya became jealous when Stan gave me the client project she wanted, and that I screwed up anyway due to a bout of morning sickness. Or that Maya had secretly coveted my boyfriend. And that really, all my trouble with Maya started because I had kept Brad a secret from her.

"We were friends in law school, but we grew apart into different people," I said, giving a little shrug and taking a sip of my drink.

Brad's eyes narrowed slightly at my pat answer, but he wasn't going to press. "And how do you like it there now that she's gone?"

"Honestly, still not so much. It's no secret in our office that I don't have any work. And Mark doesn't seem to like me, although I haven't done any work for him so that he can even assess my qualifications."

"Yeah, I know. He was asking about you during lunch today," Brad said, his eyes briefly flitting away from me as he seemed to scan the bar, a pause long enough for my stomach to drop. He looked back at me, his eyes intense. "He wanted to know if we worked together before. I told him yes, and that you were one of the best attorneys at Levenfield, and how people were shocked when you left."

I blinked a couple times. I knew he had promised to put in a good word for me, but it was different to hear his praise in such direct terms. Also, I wondered what Mark's reaction was, but I wasn't going to ask. Everything still felt too tenuous.

Brad continued. "I suggested you help us with working on the new Moonstruck facilities. Now that they've acquired Imogen, they want to build a new campus. I mean, you're the only other real estate partner there. Mark and Adeline may have worked on this deal, but you know both corporate and real estate. And you didn't do anything to make Mark distrust you. It's just the type of guy he is. He couldn't stand Maya. Apparently, she had a reputation for looking out for number one at the expense of her colleagues."

Brad raised his eyebrows and, without meaning to, I felt myself nod. Maybe even without the complications of my secret pregnancy and relationship with Matt, everything would still have turned out the same between Maya and me.

"And because she was the one who recruited you," he continued, "you unfortunately got associated with her. Also, since you were originally corporate and then suddenly moved into real estate, he's not sure what to make of you."

"Fair enough. But he could at least try to work with me and then make up his mind."

"Yeah, agreed. I think it's unfair that he didn't include you on the Moonstruck-Imogen deal. Once he gets to know you and sees your work, he'll come around. Despite his suspicious outlook, he's a pretty decent guy."

Brad gazed at me, and I looked down at my drink.

"What lawyer isn't paranoid?" I answered, tapping my finger on my wine glass and hoping Brad's prediction was correct. "That said, I'm happy to help out in any way I can—I'd love a chance to prove myself."

"I don't want you to leave," he said, his voice low. "You're all I have here."

I felt the tips of my ears burn red. *Does he mean in the real estate department? At Gilchrist? In San Francisco? Or in his life?* I assumed the smallest and safest option.

"Great, but perhaps don't give me *too* much work. I've gotten used to this life of leisure now." I took a sip of my wine and then smiled so he could see I was joking.

"You don't say? And what have you been doing with this newfound leisure time?" Brad leaned back and stretched his legs alongside the table, settling in to hear a good story.

I told Brad about my new cooking skills, which he teased me about along with my vegetarianism. I also told him how I was trying to learn more about wine, to which he responded, "Then let's get another round. All in the name of research."

He also asked what I had been reading, and I admitted, "Not much."

"That's too bad. You were always reading something interesting."

That night when I went home, I selected something from my dusty book pile to take to bed.

When Matt came over the next night, while we ate dinner on my sofa, I told him about my drinks with Brad. If Matt thought it odd that we had had drinks rather than lunch, as he had suggested, he didn't give any indication.

"That's wonderful, baby," he said. "Does it make you feel differently about staying?"

"For now, yes. I want to see how things play out."

He stood up to put his plate in the sink and held out his hand to take mine. "So what do you want to do tonight? Should we see what's on Netflix?"

I thought about the book I'd started the night before, but said, "Sure, whatever you want."

***

Later that week, Brad and I went to lunch, and this time we kept our conversation strictly professional. Brad looked tense and said, "I'm reviewing all the final documents from the Moonstruck-Imogen deal, and I was wondering if I could ask your advice."

"Of course."

When we returned to work, I followed him straight into his office.

"This is supposed to be the final acquisition contract, but it's missing some real estate provisions," Brad said, his forehead creased with worry. "Do you know anything about it? This can't be the final one, right?"

I took it from him and looked at it. Brad was right—the real estate clauses were missing. "Maybe the paralegal gave you the wrong document? Let's compare it to what was filed."

We looked it up on the server, and then compared it to the SEC filings. It was the same document.

"I don't know, Brad. Mark was in charge of this deal. I would ask him."

"Fantastic," Brad said. "Just what I need when I only just got here."

"I'm sorry. I admit I don't envy you." I grimaced. "Good luck."

He ran his hand through his hair. "Thanks. I'll need it."

***

Sunday night I received an email from Mark to have me join their Monday morning team meeting for Moonstruck. I was tempted to email Brad to see if this was his doing, but it obviously was. That Monday, I was the first to arrive in the conference room and then the rest of the team trickled in—Emma, Rachel, and then Brad. Brad said, "Good morning," to me, but didn't say anything else as the two associates, Emma and Rachel, were also sitting there. Adeline soon followed, and I saw her pupils dilate briefly when she saw me.

"Good morning, Adeline," I said, hoping I sounded friendly.

"Good morning," she said, and then quickly turned her attention to Emma.

The three associates seemed confused by my presence in the room, as no one engaged me in small talk, not even Brad, which probably added to the awkward atmosphere. When Mark arrived, he immediately launched into the meeting by assigning tasks to the associates. He never addressed me except to say that he was expanding the team, which gave the impression that he had done so begrudgingly.

Nothing was specifically mentioned about the error in the Moonstruck-Imogen contract, but I assumed I was there because they had screwed up. So, during the meeting when Mark asked Adeline to put together some letters to the zoning board, I spoke up, cautioning Adeline to be very thorough. "We can't afford to leave anything out," I said.

"I trust Adeline will be thorough," Mark said brusquely, responding on Adeline's behalf, and then continued quickly going through his list. Maybe he was simply expressing confidence in her, but still, my skin prickled during this exchange.

After the meeting, as we were leaving, I tried to approach Adeline. "If you need any help, Adeline, please let me know," I said.

She said a curt, "Thank you," and then rushed out the door to follow Mark down the hall. Just as Rachel's unexplained attachment to me sometimes unnerved me, Adeline's constant fleeing had the same effect. While I was heading back to my office, Brad caught up to me and said in a low voice, "Can we talk in my office?"

"Sure," I said, and walked the few extra steps to his door.

He closed the door behind us, and when we sat down, he said, "I talked to Mark about the acquisition contract. I could tell from his face that an error was made, something we had to talk about to the client. So I insisted that, going forward on this real estate project, you work on a large part of it. I know Mark and Adeline know the corporate side and have a relationship with the client, but I need someone I trust to help me with the real estate side. So, as you learned from the meeting, you're officially working on Moonstruck. I'd like you to be on the next conference call I have with their general counsel, Scott, so we can formally introduce you."

"Of course. God, that's awful about the contract." But after all my attempts to ask Mark if corporate needed assistance, I couldn't help but feel the tiniest bit of schadenfreude. "I'm surprised something like that happened. Seems like someone accidentally just hit a delete key at the last minute."

"Yeah, Mark was in shock. It was an amicable deal, so he doesn't think it will change anything. But it still needed to be pointed out to Scott, and it could shake client confidence." He swallowed. "And that's something that doesn't bode well for me either."

"Whatever I can do to help, just let me know."

"Let's start with moving this new project forward. Do you have time?"

"I'm all yours." The old Jae never would have uttered those words in the office, but this new Jae, colleague of Brad Summers and nothing more, had effectively compartmentalized LA Jae and San Francisco Jae. The Brad Summers affair was tucked into a box with the lid closed on the highest shelf possible. Not completely forgotten, but definitely out of sight.

CHAPTER TWENTY-SEVEN

It felt good to be busy again. That week was Thanksgiving, but rather than going home to Los Angeles, I stayed in San Francisco to work and learn everything I could about Moonstruck and the new campus project. Matt offered to stay in town for Thanksgiving so we could celebrate together, but I knew his sister and family really wanted him to join them in Oregon. And since I planned to work over the weekend, I didn't want to ruin his long weekend as well. When he kept asking me if I was "sure," I joked back at him, "Besides, as a vegetarian, I don't get that excited about a holiday centered on eating turkey."

Thursday I worked from home, but Friday I went into the office. It was easier to access files from the server at the office than it was from home, and I knew it would be quiet. I arrived around nine o'clock and was the only person there. Later in the morning, a few others trickled in. As they walked by my office in their casual garb, we waved and said, "Hello." But it was clear they were just doing a drive-by to check in on something before heading to their holiday-weekend plans. By noon I was alone again, and it wasn't until late afternoon that I heard the elevator doors open.

"Hey," Brad said as he passed my office. "What are you doing here?"

My head jerked up at his voice and his presence in my doorway.

"Hey, yourself," I said as I put my hands under my desk and pressed them on the top of my thighs to steady myself in my nervous surprise. "Getting up to speed on Moonstruck. What about you? I thought Ivy was up here for Thanksgiving."

"She is. She's with my parents. They're taking her to the Academy of Sciences so I can take care of some things here."

"Oh." I nodded. "Hopefully it won't take too long. Good luck."

Brad paused for moment, then said, "Guess I should get to it."

I turned my focus back to the SEC filings I had been reading, but my concentration was broken. All of my recent encounters with Brad had been in public places, and during the last week, the routine of office life and others present had allowed me to push him into the professional compartment in my mind. But now that we were in the office, just the two of us, alone, breathing the same air, I found the lid on that box starting to rattle. I thought about running out to Starbucks but was scared to leave the confines of my office.

Fifteen minutes later, I received an email from Brad.

> What are you reading?

It might as well have said, What are you wearing? because my reaction was an accelerated heart rate and a sudden surge of longing. My fingers hovered over the keys for a second before I typed, I'm reading the SEC filings from the

Moonstruck-Imogen deal. Almost finished, so I'll probably head home soon.

Brad wrote back: So soon? Is it anything I said?

That was it. I had to get out of there. Whatever else I wanted to read, I was going to read it at home. I opened the couple remaining documents from the server and hit print. Since they were contracts, I sent them to the fast printer in the copy room, and I could hear the whir of the machine zipping them out. When it stopped, I got up to collect them. As I was lifting them from the tray, Brad walked by, holding a cup of coffee. He must have just been coming out from the kitchen.

"Hey," I said, hurriedly piling the stacks in my arm. "So I'm going to take off. Enjoy the rest of your weekend."

"Oh, okay. You too." Brad lingered in the doorway. I didn't trust myself to pass him, so I just stood there awkwardly as I waited for him to move. Instead, he moved into the copy room. "Are you okay?" he asked, his eyes fixed on me, his voice low and soft.

I nodded and found I was holding my breath. One, two, three . . . another step closer to me, I felt I was going to combust. Brad set down his cup. He must have read my expression because what at first had appeared to be a look of concern now matched my intensity. The two of us being like magnets, Brad was suddenly in front of me, both hands behind my head, tangled in my hair, and his mouth firmly on mine. In my shock, I let go of the papers. My lips, remembering his touch, kissed him back, and soon my hands were running down his back.

"Jae," he whispered. He put his hands on my waist and in one move lifted me onto the counter. "God, I've missed you."

"I've missed you too," I said in a small voice that I couldn't believe was mine.

His lips were back on mine, and his hands started to move

up my skirt. When his hands reached my hips, I pushed him away.

"We can't," I said. "I have a boyfriend."

Brad looked momentarily stunned, but then leaned back in and started kissing my neck. "This is different, you and I," he said softly in between his kisses.

"No," I said more forcefully, in that moment overwhelmed by every emotion from the past seven years. "We can't." Out of nowhere I started crying. "We can't because last time you got me pregnant, and then you ignored me."

Brad pulled back. "Pregnant? What are you talking about?"

My tears became choking sobs as I said, "Before I moved. I was pregnant. I tried to tell you, but you wouldn't talk to me."

"I don't understand. Where's the baby?" He stood there frozen, his eyes wide and his expression full of confusion.

"I miscarried. I miscarried when you said you were moving here."

Before he could respond, I jumped off the counter and ran back to my office. I grabbed my laptop and purse before he could follow me, and I headed to the elevator bank. While I was standing there willing the elevator to come faster, Brad walked up to me holding the contracts I'd dropped in the copy room.

"You forgot these," he said, holding them out to me.

I could see him in my peripheral vision and grabbed the papers, not making eye contact. The elevator doors opened, and I stepped in.

"Is it true?" I heard Brad ask, his voice still in shock.

"Yes," I said, looking up.

Our eyes locked and the doors closed.

***

When I got home, I was relieved Matt wouldn't be back until Sunday night. It was only four o'clock, but I opened a bottle of wine and took it to bed. I also shut off the ringer on my phone. I knew Matt would be worried, but I would apologize in the morning. For the moment, I needed to feel the entire weight of my actions sink in before I trusted myself to talk to anyone.

That night I grieved. I grieved the young woman I had once been who held so much promise. I cursed the choices she'd made that caused her to ruin her best years, that cut her off from friends, that stopped her from finding a suitable life partner. I apologized to her and thought back on the points at which I could have said no and been on a completely different path. I grieved for my baby. The baby who maybe knew what a complicated life she would be getting into and decided she would rather die than be part of my twisted story. I grieved my relationship with Matt. He was a good man, and I had gone and kissed a bad man because I couldn't help myself. I hadn't decided yet whether to tell him. But now things had changed, and there would always be a secret between us. I was no better than Brad.

The wine allowed me to pass out, and I woke up around three o'clock in the morning. I had fallen asleep while it was still light out and woke up in the dark, alone. It seemed fitting. From my high-rise window, the entire city appeared to be asleep. I had no answers when I woke up other than I knew I could no longer stay at Gilchrist. I couldn't work with Brad. I thought of just resigning without another job—saying I was taking time to deal with some family issues or to travel. Having no one to spend money on other than myself, I had enough saved to not work for a year or more. Travel seemed like the best option because I could immediately leave San Francisco. Then maybe I'd move back to LA. Or better yet, maybe back to Boston. Or I could run away to Paris? But all those options sounded exhausting. And what did it matter? I couldn't escape my mistakes or myself. So I went back to sleep.

When I got up in the morning, I decided that I wasn't going into the office as I had planned. My future—at Gilchrist and in general—was limited. So instead, I stayed in my apartment, reading and watching television, mindlessly channel surfing. Because I didn't want to be crueler to Matt than I had already been, it was time to check my messages and emails. There was a missed call and text from Matt.

> Sorry I missed you. Hope you didn't work too hard today. Love you. Talk to you tomorrow.

And after that message from Matt, there were ten from Brad in varying degrees of urgency: Jae, I'm sorry. Can we talk?

I responded to Matt and ignored Brad. I had proved myself to be an unworthy girlfriend, and I felt the guilt in my fingertips as I texted Matt back.

Around nine o'clock that night, when I was half sleeping and half watching a movie, there was a knock at the door.

That was strange; the doorman usually called up to let me know I had a visitor. I hesitated but then thought it could be a neighbor with an emergency. Suddenly alert, I stood up and answered it.

"Jae!" Brad said, relief evident on his face. I wanted to slam the door.

"What are you doing here? How did you get in? How do you know where I live?"

"I was worried about you. I followed someone in. Your contact info from work. Can I come in?"

"No, you can't come in," I huffed. "I don't want to talk to you."

"I don't care." Brad came in, brushing past me. "We have to talk."

The back of my neck prickled. "What if Matt's here?"

"He's not. You told me he's visiting family."

Brad walked straight into my living room, shook off his jacket, and draped it on a chair. "I should've followed you yesterday. You were so upset, and I should've tried to talk to you. I was in shock. I'm sorry. I've been an idiot and a jerk, and we need to hash all this out before Monday morning."

I stood there, still holding the front door open.

"Jae, there are things to say." He sat down on the armchair. "So let's do this. No more secrets. No more doing the wrong thing, or trying to do the right thing and not communicating."

I closed the door reluctantly. There were things to talk about. Though he didn't deserve to know, this time, I wanted to tell him my plans.

I sat down on the sofa across from him. "Don't worry. I've made my decision, and it won't affect your life. You won't see me anymore."

Brad narrowed his eyes. "What do you mean?"

"I'm going to give my two weeks' notice. I'm going to take some time off and travel. I haven't been on a vacation in a long time." While I hadn't yet decided on a particular course of action, as soon as the words left my mouth, I knew that was what I wanted to do.

"You can't quit because you don't want to work with me. I'll quit, okay?"

"You can't quit. It's your client. It will ruin your career. Plus, you have dependents. I don't." *I have nothing,* I almost added.

"None of that matters right now," he said, anguish in his voice. "My job is not important to me. *You're* important to me.

And I don't want . . ." He paused and leaned forward, looking deeply into my eyes. "I'm not going to let you run away again."

"Oh?" I laughed bitterly. "*I'm* important to you? When did that happen?"

"You've always been important to me. But I was an idiot, and I'm going to stop being an idiot right now."

"I'm not sure how you're going to manage that. Have you ever heard the expression 'too little, too late'?"

"Yup. I deserve that. And it's good to see you still have a sense of humor." He changed his tone and said gently, "I was worried about you last night. When you said you miscarried—"

"Don't, Brad. Please. I can't handle this right now." I could feel the tears starting to brim my eyes. My grief was still too raw, and I was too emotionally fragile to handle the conversation that Brad wanted to have, even if it had been a long time coming.

Brad got up from the chair and sat next to me on the sofa, putting his hand on my back and rubbing it in circles. I shook him off.

"Okay." He dropped his hand. "But I want to say that I'm sorry. I can never express how sorry I am. I let my pride and hurt get in the way of letting you tell me about the pregnancy, and I hate myself for it. I hate that you were alone, and it was my fault. You're never going to be alone again."

"What do you mean I'll never be alone again?" I bristled. "I'm not alone. I've been with Matt. And he was there for me when I miscarried."

"You're not in love with Matt."

I narrowed my eyes at him.

"You're in love with me," Brad said quietly, his eyes on mine.

"You're more deluded than I thought," I said, feeling the heat rise in my cheeks and my heart banging against my chest. "I don't know what we're accomplishing here. I'm quitting on Monday, and we're going our separate ways. This time for good."

"No. You can quit Gilchrist if that's what you really want for you. But this"—he pointed between us—"we're doing this for real." Brad reached into his pocket and pulled something out. "This," he said, holding up an antique-looking platinum band with diamonds in one hand, and reaching for my hand with his other, "was my grandmother's wedding ring. It's a promise ring . . ."

Before he could continue, I snatched my hand away and jumped up. "No! What is wrong with you? You're! Still! Married! And I have a *boyfriend*."

"I told you, I'm getting a divorce. This is happening. I was stupid and scared back then. Kathryn has manipulated this marriage from the beginning, but I'm older and smarter now, and she can't win this one. She's still seeing the ex-con. She's brought him into our house, and he's met Ivy. No court is going to give her custody. Plus, she's been having this affair for years." He shook his head gravely. "I apologize for everything I've put you through, Jae."

"I don't care anymore," I said, feeling beaten. "I forgive you. There. Now we should go our separate ways."

Brad stood up and touched my cheek, rubbing it with his thumb. "Like I said, I was worried about you last night. I can't imagine my life without you."

I wanted to say that I could imagine my life without him. But it wasn't true, and we both knew that.

Brad took my silence as his cue and kissed me, tenderly at first, and then with more urgency. This time I let him. I let him all the way to my bed, where he spent the night.

CHAPTER TWENTY-EIGHT

I had promised Brad that I would hold off on my resignation, but there was one action I needed to take immediately. When Matt returned from Thanksgiving, I did the honest but awful thing to do and broke up with him. As we sat on my sofa, I told him that I loved him and thanked him for being there when I needed someone. Then I told him everything—about my affair with Brad in Los Angeles, why I fled to San Francisco, and the kiss with Brad at the office over the weekend. I tried to be as straight with him as possible, and my chest constricted as I watched Matt's face fall with every word I said, and he only interrupted my story to repeat my own words back to me in disbelief.

"He was married?"

"He was the father?"

"You kissed him? At work?"

And when I was finished, Matt's anguish turned to anger. "Why didn't you tell me all this before? Why did you let me believe that this new guy at work, this *friend*," he practically spat, "was actually your *ex-lover*?"

I didn't defend myself because there was no excuse.

"You deserve better than me," I said.

The way his eyes flashed and his jaw clenched, Matt didn't have to say anything for me to know he agreed. When he walked out my apartment door, slamming it behind him, I knew he was completely closing me out of his life for good.

When I had said, "I love you" to Matt, it was true—I loved Matt, but I wasn't in love with him. I hated hurting him, and I vowed that I would never keep another secret for as long as I lived.

Suddenly, I wasn't with Brad, and I wasn't with Matt. Though I felt free, I also felt a bit numb. Even though I had slept with Brad and he said he was divorcing Kathryn, he was not divorced yet. For the sake of my sanity, I needed to keep him at an emotional arm's length, and I wasn't going to make him any promises.

***

At our Monday morning meeting for Moonstruck, I tried to make sure I was the last to arrive so I could avoid having to make small talk or even eye contact with Brad. Thankfully, Mark arrived soon after I did, and he started the meeting right away.

"First things first," he said, "I assume you've all seen the email regarding office security this morning." That morning, a firm-wide email went out reminding us to lock our computers and change our passwords often for security reasons.

We all nodded.

"Good," he said. "Please take this reminder seriously. It was sent out because we've had a security breach in our own office."

Finally, I had something that made me forget my drama with Brad over the weekend. "Oh no! That's terrible," I said. "What happened?"

"One of our computers was compromised, and an important document was altered."

"Recently? How did that happen?" I asked. *And why does no one else seem as shocked as me?*

Mark glanced over at Adeline, and then back to me, before he said, "The acquisitions contract for the Moonstruck-Imogen deal was edited from Adeline's computer, but not by her. She was out and had her computer locked for the night."

I looked at Adeline. "How did that happen?"

"I don't know," Adeline said, and glared back at me.

What is her problem? I thought. While I could understand that she was angry at being hacked, I didn't know why her eyes were shooting daggers at me.

Mark said, "We're investigating with the technical team to figure out what happened."

"That's good," I said, and since I seemed to be the only person responding, I guessed that Brad must've already known, and again I felt like I was the last to be briefed. So much for being part of the team.

After the meeting, I went to the kitchen to make myself a cup of green tea, both needing the caffeine and hiding out from Brad. But my quiet moment was interrupted by Adeline entering the kitchen.

I greeted her politely, "Hi, Adeline."

She gave me a curt nod.

Willing myself to be friendly, even though I knew she disliked me, I said, "That's awful about your computer."

"Yeah." She busied herself with making a cup of coffee.

I put a teabag into my hot water, and rather than stand there together in awkward silence, I asked, "How did something like that happen? Are you sure you locked your computer?"

"Yes, I'm sure," she replied, each syllable with a bite.

Shocked by her angry tone when I was just trying to sympathize, I looked down at my tea. "Well, sometimes when we're working late, we forget things."

"But I wasn't working late," she said defensively. "I wasn't even here."

I didn't respond. I knew my last statement sounded critical, but I was tired of dealing with the petty interpersonal politics at Gilchrist. Clearly, there was no making amends with her. In my head, I started drafting my resignation letter.

Suddenly, Adeline's voice turned ominous. "Be careful, Jasmine."

I stopped stirring my tea. "'*Be careful*'?" I repeated back.

Is she talking about the hacking or something else? I silently wondered.

"I know, okay. Let's just say, I know. Others know too. So I would be very careful if I were you."

My blood ran cold. *She knows. Of course she does. Of course, everyone knows about me and Brad.*

I still managed to say, "You know what?"

She gave me a petty shrug, swung on her heel, and took herself and her coffee out of the kitchen.

I made a beeline to Brad's office and entered without knocking, closing the door behind me. "Everyone knows," I said, marching up to his desk.

"Everyone knows what?" Brad looked confused.

"About us," I said coldly, trying to fight my panic.

"How can anyone know?" He shook his head, and so I related what happened in the kitchen. Brad seemed to whiten and told me he would take Adeline out to lunch.

That afternoon, I picked at a salad alone in my office and looked at job listings while waiting for Brad's report. When he returned, he said that he didn't think she knew anything about our relationship, but I still wasn't convinced.

***

Later that week, to make matters worse, Mark had a talk with Brad and me. During the investigation of the hacking incident, security cameras had caught us kissing in the copy room. Just when I had reached a possible turning point with Mark, I gave him an actual reason to distrust me. I was mortified. Brad was less so, perhaps because Mark was his friend, and they had a history that predated law firm life. Brad told me not to worry, as it wasn't the first time anyone had ever kissed at the office.

"But Mark knows you're married," I said.

"Yeah, but he also knows my situation and that we're getting a divorce. And even if he didn't, my relationship with Scott is stronger than Mark's. He's not going to get on my bad side."

The Brad I was meeting now was a different Brad from the one I knew in Los Angeles. The younger Brad was unsure and overwhelmed. This older Brad was determined and decisive. He took charge. He knew what he wanted. And what he wanted was me. He frequently asked me out to dinner, though I declined. He sent me flowers, which I gave to my doorman for his wife. He flew back and forth between San Francisco and Los Angeles for hearings and court dates and did whatever he could to hasten his divorce proceedings. Despite his assurances that Kathryn didn't have much standing, she still seemed to want to drag out the process, probably to see how much money she could come away with. And when he tried to bring up the ring again, I refused to talk to him. After all the heartache I'd been through with him, I wasn't going to accept any promises until Brad was finally divorced.

I took a weekend to visit my family in LA for Saffie's bridal shower. When my mother saw me, she said, "Oh, honey, you've lost weight." From the concern on her face, I could tell it wasn't a healthy-looking change. All weekend, Saffie tried to push cookies and various desserts at me, explaining, "As my maid of honor, you're not allowed to be skinnier than me at my wedding." It was her way of expressing that she, too, was worried about me. My father inquired about how things were at my new firm. I was semi-honest and told him, "Not great." Though I had never asked him for favors before, when he asked me if I'd like him to ask around about in-house jobs, I said, "Not yet, but maybe."

When I returned to Gilchrist, I checked in on Rachel, who was doing some research work for me, and I invited her out to lunch to see how everything was going. At the restaurant, I ordered a sandwich, and Rachel ordered the same. "Normally, I never eat carbs," she commented, and then proceeded to eat the entire sandwich and chips.

"You must've needed it," I said lightly, and smiled.

Rachel smiled back shyly and blushed. That hint of vulnerability was a first for her.

Back at the office after lunch, I entered the bathroom and heard a gagging sound from one of the stalls. It stopped me for a second, and I wasn't sure whether the person wanted privacy or companionship. But while I dawdled, Rachel came out of the stall looking bleary eyed. Over her retching, she must not have heard me come in.

"Rachel, are you okay?"

She nodded weakly and walked over to the sink, where she washed her hands and then stuck her head under the spout to rinse out her mouth.

"Are you sick?"

She shook her head. "No. You know how it is."

"No, I don't know how it is. If you're sick, you should go home."

"I'm not sick," she repeated.

Then I remembered my own early days. "Oh, I see. Can I get you anything? Saltines?"

She shot me a dirty look. "How will saltines help?"

I had overstepped the partner-associate boundary line, but by then I had also ceased to care. "You know? With the nausea."

"I'm not nauseated. I was just throwing up that sandwich."

"Oh no. Food poisoning?" I swallowed, worried, since I had the same sandwich.

"No." Rachel looked at me strangely. *"Carbs."*

Now we really were outside the boundary line.

"I'm not sure I understand," I said, even though I felt like I was reliving walking in on Maya and Denise's conversation in the kitchen.

"It's okay. I heard you before in the bathroom when you started here. Maya explained that you were a recovering bulimic. That's why you look so great." She looked at me with her bloodshot eyes and sighed. "It's exhausting, though, isn't it?"

I hesitated, not sure if I was going to cry or laugh at the absurdity of that moment.

"Rachel, I'm not bulimic," I said carefully. "I was pregnant." I met her eyes in the mirror, and saw her surprise and confusion. "Let me know if you need anything." I gave her a sympathetic look and left.

When I got back to my office, I closed the door and sat down at my desk. I stared out the window and shook my head. Maybe I should've stayed with Rachel and tried to assess whether this was a one-off incident or something more serious; but the expression on Rachel's face told me the kindest act was to give her a minute to herself.

I wasn't even mad anymore at Maya. Besides, now she had a good reason to be pissed at me, since I ultimately broke her friend's heart. And really, what was I still doing in San Francisco? I had no life, no real career, and no friends there. For a brief moment, things looked up while I was with Matt, but then I broke up with him for a man I didn't even have. It was a comedy. Albeit a tragic one. I shook my head again, turned to my computer, and clicked over to where I'd been bookmarking Parisian rentals—and sighed.

***

Saturday night there was a knock at my door. I opened it to find Brad standing there, holding a pizza box.

"I hope you haven't eaten yet," he said, smiling.

"No, and how did you get in?" I said coolly as I tried to ignore how good he looked in his dark crewneck sweater and jeans.

"I followed someone in. You should be worried. This doesn't seem to be a secure building."

"Clearly not." I stared at him and waited a beat. "I don't remember us having dinner plans."

"We do. I just didn't tell you about them. Whenever I try, you turn me down."

He was already at my door and the pizza smelled good, so I finally dropped my guard, stood aside, and let him in. I pulled out plates and silverware, and we had dinner. And then we had sex.

The next morning Brad said, "Let's get breakfast."

Not only was Brad waking up next to me, but he was also suggesting we go out. Since I had decided my life was a comedy (of errors), I thought, *Why the hell not?*

"Brunch it is," I said.

We walked to a nearby restaurant, with Brad still in his rumpled clothes from the night before and scruffy stubble. After we ordered, I reached out and stroked his whiskered cheek. He smiled and grabbed my hand and kissed it. We leaned across the table and kissed. When we pulled apart, I felt someone's eyes on me, and I instinctually looked in that direction. It was Maya looking surprised to see me and that I was kissing someone who wasn't Matt. To her credit she mouthed "Hi" and gave me a small wave. I mouthed "Hi" back and also gave her a small wave before refocusing on Brad. He looked over at Maya and asked me, "A friend?"

"Yep, a friend," I said, vaguely hoping that maybe one day that could be true again, though knowing deep down that Maya and I had both burned that bridge.

I didn't elaborate, and Brad must have guessed something shifted because he didn't question further. Our having breakfast and acting like a couple in public brought back memories of the last time we did so in San Francisco, uncomfortably reminding me of the disastrous trajectory of the last seven years.

After breakfast, which I ate quickly and silently after seeing Maya, Brad and I were standing outside the restaurant, and he asked, "Now what?"

"I'm going to go home."

"And then?"

"And then nothing, Brad. I'm going home and doing nothing."

"I'll walk you there."

I shrugged my assent and started walking, Brad beside me.

When we got back to my place, he asked to come up to grab his jacket from last night. In my apartment, he asked, "Are you sure you don't want to do anything today?"

"I'm sure," I said, willing him to leave, needing to be alone with my thoughts.

"Can I take you to dinner tonight?"

I looked at him, exasperated. "What are we doing?"

Evading my real question, which was about our relationship, Brad said cheerfully, "What we are 'doing' is I'm picking you up around five tonight. Be ready." He kissed my cheek and walked out the door.

But it didn't matter if we went to dinner. The look on Maya's face had hurt, reminding me I had no business being in San Francisco. I was resigning, and I would tell Brad that night. But having learned my lesson, this time I didn't plan on telling him where I was going.

When Brad arrived at my place later that day, he had a bouquet of roses and a bottle of champagne. "This is a little extravagant for a Sunday night," I commented.

"We have things to celebrate," he said, his eyes twinkling happily.

I didn't agree, but I drank a glass of champagne anyway, silently wondering about his strange mood. We put the remaining champagne in the refrigerator and the roses in a vase, and then Brad drove us to the Marina district where we circled the streets for a few minutes, looking for parking. It wasn't dark yet, but the light was fading. When he finally slipped the car into a spot, he took my hand to lead me to the restaurant. I hadn't even bothered to ask which one. On the way, we found ourselves walking through the Palace of Fine Arts.

"I didn't know there was a restaurant around here," I said.

"There's not," he said.

He didn't explain and I didn't ask, and he led us to the spot where he had taken a photo of me years ago. We paused and admired the lagoon and the pink-and-silver sky. I wondered if he remembered us standing there before. "Beautiful, isn't it?" he said, breaking the silence.

"Mm-hmm." The beauty and the memories there filled me with emotion, and I didn't trust myself to speak.

"I remember being here with you seven years ago. It seems like another life." He turned to me and took my hands so

I would turn to face him. "I'm so happy to be here with you again," he said, giving my hands a gentle squeeze. "Kathryn and I both signed the final divorce papers and filed them with the court. That's it. It's final. And though it might seem too soon . . ." Brad quickly reached into his pocket and pulled out the ring he had tried to give me before. "This isn't a promise ring now. This is an engagement ring." He slid down onto one knee. "You are the only woman I have ever loved, but I made your life hell for seven years. Please let me make it up to you for the next seventy. Jasmine Phillips, will you marry me?"

My heart and mind raced.

The ink was barely dry on his divorce. Did he really think I would say yes? Besides, I was leaving San Francisco. And what took him seven years to do this? He was deluded, selfish, and a cheater. He was also the only man I had ever felt truly myself with, who made me feel alive, and had my whole heart. And, damn it, I was still in love with him.

I looked away from him, and up toward the soft glowing sky and then across the dark lagoon. I swore I saw myself standing there on the other side in my peasant blouse and jeans from years ago and a younger Brad in his jeans and leather flip-flops. They nodded at me, and I found myself nodding.

"Yes?" Brad asked tentatively.

I looked at this Brad, a little older, a little wiser, and on one knee, and continued nodding.

Taking my nod as a yes, Brad jumped up, put his hands through my hair, and kissed me. When we pulled apart, I looked back to where I thought I saw our younger selves, but the image or hallucination had vanished. It seemed fitting.

The younger version of me thought that love was simply a matter of Brad's choosing me, but he was struggling with life's complications. The two of us here years later had changed into different people, hardened by our questionable choices, and mature enough to know that not all love stories were a romantic ride, but it seemed Brad was willing to try.

While I didn't want to look back anymore, I still had to ask myself: Were the two of us standing there in that moment finally the real couple?

EPILOGUE

"Jae, honey, let me take that." My mom, who never carries anything, cheerfully relieves me of the cutting board I'm holding with various cheeses on it and walks with it to the patio table, where my dad is opening a bottle of wine. They are visiting from LA. I'm in my third trimester, and I think they are hoping to be here when the baby is born. Brad is chatting amiably with my dad, Saffie and her new husband, and some of our friends we invited to dinner. Ivy, who lives with us full time, is running around the lawn with some other kids in the neighborhood.

We bought a house in Yountville, in Napa County. We are both still working at Gilchrist, but I mostly work from home, and Brad goes to the office only three days a week. He is relieved my parents are here in case I go into early labor. I rub my belly and like to think this is my same baby. That she never died. She just decided to go away for a while and return under better circumstances. Her name is Rose, and I thank her every day for coming back to me.

After Brad proposed, I told him later that night that I still needed some time to think it over. He was disappointed but understood. "I've waited this long," he said, "and I'll wait for however much longer you want me to." Though our affair had been long, his divorce was too fresh, and I needed time to process it all. So while I didn't resign from Gilchrist, which had been my plan, I did decide to take a trip to Paris, a city I love. Alone with my thoughts and no physical reminders of my past with Brad, I spent my days walking through the neighborhoods of Paris, revisiting sites from my junior year abroad, and journaled in various cafés, trying to make sense of the last several years of my life.

One afternoon in a café, I heard a song for which the lyrics roughly translated were, "The heart is hard to understand; but I listen to it anyway." And I realized that is my relationship with Brad. He is the one I love. There's never truly been anyone else because he's the only one I've ever wanted. Whether he was a good or a bad man wasn't the right question; he was imperfect, as am I. He was trying to make up for our past, and I owed it to myself to take this chance.

When I returned to San Francisco, I officially said yes to Brad's proposal. Brad put his arms around my waist, and I thought he was coming in for a kiss, but instead, he picked me up and spun me around, while repeating, "Yes, yes, yes!" I laughed in surprise, until he finally set me down and said, "I love you, Jasmine Phillips," and we kissed, and then celebrated the best way our bodies knew how. I asked that we not announce our engagement until after Saffie's wedding. And because I no longer had a secret scarlet *A* burning inside me, I invited Brad as my date, officially making our relationship public.

Today, I'm surrounded by family and new friends. I have a home, a career, and soon a daughter. Sometimes I feel undeserving of this happy ending, considering how I arrived here, and, now and then, I worry that my happiness is precarious. But I was miserable for so long that I have to think there is a reason for everything. While I don't condone my earlier mistakes, I have learned to always be forgiving toward others, that things are never black and white, and that love and happiness sometimes lie in subtle shades of gray.

ACKNOWLEDGMENTS

Writing this page is always my favorite, making me feel oh-so-lucky for the incredibly supportive cast of characters in my life that helped get this book out into the world. So let's get this big ol' gratitude party started . . . A huge thank-you to:

First and foremost, Kristin Mehus-Roe, Ingrid Emerick, Christina Henry de Tessan, Georgie Hockett, Kristin Duran, Abi Pollokoff, Rachel Marek, Emilie Sandoz-Voyer, and Aidan Davis, and those whom I haven't yet had the pleasure of meeting at Girl Friday Books—without them, this book wouldn't exist. I appreciate all your expertise and the care that you put into my titles, and for always patiently answering my many questions.

To Corrine Moulder and Andrea Kiliany Thatcher at Smith Publicity for your extroverted enthusiasm in spreading the word for this introvert's books.

To my editors and beta readers, especially Charlotte Hayes-Clemons, Annie Tucker, Chrissy Wolfe, and the team at The Spun Yarn, who read and helped shape this story with their insightful commentary.

To Kari Bovée and Kristin Noel Fischer for our monthly writer calls.

To the NorCal WFWA group, with special thanks to Lisa Carnochan for coordinating our get-togethers.

To these incredible mentors and fellow women's fiction authors: Emily Belden, C. D'Angelo, Allison Larkin, Densie Webb, and Andrea J. Stein (whom I first met on Instagram and is now my sister-in-publishing at Girl Friday!) for your wisdom and friendship.

To all my friends and family who provided input or supported me while writing this book. Shout-out to my book-club ladies for your friendship and our discussions about others' books over all these years. To the American Writers Museum and its incredible Chicago Council members—Olivia Luk Bedi, Heather Grove, and Kathryn Homburger Mickelson—I always have so much fun during our spirited book talks.

To Melissa Amster of Chick Lit Central, whose excellent taste in books, movies, and television series provides much inspiration for (and sometimes necessary distraction from) my own work.

And to Maryam Ghaffari-Ragan and Beata Osmondson for being the best ride-or-die besties a gal could have.

To my parents, Catherine and Richard Terry, without whose own law-office romance I would not exist, and for our trip to Paris this year, which inspired Jasmine's travels. To my brother and sister-in-law, and my extended family for always being such great cheerleaders. To my husband, who indulges me in all my agonizing-over-comma-placement glory—you're a good man.

To my readers, for whom I'm so grateful. So many of you were curious about Jasmine from *The Trials of Adeline Turner*, and your questions pushed me and helped create this book. I hope you enjoyed it!

ABOUT THE AUTHOR

Photo by Sarah Deragon

Angela Terry is the award-winning and Amazon bestselling author of *Charming Falls Apart* and *The Trials of Adeline Turner.* She is an attorney who formerly practiced intellectual property law at large firms in Chicago and San Francisco. She is also a Chicago Marathon legacy finisher and races to raise money for PAWS Chicago—the Midwest's largest no-kill shelter. She resides in San Francisco with her husband and two cats, enjoys throwing novel-themed dinner parties for her women's fiction book club, and is currently working on her next novel.